Shelving Doubts

BARBARA HINSKE

Also by BARBARA HINSKE:
Coming to Rosemont, the first novel in the *Rosemont* series
Weaving the Strands, the second novel in the *Rosemont* series
Uncovering Secrets, the third novel in the *Rosemont* series
Drawing Close, the fourth novel in the *Rosemont* series
Bringing Them Home, the fifth novel in the *Rosemont* series
The Night Train
The Christmas Club
Available at Amazon in print, audio, and for Kindle.

UPCOMING IN 2020
Guiding Emily, the first novel in a new series by Barbara Hinske
The seventh novel in the *Rosemont* series

I'd love to hear from you! Connect with me online:
Visit **www.barbarahinske.com** and sign up
for my **newsletter** to receive your Free Gift, plus Inside Scoops, Amazing Offers, Bedtime Stories & Inspirations from Home.
Facebook.com/BHinske
Twitter.com/BarbaraHinske
Instagram/barbarahinskeauthor

Search for **Barbara Hinske on YouTube** for tours inside my own historic home plus tips and tricks for busy women!
Find photos of fictional Rosemont, Westbury, and things related to the Rosemont series at **Pinterest.com/BarbaraHinske**.
bhinske@gmail.com

Library of Congress Control Number: 2019909401
ISBN-13: 978-0-9962747-7-7
ISBN-10: 0-9962747-7-4

Casa del Northern Publishing
Phoenix, Arizona

Dedication

To librarians everywhere—with a special thank you to Heather Kendall. You are essential to the heart and soul of our communities and hold the keys to a better life for everyone that comes through your doors.

Chapter 1

Maggie Martin nodded at the group of students draped over the low stone wall flanking the concrete steps leading to the impressive portico of the administration building. She envied them the luxury of being free to bask in the sunshine on this surprisingly mild autumn day in December. The president of Highpointe College did not have time to spare, however. Maggie unbuttoned the jacket of her trim black St. John suit and stretched her shoulders. Quickening her pace, she sprinted up the steps and into the four-story red brick structure that was a fine example of Gothic architecture. The ivy on the façade, now resplendent in autumn colors, made her wistful for her favorite perch at the bottom of Rosemont's garden. She couldn't remember the last time she and her devoted terrier, Eve, had sat at the edge of the woods, Maggie savoring her morning coffee while Eve scented for squirrels. She sighed. She had no time for any of that now.

The heels of her Stuart Weitzman pumps clicked on the polished marble hall as she rounded the corner and headed for her office. The sign over the double doors to her suite—"Office of the President" in elaborate brass letters—still sent chills down her spine. She'd been through doors like these hundreds of times when her late husband, Paul Martin, was president of Windsor College, but she had never imagined that she would fill such a position.

She swallowed the lump that had formed in her throat and pushed open the door to the inner reception area. "That went better than expect—" the words froze on her lips.

Josh Newlon, the graduate student who worked part-time as her assistant, sat at the desk outside her office door, head in his hands.

"Are you all right, Josh?"

Josh moaned and rocked back and forth.

Maggie slung her purse and the folio she carried with her everywhere into a chair next to the desk. She leaned toward Josh. "What's wrong?"

Josh dropped his hands to his desk and turned wide eyes to hers. "My dad," he began and choked on the words.

"Something's happened to your dad?"

Josh drew a deep breath. "He's had a heart attack."

Maggie's eyes encouraged him to go on.

"He's in the hospital, but it's touch-and-go. I just got off the phone with his nurse. He may not make it. She told me I should come if I want to see him before he passes."

"I'm so sorry, Josh! You have to go to him."

"It's four weeks until exams." Josh shook his head.

"Don't worry about that. We'll grant you a compassionate leave to give you more time." She leaned against the edge of his desk. "Your dad lives in Atlanta, doesn't he?"

Josh nodded.

"Have you checked flights?"

Josh pointed to his computer screen. "I can get there late tonight on a flight that leaves in five hours."

"Perfect. Have you booked it?" Maggie reached for her wallet. "Do you need help paying for the flight?"

Josh held up his hand. "I can afford it. I was waiting for you to get back to ask for the time off."

"Of course, you can have time off! Book that flight and pick up your backpack. I'll take you to your apartment to get your things and then I'll drive you to the airport."

Relief washed across his face. "You don't have to do that," he said. "I can take an Uber."

"You'll do no such thing. You'll be on your own once you get there. The least I can do is support you on this end. Now book that flight and let's get going."

Josh turned to his computer screen and began to type. "You remind me a lot of my mom," Josh said softly.

Maggie's breath caught in her throat. Josh's mom—his adoptive mother—had died earlier that year after a long battle with cancer. She'd heard a lot about his mom during this difficult time and knew that Josh revered her. The compliment hit home; she would take care of this other woman's child as he made his way to his dying father.

Maggie pushed the back-door release button on her SUV when she saw Josh and his dog, Dan, making their way to her across the apartment complex parking lot. The tall, dark-haired young man moved with athletic grace. The enormous black Lab at his side was an appropriate match for him. She checked her watch—they'd be cutting it close if rush-hour traffic was bad.

Josh stowed his suitcase, then opened the door to the backseat. Dan jumped in and settled himself.

Josh climbed into the front passenger seat. "It's awfully nice of you to take Dan," Josh said, gesturing to the dog who sat behind him.

"It's no trouble at all," Maggie said, leaning back to ruffle the ears of the dog who returned the attention with a slobbery lick of her hand. "He seems like a good boy."

"He really is. He's friendly with people and dogs. We go to the dog park all the time."

"I think he'll get along famously with my Eve and Roman," Maggie said. "And if not, we can board him at Westbury Animal Hospital. You know that I'm married to John Allen? The vet?"

Josh nodded. "Thank you."

"Now—before we start out—let's make sure you have everything, okay?" Maggie turned in her seat to face him. "Driver's license?"

Josh nodded.

"Plane tickets?"

Josh nodded again.

"Cell phone and charger? Any medications? Clothing and a warm jacket—it might turn chilly—you never know."

Josh nodded affirmatively to all of her questions.

"Do you have cash on you? We have time to stop at an ATM."

Josh opened his wallet and thumbed through the sparse bills it contained. He shrugged.

"It's not wise to travel without cash," she said.

He cleared his throat. "There's really not much in my account," he said. "Payday isn't until next week. I've got my credit card."

Maggie fished in her purse on the floor behind her and pulled out her wallet. She removed two hundred dollars in twenties and pressed it into his hand. "This is all I've got on me, but it should be enough."

Josh hesitated.

"Go on. Take it. I wouldn't be able to sleep if I knew I sent you off with," she cut her eyes to his, "eight dollars to your name."

Josh cleared his throat and put the money in his wallet.

Maggie started the car. "We'd better be on our way."

"My car's parked in the admin lot," Josh said. "We're not supposed to park there overnight."

Maggie smiled at him. "Don't worry. We won't tow you. I think I've got enough clout to prevent that from happening."

Maggie tuned into NPR and concentrated on making her way through the rush-hour traffic. The soothing voice of the radio personality filled the space. They made the trip to the airport in good time.

"I'm so very sorry that this is happening to you, Josh. Especially so soon after losing your mother."

Josh turned his face to the window. "I guess I'm going to be an orphan again."

"So your birth parents died? That's why you were adopted?"

"Yes."

"That's really hard." Maggie pulled to the drop-off curb for departures. "Would you like me to contact your professors and arrange for extensions on your assignments? I'll do whatever I can to help you."

"I haven't even thought about that."

"Why don't you decide after you see how things are when you get there?" Maggie suggested. "Will you let me know how it's going?"

"I will."

Dan let out a sharp bark.

Josh leaned over the seat and put his arms around the dog's neck. "You be a good boy, you hear? I don't want you making any trouble for Ms. Martin."

"We'll all be fine. Don't worry about things here." Maggie squeezed his shoulder. "I'll be praying for you and your dad."

Josh nodded. He stepped out of the car and retrieved his luggage. "Thanks for everything," he said before he closed the passenger door.

Maggie watched him square his shoulders as he walked into the terminal. She eased away from the curb and checked the clock on the dashboard. It was her night to rock Julia. With a bit of luck, she'd only be a few minutes late getting to Susan's.

A colicky baby was difficult for any parent, but with Aaron working long hours in his new medical practice, Susan shouldered most of the burden on her own.

At least she had assistance. Maggie smiled as she thought about the group of friends who stepped in to help her daughter in the early evenings when Julia was her fussiest. Gloria Vaughn, Tonya Holmes, Joan Torres, Beth O'Malley, and Judy Young were regular fixtures around Susan and Aaron's home these days. They rocked, bounced, and cuddled the baby while Susan took a shower, made dinner, or ran errands, giving her a much-needed break. Tonight was Maggie's assigned night.

Maggie pulled into the driveway of the two-story brick home and retrieved her phone from her purse. She texted Susan: *I'm here. Sorry I'm late.*

Susan's text came immediately back: *I'm coming!*

Chapter 2

Maggie approached the front porch. She'd been thrilled that Susan and her husband had decided to leave California. Having at least one of her two children—and a grandchild—nearby in Westbury was something she'd longed for. She looked up at the traditional symmetry of the house. It would be a fine place to raise a family.

Maggie stepped to the door as Susan flung it open, a red-faced Julia in her arms. Even with no makeup and her hair corralled in a sloppy topknot, Susan exuded an effortless beauty. Maggie reached for her granddaughter when a loud stream of barking erupted from Maggie's car parked in the driveway.

"Did you bring a dog with you?" Susan stepped onto her porch and peered toward the car.

"Yes," Maggie replied. "I was running late and didn't want to take the time to drop him off at Rosemont, so I thought he could wait in the car while I spent time with Julia." Maggie swayed with her granddaughter in her arms.

The barking continued unabated.

"That's a big dog. It's not Roman, is it?"

Maggie shook her head.

"Did you get a new dog?" Susan turned wide eyes on her mother.

"No. Dan—that's his name—belongs to my administrative assistant, Josh. His father had a sudden heart attack. He got the call this afternoon at work. I just dropped him off at the airport. He didn't have time to make arrangements for his dog, so I offered to take care of that for him."

Susan started for the car. "That's so nice of you, Mom. Are you going to board him at the animal hospital?"

"If he doesn't get along with the crew at Rosemont," Maggie said, "I figured John would know how to handle all of it."

"That's one advantage of being married to a veterinarian." Susan peered into the car, and Dan pressed his wet nose against the window, his tail wagging furiously. "You can't leave him out here. Why don't we bring him inside with us?"

"You're sure you don't mind?" Maggie asked, bringing Julia to her shoulder and rubbing the crying baby's back.

"He's a black Lab, isn't he?"

Maggie nodded. "He was perfectly behaved the entire way to and from the airport. Josh says he's very friendly."

Susan opened the car door a crack and slipped her hand under his collar. Dan thanked her with a slobbery kiss.

"Okay, boy, you're coming with me."

She opened the door all the way and Dan hopped onto the driveway. "Good grief! He's enormous," Susan said.

Dan walked with Susan to her front door in dignified fashion.

Maggie followed them inside, Julia screaming in her ear. Maggie knelt down on one knee and turned Julia to face Dan. "See the nice doggie?" she cooed to Julia. "He's like Roman. And Eve. At Grandma's house."

Dan sat and put his face close to Julia's. He ran his eyes from Maggie to Julia.

Susan took a step toward them. "I don't want him licking her face," she began.

Julia took a deep breath and stopped crying.

Dan remained motionless.

Julia stared at him, transfixed. Her breathing calmed.

Susan froze. She and Maggie looked at each other.

"OMG," Susan whispered. "This dog made her stop crying."

"I think so."

Julia yawned and her eyelids grew heavy.

"Let's put her in her crib," Susan suggested. She led the way to the nursery, a sea of soft pink punctuated by an array of plush gray elephants of every shape and size.

Dan followed on their heels.

Maggie placed her drowsy granddaughter in the center of the crib.

Dan stuck his nose through the slats of the crib and sniffed.

Julia was sleeping peacefully, her breath coming at even intervals.

Dan stepped beneath the crib, circled three times, then settled down, head resting on his outstretched paws. His soft eyes shifted between mother and grandmother. Dan lifted his tail slightly and moved it, almost imperceptibly, as if he were aware that any sound might wake the baby.

Maggie covered her mouth with her hand to suppress a laugh. She and Susan backed out of the doorway and tiptoed down the hall to the kitchen.

"He's like the nanny dog in Peter Pan," Susan said.

"He most certainly is. Maybe we should get him a white frilly bonnet, like Nana had."

Susan smiled. "What a weird coincidence. I've been reading about the calming effects of dogs in the home. Aaron and I are considering getting one. I thought that a dog would help me cope with a colicky baby. I never in my wildest dreams thought a dog would comfort Julia."

"This is remarkable. I was feeling awful about being late—I figured you'd be frantic by now. That's why I didn't stop to drop Dan off first."

"Good thing you didn't. It all worked out beautifully. Why don't you leave him here, with us, until your assistant gets back?"

"I suppose that'll be fine. I've got his food in the car. I'll bring it in before I leave. And if Dan becomes a problem, just call and John and I will take him off your hands."

"I'm pretty sure that won't be necessary."

"Did you have something you wanted to do while I'm here? An errand to run?" Maggie asked.

"No. I'd just like to talk to you for a few minutes. I've been worried about you. You're working long hours at the college, just like you did when you were mayor of Westbury. I thought this new job was supposed to be *less* demanding."

"In many ways, it is. I love being president of Highpointe." Maggie stepped out of her high-heeled pumps.

Susan lifted a lid and stirred a large pot on the stove. The heady fragrance of cumin scented the steam that rose from the pot. "This chili is done," Susan said. "Join me?"

"I'd love to." Maggie took two bowls from the cupboard while Susan placed crackers on the kitchen table. "This smells fabulous."

"I started it earlier. I've become very fast in the kitchen these days." Susan ladled a large serving into a bowl and handed it to Maggie.

At the table, Maggie crushed a handful of crackers into her chili. "In this new job, I don't have to deal with criminal activity so that makes it less stressful. I couldn't be happier."

"I'm relieved to hear it. Aaron and I are so glad that we moved to Westbury. We love it here, and I'm thrilled to be living near you again." Susan perched on the counter stool next to Maggie. "I want you to have a long life—I want Julia to know her grandmother—and I want you to be involved with all our children." She took a spoonful of her chili.

Maggie froze, her spoon halfway to her mouth. "Are you trying to tell me something?"

Susan choked and sputtered. "You mean—are we pregnant again?"

Maggie nodded.

"Good grief, no." She looked at her mother and they both burst out laughing. "I want more children, but not this soon. I've got my hands full with Julia."

"I can't argue with that," Maggie said. "It'll happen when the time is right."

Chapter 3

Sunday Sloan stepped onto the sidewalk and wove her way through the throng of people exiting the tube station. A tendril of long blond hair escaped her signature bun, and she tucked it behind her ear. Once out of the flow of pedestrians, she pulled her phone from her backpack and tapped in the address of the rare bookstore. The phone showed a ten minutes' walk from where she stood.

She turned in the direction indicated, pulling the hood of her down parka up to shield her from the mid-December drizzle and set out at a brisk pace. London's legendary bookstores had been calling to her since her student days at the Rare Book School. What a stroke of luck to have been granted a scholarship to attend RBS the year after she'd received her master's in library science! Her course work at RBS had given her the necessary edge over other candidates, and she'd secured a position as a librarian at Highpointe College, with responsibility for their rare book collection.

Sunday wrapped her arms around her body and bent into the stiff wind, ignoring the steamy windows of cozy tearooms and intriguing antique shop displays as she made her way to her target. She loved to window shop, but she was on a mission.

I should be getting close, she thought, slowing long enough to note the street number of a rare coin dealer as she passed. Blythe Rare Books should be on the next block.

Her pulse raced. When she was younger, her classmates had teased her about the obsessive interest she showed in old books. While everyone else was playing computer games, she was researching ancient printing techniques and conservation methods. Now that she'd landed a job that paid her to indulge her great passion, she felt like the luckiest person on earth.

She drew to a stop outside a shop with a worn wooden door. The name on the window, in scratched gold lettering, told her that she had arrived. She took a firm hold of the door handle, and despite the inclement weather, paused to take a deep breath and compose herself before entering the shop.

An old-fashioned bell tinkled as she stepped over the threshold. She stopped inside the door, allowing her eyes to adjust to the dim lighting inside, and inhaled deeply, savoring the musty smell of old books.

"Good day, miss," someone said.

Sunday turned in the direction of the voice and smiled when her eyes settled on a short, balding man with enormous glasses perched on the end of his nose. "Hello," she said. She pushed the hood away from her face, her hazel eyes taking on a violet cast in the low light.

"Wicked day out there," he said. "I like it better when it snows. It's horrible when it's half a degree too warm for that. Come in and stand by this heater for a bit." He motioned her over to a radiator in the corner of the shop.

She did as instructed and held out her hands to the warmth emanating from the metal coils.

"What brings you to me on a day like today?"

"I'm in London for a conference and I had the afternoon free. I heard about your shop and wanted to see it for myself."

He straightened and pulled his glasses onto the bridge of his nose, peering at her over the top of them. "American, aren't you?"

"I am."

"What conference are you attending?"

"One on library science," she said. "I'm a college librarian."

"And they mentioned my shop at the conference?"

"No," she replied. "One of the other attendees at the conference mentioned your shop, but I first heard about you when I attended classes at the Rare Book School."

"Ah—yes. In Virginia?"

"That's the one."

"Quite a program, isn't it?"

"It most certainly is," she said, pulling her hands back from the radiator and turning away from him to inspect the shop.

"Do you have an area of interest?" he asked.

"Nineteenth century," she said. "English language."

He nodded. "You're in luck. Our collection is huge—the best in England. This way," he said. "Searching for any particular title or author?"

"I'm on the lookout for a few items," she said, "but I think I'd just like to browse."

He showed her to a ten-by-ten-foot alcove that jutted out from the center of the shop. "There may be a few more titles scattered about," he said, "but our main selection is in here." He switched on the overhead lights, and Sunday's right hand fluttered to her heart involuntarily. The soft yellow glow illuminated a wonderland of treasured tomes, tightly packed from floor to ceiling, lining the alcove walls and the rows of bookcases sandwiched between.

"If you don't find what you're looking for, let me know. I may be able to locate it for you."

Sunday was unable to tear her eyes from the shelves in front of her. "You've certainly got a large selection." Her voice was breathy.

"Thank you. Browse to your heart's content," the man said. "Since you're a librarian and graduate of RBS, I'm confident you know how to handle a rare book?"

Sunday shook her head vigorously in the affirmative.

"I'll be up front if you need me," the man said as he retreated in the direction that they'd come from.

Sunday set her backpack on the floor and shrugged out of her parka, folding it over her arm. As thin as she was, she was still barely able to make her way between the bookcases. She inched her way up and down the crowded aisles, admiring the collection. This was no dusty refuge of neglected titles.

She stopped short when she spotted a tooled red Morocco leather version of a lesser-known work by Alfred, Lord Tennyson. *The Princess* had been published several years before Tennyson was named Great Britain's poet laureate in 1850. She knew this because Highpointe's collection of rarities also contained a copy of the work.

She took the volume from the shelf. The book was in excellent condition, just like the one back in Westbury. She opened the front cover. It was also a first edition. The top edge was gilt, and the other edges were unfinished.

She stepped into the main room of the shop and took a seat at a small table. She placed the volume on the desk and carefully opened the book, turning the pages one by one. She noted a few scattered pencil marks, similar to the book in Highpointe's collection. The blood in her temples began to pulse.

She turned the pages as quickly as she dared until she came to page [ix]-8. Her fingers froze. The upper-right corner of the page was torn from the top, a distance of about six millimeters, at a thirty-degree angle. Exactly like the tear on page [ix]-8 in the copy of the book housed at Highpointe.

Sunday's breath caught in her throat. This volume—the one on the table in front of her, in an obscure bookshop in London—had to be the volume that she'd inspected only a year earlier when she'd started her new job at Highpointe.

———

The bald proprietor stood, placed both hands on his lower back, and stretched. The box of books dropped off for appraisal today held nothing interesting. He'd offer fifty pounds for the lot. If that wasn't enough for the hopeful heirs who had brought them in, they were welcome to take them elsewhere.

He glanced into the shop and noticed the young woman, seated at a small table, carefully examining what looked to his trained eye to be a red Morocco leather volume. His pulse quickened. He'd sized her up as an impecunious librarian, but maybe he'd been wrong. A nice sale might be in the offing after all.

He straightened his tie and approached her.

"Have you found something of interest?" he asked, bringing his hands together at his waist.

Sunday started and brought her head up quickly. She met his gaze but didn't smile.

"What've you got there?" he asked.

Sunday shut the book and held it out to him.

He took the volume and held it up. "Ah … yes. The Tennyson. A lovely piece. Such an elaborately tooled fleuron pattern in gilt on both boards." He turned the book to show both sides. "A real treasure, this. You've got a good eye."

She cleared her throat. "Thank you," she said and regarded him thoughtfully. Should she convey her suspicion—no, her certainty—that the volume he held in his hand had been stolen from her library? Surely the proprietor of this prestigious rare bookstore wouldn't knowingly purchase stolen volumes. Wouldn't he want to know, want to see the precious book returned to its rightful owner? She opened her mouth to speak, then stopped.

The proprietor held the book back out to her. "Here," he said. "I didn't mean to take it from you. It would make a memorable souvenir of your trip to London," he added.

Sunday recovered herself. She'd talk to the man—try to draw him out—to see what she could learn. "Yes, it certainly would." She placed the book on the table and opened it. "These patterned silk endpapers are lovely. And it's in extraordinary condition."

He nodded, rubbing his hands together. "That it is. A keepsake."

"Except for the one tear," Sunday said, raising her eyes to his.

He cleared his throat. "Yes. A minor bit of wear. Inevitable in a volume of this age."

Sunday considered this. "I've seen a fair number of perfect volumes from the nineteenth century," she countered.

"From the collection at the Rare Book School, I imagine," he said. "They would have some extraordinary volumes there."

"Not just at RBS," Sunday replied. "My own college has a rare book collection."

"How nice," he said, running his finger under his collar. "Which college did you say you're affiliated with?"

"I didn't," she said. "It's a private institution called Highpointe College. Have you heard of it?"

The man took a step back. "I'm not familiar with it," he said. The skin tightening around his eyes convinced her he was lying.

"We were lucky enough to receive a gift of a local patriarch's rare book collection."

"How lovely for the college," he replied. "Highpointe, you say?"

"Yes."

"How long ago was that?"

"Almost forty years—but the college didn't realize how valuable the gift was for nearly twenty of them. The books sat in boxes in a dusty basement until one of the librarians decided to clean out the area for storage."

He winced. "That can't have been good for the books."

"Fortunately, the basement was dry, and they didn't deteriorate. Hazel Harrington, the librarian, had the boxes brought to her office and quickly realized she had an important collection of rare books. She had them shelved in a secluded area of the library."

"When you say 'secluded,' do you mean 'secured'? Were these books under lock and key?"

"No. They were out in the open. Everyone had access to them. For years."

He stared at her. "And now?"

"They're kept in a locked room. Hazel began researching the books in her spare time and concluded that the collection was quite valuable and needed to be protected."

"Wise woman," he said, wiping his brow with a monogrammed handkerchief.

"She certainly was. It took her five years to convince the college to appropriate money to construct a rare book room. After she died, the room was named in her honor. My expertise had a lot to do with my being hired to take her place. I started a donor group called Friends of the Library to raise awareness and funds to maintain the collection she worked to protect."

"Excellent," he said. "Are you familiar with the collection?"

"I know every book in it like the back of my hand."

"Did this collection focus on any particular areas?"

"Nineteenth-century English language literature and American Revolutionary War era writings."

"Fascinating." He reached for the Tennyson, and she thought his hand shook slightly. "You wouldn't be interested in a damaged copy for your collection," he said.

Sunday reluctantly turned over the volume and stood.

15

"I've just received a large assortment of Charles Dickens, if you'd care to see them?" He stepped aside and swept his hand in front of him, guiding her to the front of the shop. "I was examining them when you came in."

She started to walk in the direction he'd gestured, then made a point of looking at her watch. "Maybe another time," she said. She turned to look at the short man and forced a smile. "I'd love to see them, but I need to head back. I have a cocktail reception to attend and need to change into something suitable."

"Of course," he said, unable to hide his relief that she'd be leaving.

"Do you have a card?" she asked.

He fumbled in the breast pocket of his vest and produced a tattered card. "Nigel Blythe, miss." He gave a slight bow as he handed it to her. "If you have an interest in the Dickens volumes, I can send you photos and appraisals."

"Or the Tennyson," she said and smiled at him.

He swallowed hard. "Whatever you'd like, ma'am, I'd be happy to provide."

Sunday tucked the card carefully into her purse and left the shop.

Nigel checked his pocket watch. Closing time wasn't for another forty-five minutes, but he didn't care. He turned the sign on the back of the door from Open to Closed and engaged the deadbolt.

He stepped to the desk in the back corner of the shop and sat down heavily. He reached for an enormous Rolodex, brimming with cards, and began rifling through them. He cursed when he came to the end of the section without finding what he sought. He really should get these loaded into a computer.

Nigel raked his fingers through his thinning hair and began flipping through his Rolodex again, more slowly this time. His fingers caught on a card stuck to the back of another. He pried the cards apart and released the breath he'd been holding. There it was.

He reached for his phone. It would be early in Westbury, but he didn't care about propriety now. He needed to call his source from Highpointe College. The Tennyson volume was a problem that they'd have to solve. Quickly.

John Allen arched an eyebrow at his wife, tucked under a throw on the sofa. "One more episode? The finale is up next," he pleaded.

"You're hooked, aren't you?" She smiled at this kind man who never ceased to delight her. Whoever thought John Allen, DVM, would be such a big fan of *The Great British Baking Show*?

"I've never made a cake, pie, or cookie in my life, but I love watching those Brits in that tent bake all kinds of crazy things. We need to find out who'll be crowned this season's Star Baker."

Maggie covered her mouth to stifle a yawn. "I could barely keep my eyes open during the semifinals. Can we wait until tomorrow night? I'm exhausted."

"You've had a long day, what with the emergency trip to take Josh to the airport and tending to Julia." John picked up the remote and turned off the television. "Tomorrow night it is," he said, pulling Maggie to her feet.

Maggie yawned again. "We'd better let these two out before we head up to bed." She scooped Eve off her lap and set her on the ground.

John stepped to the massive stone fireplace and picked up a poker. He separated the logs on the grate, sending a stream of sparks up the chimney. "It'll die out on its own."

"Thank you for making a fire whenever we're in here."

He smiled at his wife. "I know you love curling up by the fire."

"It relaxes me. Makes the cares of the day recede"

"Then I'm going to keep doing it—that's exactly what you need."

"Is it okay that I let Dan stay at Susan's? Do you think Josh will mind?"

"I'm sure Josh will be fine with it. If Dan's working his magic on Julia, then we need to leave him there. For now, anyway."

Maggie and John walked to their back door, Eve and Roman racing ahead. The dogs ran down the long, sloping back lawn to the fringe of woods at the end of the property as Maggie and John stepped onto the patio. The moon painted the grass with tall shadows outlined in silver.

Maggie shivered in the chilly night air and John wrapped his arms around her and pulled her close. She leaned the back of her head against his chest, solid and secure in his embrace.

"Dan's got a sixth sense about him. I'm convinced of it. He knew that Julia needed him."

"Like Roman with Bubbles, Blossom, and Buttercup when their mother was killed a couple of years ago. Even though they were kittens, he stayed with them and kept them warm."

"Exactly. Roman saved their lives. No doubt about it."

"What is it they say? 'Dog' is 'God' spelled backward?"

John kissed the top of Maggie's head and whistled for the dogs. "And to think that you'd never had a dog until you adopted Eve when you moved into Rosemont."

"You mean until she adopted me," Maggie corrected him with a smile.

"You're a dog lover through and through."

"An essential quality in a veterinarian's wife, I should think."

"It helps," John replied. Roman and Eve bounded up to them.

Maggie and John headed back inside and to the elegant stairway that swept along the wall to the second floor. Eve ran ahead, with Roman on her heels.

They began the ascent to their bedroom that ran the width of the house, overlooking the lawn. "Other than taking care of his dog, what will Josh's absence from your office entail for you?"

"Josh only works part-time, but he's incredibly efficient. He manages my schedule and handles all of my social media." She looked up at John. "I can keep up with it for a while. Things have been pretty calm lately. It shouldn't be that bad."

"Good," John said. "I wasn't looking forward to you working sixty-hour weeks again."

"No worries. That isn't going to happen. In fact, the only thing on my schedule tomorrow is to return a call from the new librarian."

"I can't imagine that a librarian would have an emergency."

Maggie chuckled as she turned back the thick down duvet. "That's for sure. She said she's in London right now at a conference. I'll bet that she wants to extend her time there with a few vacation days. I'll give my blessing and that will be that."

Maggie tucked her feet under the duvet and snuggled into John as he turned out the light. They were both drifting off to sleep when Roman's rumbling snore rose from the floor in the corner.

Chapter 4

Josh stuffed the wrapper from the minuscule bag of airline pretzels into his empty soda cup and placed them both in the trash bag that the flight attendant held open to him. He locked his tray table and returned his seat to the upright position. The short—and seemingly interminable—flight to Atlanta was almost over.

He withdrew the scrap of paper from his pocket where he'd scribbled the name and address of the hospital and checked them for the hundredth time. He planned to leap up, pull his bag from the overhead compartment, and push his way up the aisle from his seat in the back of the plane as soon as they reached the gate.

The plane dipped lower and he could see the lights of the city below becoming gradually larger. He watched a steady stream of cars on a highway. Then the plane jolted and bumped as the wheels touched the runway. It wouldn't be long now.

He hoped the doctor had been wrong and that he'd find his father sitting up in bed and smiling when he came into the hospital room. If the doctor had not been wrong, he prayed that his father had hung on long enough for him to say goodbye. Tears stung at the back of his eyes. He blinked hard as the plane taxied to the gate and rocked to a stop.

Josh propelled himself to his feet and opened the overhead bin, grasping his bag and removing it with one swift motion. He got no more than two rows toward the front when his path was blocked by other passengers preparing to deplane.

Irritation, followed by panic, hit him like a tidal wave. He closed his eyes and breathed deeply. What was it his mother had always told him? *There are times in life you just have to be patient and wait. You can save yourself from needless suffering if you learn to be patient.* He heard her voice in his head now. *I'm trying, Mom. I'm trying.*

Josh shuffled along with the other passengers as they made their way slowly to the exit. He used his long arms to help those in front of him retrieve their luggage from overhead bins. He accepted their thanks with a pang of guilt, knowing that he was motivated by the desire to get them out of his path more than any wish to be helpful.

When he finally emerged from the jetway, he stepped around the woman in front of him and searched for a sign that showed the way to ground transportation.

He froze when he heard her call, "Young man?" The last thing he wanted to do now was stop. He glanced in her direction and saw her struggling with the retractable handle of her bag. He hesitated and, once more, heard his mother's voice in his head. *If you can help someone, do it. Someday, you'll need help, too.*

Josh reached over and took the woman's bag from her and gave the handle a sharp pull, releasing the finicky latch. He extended the handle to its full height and set the bag back on the ground, offering the handle to her.

He turned and took off at a run before she could thank him. He wove through the busy terminal and emerged to find a long line of people waiting for cabs. He took his place at the back of the line, a growing unease circling his chest like a vice. The person at the front of the line was an elderly man in a cleric's collar.

Josh swallowed hard and stepped up to the man. He opened his mouth to speak and his eyes swam with tears.

The man looked at him and leaned over to take his arm. "Do you need my spot, son?"

Josh nodded, unable to speak.

The chaplain opened the door of the cab at the front of the line and Josh got into the backseat.

"Where are you going?" the cleric asked.

Josh fished the scrap of paper out of his pocket and showed it to him. The man smiled broadly. "Emory University Hospital," he told the driver. "That's where I'm headed. Mind if I join you?"

Josh slid over on the seat.

"I'm Reverend Anderson," the man said, offering his hand.

They shook and the chaplain brought his left hand to cover Josh's. "Would you like me to say a prayer for someone?"

Josh struggled to find words.

The chaplain waited patiently, holding Josh's hands in his strong grasp.

Josh cleared his throat. "My dad—my dad's had a heart attack. I'm on my way to see him."

The chaplain nodded.

"They told me that he might not survive—that I might not get there in time. I want to see him. One last time." His voice cracked. "I've got so much I need to tell him that I haven't said."

Reverend Anderson took a deep breath. "We'll pray that you get to see him, and we'll pray for his recovery. We'll pray for God's will to be done and for our strength in accepting it. Would that be all right?"

Josh nodded.

"One thing I know for sure, son, in all my years as a hospital chaplain, is that our loved ones know what's in our hearts without our having to say a word. Your father knows whatever it is that you want to say to him."

Josh turned hopeful eyes to his companion. "Do you really believe that?"

"I'm absolutely certain of it." He held Josh's gaze. "Now, let us pray," he said, and the two men lowered their heads while the cab carried them to the uncertain future.

The cab pulled to a stop at the main entrance to Emory University Hospital. Reverend Anderson handed his credit card to the driver as Josh reached into his wallet, grateful for the cash that Maggie had pressed upon him.

"I've got this," the chaplain said. "I was coming here anyway." He waved away the twenty-dollar bill that Josh held out to him. "I'd like to take you to your dad's room. This is a huge hospital and it's easy to get lost. Would that be all right?"

"I'd be grateful," Josh said. His hand shook as he put the bill back into his wallet.

"Whatever awaits you," the chaplain said, "God will be with you. Don't be afraid."

The two men stepped through the automatic doors and Reverend Anderson took Josh's elbow and steered him along a series of corridors to a bank of elevators. They rode the elevator to the cardiac ICU in silence.

Reverend Anderson led Josh to the nurses' station and nodded to the woman seated behind the computer monitor.

"Hey, Reverend," she said as the chaplain stepped back and the nurse turned her attention to Josh. "How can I help you, hon?" she said in a thick Southern drawl.

"I'm here to see Kevin Newlon. I'm his son." Josh fumbled for his paper. "He's in room—"

"I know where he is," the nurse said, raising quickly from her seat. "Your daddy's been asking for you," she said. "We told him you were on your way and would be here shortly." She cut her eyes to the chaplain and a knowing look passed between them.

"He's been waiting for you. Before he goes," she said gently. "Are you ready for this?"

Josh turned his palms up and shrugged.

Reverend Anderson stepped forward and grasped Josh's suitcase. "I'll take charge of this. Go to your father, and I'll be right here if you need me. If you want me to come in to pray with you, I can do that."

The nurse put her hand on the small of Josh's back and walked him to a room across from the nurse's station. The door stood slightly ajar. The overhead light was off, but the room glowed with the red, green, and white lights from the monitors hooked up to the still figure lying in the bed.

"He's got somethin' he's determined to say to you, son," the nurse said softly. "Best let him unburden himself straight away. That'd be the kindest thing you could do for your daddy right now."

Josh swallowed hard and nodded. He didn't know if he could find his voice right now, anyway.

The nurse led Josh to the bedside. "Look who's here, Mr. Newlon," she said in a voice that could be heard above the beeping monitors. "Your son's just arrived. Came right from the airport."

His father's eyelids fluttered open and found Josh's face leaning over the rail of the bed. A smile flitted across his lips.

Josh touched his father's fingertips, taking care not to dislodge the tube protruding from his hand. "Hey, Dad," he croaked. "I got here as fast as I could."

His father pressed his fingertips into Josh's palm and moved his lips.

Josh bent over until his ear was inches from his father's mouth.

"Kept a secret," the dying man whispered. "All these years. Promised your mother. We were wrong. Horrible to you."

Josh swiveled his head and looked into his father's eyes. "You and Mom were wonderful to me," he said, choking on his tears. "You took me in and gave me the happiest childhood I could ever have imagined."

His father's eyes conveyed an urgency and Josh stopped talking.

"Birth mother didn't die. She was unmarried and gave you up for adoption."

Josh stared at his father. "So—so I wasn't an orphan?"

"Needed to know," he gasped

"Is she still alive?"

His father's eyes became unfocused and his shallow breathing slowed.

Tears rolled down Josh's cheeks as he watched monitor blips elongate. He pressed his lips to his father's forehead. "It's all right. You didn't do anything wrong. I love you, Dad. You and Mom were the best."

The lines on the monitors flattened.

"I'll always love you," Josh whispered, resting his forehead against his father's.

The nurse noted the time and stood respectfully at the foot of the bed.

Josh finally stood upright and looked at her.

"He's gone," she said, answering the question in Josh's eyes. "You did good to let him say what was on his mind. He was holding on for you."

Josh nodded and brought his hands to the sides of his face.

"What happens now?" Josh asked.

"We'll help you with the next steps," she said. "Don't you worry. There's time for all that." She leaned over and gently closed his father's eyes. "You can stay with your daddy awhile yet. Would you like me to get the chaplain for you?"

Josh nodded.

The nurse silenced the monitors and stepped out the door.

Reverend Anderson entered the room. "I'm sorry, son," the chaplain said.

"He waited for me," Josh said in anguished tones. "Just like the nurse said. He'd been keeping a secret from me all my life and needed to tell me before he could die."

"That happens. More than you might think."

"But it doesn't matter," Josh said. "I don't care. I love him." He ground the heels of his hands into his eyes. "I hope he knew that. I can't stand the thought that he died thinking he'd done something wrong to me."

The chaplain put his arm around Josh's shoulders.

"You did a kind thing by letting him release this secret before he died. You gave him peace."

Josh straightened his shoulders. "I tried to tell him that what he said didn't matter, I don't care about it, that I love him. I just don't know if he heard me."

"He did. You can be sure of it."

"Can we say a prayer over him before I go out there to make arrangements?"

"We most certainly can."

The two men stood at the bedside and bowed their heads.

"Heavenly Father," the chaplain began, taking Josh's hand and filling the silent room with his supplication.

Chapter 5

The cell phone resting on her lap began to vibrate. Sunday grabbed her purse from the floor at her feet and leapt from her seat. She slid past the two conference attendees between her and the aisle and made her way quickly to the exit. She swiped the screen and brought the phone to her ear just before the call went to voicemail.

"Sunday Sloan," she said breathlessly.

"Hello, Sunday. It's Maggie Martin."

"President Martin. Thank you for returning my call."

"I hope I didn't get you at a bad time?"

"I was in a lecture," Sunday replied. "I'm at the International Collegiate Libraries Conference in London."

"Are you enjoying yourself? How is the conference?"

"I'm loving it. Thank you so much for approving my trip. I've learned so much that I can apply at Highpointe," she gushed. "It's been great."

"I'm glad to hear that," Maggie said. "How's the weather?"

"Nothing to write home about, but I'm still enjoying myself. London is a fantastic city."

"Good. It's one of my personal favorites."

The line went silent.

"Thank you for checking in—" Maggie began.

"There's something else," Sunday cut in, surprised at the volume of her own voice. "I, um, I didn't call just to thank you—although I am grateful," she rushed to add.

"I know you are. So what's up?"

"I'm walking through the conference center lobby to a quiet corner," Sunday said. "I don't want to be overheard."

Maggie sat up straighter. What could this pleasant young woman need to tell her in private?

"I've discovered something—unsettling—while I've been here."

"Really?"

"I visited an antiquarian bookstore yesterday afternoon. It's one of the most prominent rare bookstores in the world."

Maggie's brows drew together. What in the world could be unsettling about that?

"They have a large collection of nineteenth-century literature—like we do at Highpointe. I wanted to browse their offerings to see how our collection compared to what the proprietor offered in his shop and whether they had any volumes we might need to fill out some of our incomplete sets."

"Does Highpointe have any money in the library budget for the acquisition of rare books?"

"No," Sunday said, "but the Friends of the Library set aside a small amount to acquire volumes that would complete some of the sets. The acquisitions would make our holdings more valuable."

"I see."

"I was searching for those books when I came across a very rare Tennyson. It's a beautifully bound first edition." Sunday paused.

"And you want to discuss its acquisition by the college?"

"No. I think the college already owns it. That very volume."

Maggie leaned back into her chair. "What do you mean?"

"I was surprised to find another copy of it in the shop, so I went through it, page by page. I wanted to assess the condition of it and ask the proprietor how much he was selling it for. I thought that would give me a better idea of the value of our volume."

"That makes sense."

"One of my projects is to figure out what exactly Highpointe's collection is worth so we can get it insured," Sunday continued with a note of pride in her voice.

"Good idea. Well done. So, what do you mean about the college owning that volume?"

"I think the copy in the shop was stolen from the Highpointe Library."

"What?" Maggie leaned across her desk. "Why do you think that?"

"The copy in the shop had a distinctive tear in the upper-right corner of one of the pages. Exactly like the tear on the same page of the Highpointe copy."

Maggie was silent, taking this in. "Is it possible that the tear was some sort of production error?"

"No. This tear was made by hand. My coursework at the Rare Book School taught me how to tell the difference between machine error and handmade damage." Sunday took a deep breath. "This defect could only exist on one copy of this book. That copy belongs to Highpointe College."

"The book in the shop is from Highpointe?"

"I lay awake most of last night thinking about this. There's no other explanation. That rare book was stolen from Highpointe."

"Do you have any idea when?"

"I finished cataloging our collection at the end of last January. I remember spending a fair amount of time on our Tennyson. It's absolutely beautiful—a little work of art. Our copy was on the shelf in January."

"Was that the last time you saw it?"

"I—I'm not sure. Construction of the rare book room was completed at the end of February and the books were all moved into the secure room by the middle of March."

"Did you see it after it was in place in the new room?"

"No. That was when the head librarian went out on medical leave for four months. I was working fourteen-hour days, covering for her." Sunday let out an anguished cry. "I didn't have time to check on individual volumes. We got the books moved and locked the door. That was it."

"That's understandable," Maggie said. "Nobody's blaming you."

"I know, but I should have checked—at least on the most important volumes in our collection."

"Who moved and shelved the books?"

"Volunteers—members of Friends of the Library. I trained them and gave them detailed shelving plans. They turned in checklists to me when they were done with a section. I thought it all went very smoothly. I never imagined there would be a problem."

"Of course not. Why would you?" Maggie tried to reassure the distressed young woman on the other end of the line. "So a lot of people had access to the books at that time?"

"Yes."

"Did anyone express interest in the Tennyson during this time frame?"

"Not that I remember," Sunday said.

Maggie drummed her fingers on her desk. "You're telling me this would have been an easy crime to pull off—that it'll be tough to catch the perpetrator."

"I'm afraid so." Sunday's voice cracked. "I wasn't sure what to do next."

"Have you told anyone else? Any of the other librarians?"

"No." Sunday hesitated, then continued. "I—I didn't think it wise. The shop had it priced at three thousand five hundred pounds. I hate to say this, President Martin, but a librarian would definitely know the value of that volume."

"And they all have easy access to it." Maggie finished Sunday's thought.

"That's why I came to you."

"You did the right thing," Maggie said. "Did you alert the proprietor of the shop to your suspicions?"

"No. I hate to sound paranoid, but it occurred to me that he might not be innocent in all of this."

Maggie was nodding her head in agreement. "Again, you did the right thing. Your instincts are dead on. We shouldn't alert him of our suspicions until we've verified that our volume is missing."

"So you want me to keep quiet about this until I get home and check on our copy?"

"When do you return from the conference?"

"The closing reception is tonight. I planned to spend another four days in London, sightseeing. I'll be home at the beginning of next week. Do you want me to change my plans?"

"No. Continue with your vacation." Maggie smiled. "It's not often that you'll find yourself in London on business. I'd hate to see you miss out on that."

"Would you like to go into the rare book room to look for it yourself? I can tell you where it should be shelved."

Maggie considered this. "I've never been in the rare book room before, so I think that would get noticed. I've been around college campuses most of my adult life, and the gossip mill runs rampant on them. Highpointe is no exception."

Sunday sighed. "You're right about that."

"If we do have a thief in our midst, I don't want to alert him or her that we may be onto them. The remaining collection is locked up and everyone who goes in or out of the rare book room has to sign a log, correct?"

"Yes."

"I don't think we need to worry about the other books."

"What if the bookstore sells the volume that I believe is ours?"

"If you're right, it's been in his store for months. There may not be many buyers for it at that price. At any rate, it's a risk we'll have to take. Let's make sure our volume is missing, first, before we raise a hue and cry."

"Okay," Sunday said, swallowing her reservations.

"Put this out of your mind and enjoy the rest of your visit. Be sure to have high tea at one of the hotels. It's a lovely treat."

"I've had reservations at the Ritz since before I left home. I'm so excited about it."

"The Ritz? It's the best. You can't cut your trip short and miss that. Thank you for offering, though."

"I have to admit—I'm very excited about the rest of my time here."

"We'll get to the bottom of this as soon as you get back." Maggie consulted her calendar. "I've got appointments on my calendar all of next week. I'd like to talk to you—privately, away from campus—if and when you've verified your suspicion."

"I'll be in my office by six Tuesday morning. I'll have the answer by six fifteen."

"Good. I'm going to give you my cell phone number. Will you text me as soon as you know something?"

"Of course," Sunday said.

"If that Tennyson is missing, can you come by Rosemont Tuesday evening? We can discuss things in private there."

Sunday drew in a deep breath. *Rosemont?* She'd driven by the legendary estate that was the home of their college President—seen its imposing stone walls and gabled roof; its mullioned windows and multiple chimneys. Her passion for late-nineteenth-century architecture was almost as strong as her love of rare books. She flushed, suddenly realizing that a part of her—and it wasn't a small part, either—was secretly hoping that the Tennyson was stolen so she could get a glimpse inside that stately home.

"Sunday, are you still there? Would that fit your schedule?"

"Yes—of course. I'll text you Tuesday morning."

"Good. Thank you for bringing this to my attention. Have fun on the rest of your trip."

Maggie disconnected her line and leaned over her desk, head in hands. Good grief—was she to be involved in yet another criminal intrigue? Wasn't her day supposed to be consumed with budgets, fundraising, and mediating disputes between academic departments?

She dropped her hands and turned to the oversized window behind her desk. The wide expanse of the quadrangle filled her view. A brisk wind sent the fallen leaves chasing each other until they were out of sight. A smile stole across her lips. She had to admit—a bit of intrigue got her blood pumping. She replayed the conversation with Sunday in her mind. It seemed improbable that their volume of the rare Tennyson work had been stolen. Most likely, the young librarian would return to find the volume securely in its place. Maggie would receive a text that her suspicions had been misplaced, and all would be well.

Maggie looked up as the temporary assistant filling in for Josh knocked on her office door.

"Your four o'clock is here."

Maggie leaned toward the calendar on her desktop.

"Dean Plume," the assistant said. "You requested that I make an appointment with him."

"That's right," Maggie said, smiling at the young woman. "I forgot. Please send him in." Maggie rose and met Dean Anthony Plume with an outstretched hand as he entered her office.

"Thank you for making time to stop by on such short notice," Maggie said.

"I'm happy to, President Martin," he replied. "I hope you don't have any issues with the English Department."

"Not at all." Maggie drew him to a pair of chairs positioned by the large window overlooking the quadrangle. "And call me Maggie. We've known each other too many years for such formality."

Anthony smiled at Maggie as he took his seat. "That we have. How many years has it been?"

"At least twenty," Maggie said. "We knew each other before Paul was president of Windsor College."

"Time flies, doesn't it? Seems like yesterday that you and your husband were at Windsor. And now look at you—president of Highpointe."

Maggie brushed a strand of hair out of her eyes. "Sometimes it all seems surreal to me—how quickly life can change." Her expression was serious. "I asked you here today for two reasons. First, I want to thank you for your support of my candidacy for this position. I know that you were a strong advocate of my appointment. I appreciate that."

"It was nothing."

"I know that isn't true. President Lawry said that you were my champion. I didn't think you knew me that well." She tilted her head. "We had only occasionally spoken to each other."

"I was always aware that you were"—he paused, choosing his words—"very much involved in the good things that Paul did at Windsor."

Maggie gave him a wry smile. "It's nice to know, after all these years, that my contributions weren't invisible."

"They weren't. Not to me." Anthony drew in a deep breath. Truthfully, he had never paid much attention to this woman when Paul Martin was alive. The retiring president, Maggie's predecessor, had never been an enthusiastic supporter of Anthony's. Her candidacy had been a way to get someone who might be more favorable toward him into the position. "You underestimate yourself, President—Maggie," he said. "I knew that you were the driving force behind most of Windsor's fundraising success." He shifted in his chair. He had made this up on the spur of the moment and hoped she would be flattered.

"I was the only driving force, most of the time," Maggie said with a rueful smile. "Still—I want you to know how much I appreciated your support."

"You're welcome. I hope you're enjoying your new position and not cursing me for helping get you into this mess?" Maggie laughed. "It's not a mess and I love this job. It's the most fulfilling thing I've done in my professional life—after helping to untangle the fraud in Westbury town government."

"You have a lot to be proud of on that score." Anthony relaxed back into his chair. "You said there were two reasons for our visit?"

"Yes," Maggie leaned toward him. "I have a favor to ask of you."

Anthony smiled and hoped he didn't look gleeful. Doing favors for the college president—having her in his debt—could only be a good thing for him. "Of course. I'd be delighted to help you however I can."

"Good. I think this will be right up your alley. I believe you'll enjoy it."

Anthony raised an eyebrow.

"I'd like you to become a member of the Friends of the Library."

He swallowed hard. "Is that the citizens group that holds read-a-thons in the community to promote literacy and used books sales to raise money for the library?"

"Among other things, yes."

"Why do you want me to join? Aren't the members local schoolteachers and a few retired librarians?"

"At the moment. I want to elevate the group and their mission. The librarian that runs the group is Sunday Sloan. Do you know her?"

He nodded. He knew about Sunday Sloan.

"She's got great plans for the library. I think she deserves to have a more"—Maggie paused, searching her brain for the right word—"robust and knowledgeable group to work with within the Friends of the Library."

"Are any other faculty members involved?"

"No." Maggie crossed her right knee over her left. "That's why I thought of you. Who better than the dean of English and Literature?"

He rubbed his chin with his hand. He could see advantages to being part of this group. "I'm sure I could make the time," he replied.

"I appreciate this, Anthony. I won't forget it. I know how busy you are. Our rare book collection may be a very valuable asset to the college. I'd like you to become intimately familiar with it and involved in its management. Sunday will benefit from your participation. She's got far too much on her plate to deal with this without help."

"You want me to assist her without ruffling her feathers? She's not to know you think she needs help. I'll just be a member of the Friends."

"Well—" Maggie looked at him over the top of her glasses. "That's one of the advantages of getting you involved this way. No point in upsetting anyone."

"Consider it done," Anthony said. "I'm glad that you remember the crazy politics of college administration."

"That's one thing I learned from Paul that I'll never forget." Maggie stood and smoothed her skirt. "I'll contact Sunday and have her put you on the roster for the next Friends of the Library meeting."

"I'll look forward to it." Anthony moved to the door. "Don't hesitate to call me whenever you need anything, Maggie. I'm here for you."

Chapter 6

Tim Knudson took the short flight of steps to Haynes Enterprises two at a time. His high spirits made him feel like a kid again. He couldn't wait to share the good news with Frank Haynes.

He paused as he put his hand on the door handle. If someone had told him a year ago that he would count Frank as one of his best friends, he would have told them they were crazy. Working together to manage the properties owned by the Westbury town workers' pension fund had fostered a respect between the two men that had grown into a deep friendship.

Tim pulled the door open and stepped across the threshold.

Loretta cut her eyes to him from the bank of three computer monitors perched on her desk in the lobby.

"Where's that husband of yours?" Tim asked. "I've got some great news."

Loretta tucked a strand of her long blond hair behind her ear and pointed to the private office that opened off the lobby. She returned her gaze to the monitors as she mumbled, "In there. Go on in."

"Thanks," Tim said as he skirted the play kitchen that Frank had set up in the lobby for Loretta's youngest daughter, Nicole. He knocked, then pushed the door open without waiting for a response.

Frank was leaning his tall, lean frame over the desk, magnifying glass in hand, examining a portion of a large plat map spread out in front of him. He looked up. "I was just going to call you," he began, tapping the map with the end of the magnifying glass. "This shows that we've got the dedicated easement we need."

"The Riverside property?"

Frank nodded. "Yep. We'll be able to market this parcel of land as having access."

"That's terrific. Thanks for going through all of these old records with a fine-toothed comb."

Frank shrugged. "Just glad I can help."

Tim stepped behind the desk and put his hand on Frank's shoulder. "You've done more than just help, Frank. You've worked tirelessly to assist the town in maximizing the value of these assets," he said, gesturing to the map. "The pension fund is no longer under water. You're the driving force who made this happen."

Color rose from Frank's collar to the tips of his ears. "I need to make things right for the people I hurt."

"You've gone above and beyond what the court ordered you to do."

Frank studied his shoes. "You didn't stop in to talk about the Riverside property," Frank said. "What's up?"

"I've got terrific news," Tim said. "An investment group wants to buy all of those condos in Florida. They're doing a large land acquisition and need to include our units to make their redevelopment project viable."

"It'll be a big relief to unload those," Frank said. "Will the investor give us a fair price?"

"With your help in the negotiations, I'm sure they will."

"Of course. Anything you need. You didn't need to go out of your way to ask me that. You know I'm always willing to help. It's part of my parole, too," he stated quietly, lowering his eyes to his desk.

"You've more than satisfied your parole obligations," Tim stated firmly. "We both know that, and so does everyone else at Town Hall."

Frank nodded.

"We're all very aware that you're spending so much time working to restore the financial viability of the pension fund that you've been ignoring your own business."

"We're managing," Frank said. "Loretta's taken over the day-to-day management of the fast-food franchises and doing a fabulous job. She's better at some of it than I am," he said with a note of pride in his voice.

"I'm glad to hear it," Tim said. "Looks like she's working very hard. She barely took her eyes from her computer when I came in."

"She says she's really enjoying it. And she leaves at two thirty every day to pick up the kids after school and spend time with them." Frank stepped to the open door and looked out at his new wife, his expression of pride morphing into one of concern. "She's been awfully tired lately, though. I hope it's just the adjustment to her new duties."

"Nancy mentioned that she thought Loretta was looking worn out at church last Sunday. That's the other reason I stopped by." Tim slapped his forehead. "I almost forgot! Nancy baked you an apple pie and asked me to drop it off today."

"That's awfully nice of her," Frank said.

"I left it in the car. I'll go get it."

"I'll go with you." Frank glanced out the window. "It looks like a beautiful day. It'll do me good to stretch my legs and get some fresh air."

The two men walked to the entrance.

"Be right back, sweetheart," Frank said. "Nancy sent us an apple pie."

Loretta tore her eyes from the monitor. She smiled at Tim. "Tell that wonderful wife of yours thank you very much! And tell her not to worry. I overheard the two of you talking about me. I'm fine. Just concentrating, is all."

"Glad to hear it," Tim said. "Your husband is doing wonderful things for the pension fund. I'd feel horrible if you were paying the price."

Loretta waved her hand dismissively and returned her attention to her work.

———

David Wheeler patted the golden retriever's head resting on his thigh. He looked down at the animal who returned his gaze with raised eyebrows. "You need to go out, boy? Is that what you're trying to tell me?'

The animal wagged his tail.

David stood and interlaced his fingers, stretching his arms over his head. "I need a break, too."

He whistled over to Dodger, the one-eyed therapy dog that was his constant companion since he'd adopted him from the shelter. Dodger lifted his head from the mat where he'd been happily sleeping and got slowly to his feet.

"Let's go," David said to the eyes trained on him.

The dogs scampered down the corridor of Forever Friends and led the way to the outdoor exercise area of Westbury's popular no-kill animal shelter.

The golden retriever found his spot and took care of business, then gamboled around the fenced enclosure.

David turned to look back at the shelter as the sun set, sending long shadows across the yard and into the back parking lot. He had to admit—he loved this place. Forever Friends was the one place where he always felt at home. Now that its founder, Frank Haynes, was busy fulfilling the community service requirement of his parole by working to restore the town worker's pension fund to financial viability, David had taken on most of the operations of running the shelter.

David spotted a tennis ball along the edge of the fence. He picked it up, called to Cooper and Dodger, and sent the ball high in the air. The dogs ran and jumped, Cooper catching the ball before it hit the ground. Cooper raced to David and dropped the ball at his feet, immediately turning away in preparation for the next throw. David obliged, and the dogs took off at a run.

David sighed. He was spending too much time playing fetch with the energetic dogs. He should put Cooper in his pen and get back to the essay he was supposed to be writing for his senior honors English class. If he wanted to go to college next year, he'd have to get a scholarship.

Forever Friends provided a quiet place for him to study in the evenings, after business hours were over. He and Dodger were on site until they went home to go to bed. He wanted to be there in case any of the animals needed anything. David liked all the dogs and cats in their care, but he'd taken a real shine to Cooper and brought the dog along with Dodger into the office where he did his homework. "Last one," David said as he sent the ball sailing. "I'm not going to graduate if we keep this up."

David watched the dogs swing into action, and this time Dodger caught the ball with easy grace.

Dodger was returning with the ball when David noticed the familiar Mercedes sedan pull into the parking lot.

He raised his hand in greeting as Frank parked in his customary spot behind the building and got out of his car.

"David," Frank called. "I was hoping to see you." He walked to the enclosure and entered the code to let himself in.

He approached the boy with an outstretched hand, and they shook. Frank bent and greeted the dogs who were wagging their tails and waiting politely to be recognized.

"Who've we got here?" Frank asked.

"His name's Cooper," David said. "He came in last week."

"He's a beauty." Frank ran his hand over the animal. "I'm surprised he wasn't adopted last weekend."

David shifted his weight from foot to foot and turned his head aside.

"Is something wrong with him? Isn't he ready to go out yet?"

David sighed. "It's not that. He's great."

Cooper picked up the tennis ball and offered it to Frank.

Frank took it from Cooper's mouth and threw it for him. Frank glanced at David as the boy watched the dog in action. "You've fallen for him, haven't you?"

David lowered his gaze to his feet and nodded.

"One of the hazards of working in a shelter." Frank put his hand on David's shoulder. "You can't adopt them all."

"I know."

"And you've got Dodger. He's a great dog."

"He is. It's not that."

Frank looked at the boy he'd come to hold with fatherly affection. "What, then?"

"Since I've been working with Dodger as a therapy dog—taking him to the hospitals and nursing homes—I've learned about other dogs called service animals."

Frank nodded. "Like for the blind?"

"Yes. And more. Dogs can be trained to sense when a diabetic's blood sugar is at dangerous levels. They can help military veterans with PTSD. All kinds of specialized things." He turned to face Frank. "If Nicole hadn't gotten a kidney from Susan, she would have been a good candidate for a service dog."

"How does this relate to Cooper?"

"There's something about him, Frank. He's empathetic. I'm certain of it. He would make an outstanding service dog."

Cooper brought the ball to David and, as if understanding their conversation, sat at David's feet.

Frank laughed. "You might be right. Do you want to adopt him and—then what?"

"I've been thinking." He cleared his throat. "Maybe instead of college, I could go to service dog school with Cooper. I could learn to train him and how to train other service animals."

David's color rose, and he waved his hands as he talked. "I could start a service dog training program here at Forever Friends. There aren't any programs within a three-hundred-mile radius, but there are a lot of people in this area that could use them."

"You've verified all of this?"

"I have. We could do it here. You wouldn't have to put any more money into Forever Friends for this," he added hastily, aware that Frank's funding of Forever Friends had been curtailed since Frank's plea deal. "We could get grants. And I'm almost positive I could get a scholarship to one of the service dog training schools."

"What about your plans to be a veterinarian?"

"I've got time for that. Running a service dog training school would look good on my application to vet school. Besides, I don't have the money for college next year, anyway. Those plans will have to wait."

Frank ran his hand along his chin. "Waiting a year or two to start college isn't the end of the world. Have you talked to your mother about this? How does she feel?"

"She tells me to do what gives me life."

"And does this idea—to learn how to train service dogs—give you life?" Frank looked at the boy and didn't need to wait for his answer to know that it did.

"I think about it all the time."

"What does Grace say about it? Weren't you both hoping to go to Highpointe next year?"

"She got in on early admission, and she wants me at Highpointe, too." David kicked at the ball.

"That's not what you want?"

David shook his head vigorously no.

"Have you told her?"

"Not yet. I wanted to talk to you, first. See what you thought." David turned serious eyes to Frank. "I respect your opinion, Frank."

Tears pricked the back of Frank's eyes and he blinked rapidly. "You should pursue the service dog school. You're a natural, David. You'll be able to help a lot of people in significant, life-changing ways." He cleared his throat. "Get yourself signed up for one of those schools. See if they'll take Cooper, too."

"I can adopt him?"

"Of course. No charge."

A smiled washed over David's face.

Cooper looked between the two men and emitted a bark as if he knew his fate had been decided.

David patted his chest and Cooper rose and leaned his front paws against it, licking David's neck.

"I'll be away from Forever Friends for months at a time," David said. "That'll make more work for you, Frank. I'm sorry about that."

"Don't worry about us," Frank said. "We'll figure something out." He regarded the happy pair of boy and dog. "Actually, Sean has been begging to get involved here. Can you spend some time with him? Show him the ropes?"

"That's a great idea. He's a nice kid. I'd love to work with him."

"Then it's settled. What will you do with Dodger?"

"He's coming with us, of course. I'd never leave Dodger."

Frank nodded his approval and looked at his watch. "I'd better sign off on payroll and get going. Loretta's been running Haynes Enterprises single-handedly and is exhausted. I promised to be home in time to help Sean and Marissa with their homework."

David tapped his leg, and Dodger and Cooper fell in beside him. He and Frank entered Forever Friends, the dogs trotting at their heels.

David headed down the corridor to the right while Frank proceeded to his office at the other end of the building.

"One more piece of advice," Frank said, turning back to David. "Talk to Grace about your decision. Tell her what you told me. She's a nice girl and she'll understand."

David shrugged.

"A lot of misunderstandings are born out of poor communication. Don't let this be one of them," Frank said as he entered his office.

Chapter 7

Josh Newlon got out of the Uber, pulling his suitcase with him. He headed to his apartment and the front door swung open into the empty space.

His hiking boots sat neatly on the mat to the right of the door. His easel was folded and strapped to the satchel that contained his paints. The canvas he was working on leaned against the wall. A faint odor of burnt coffee hung in the air. Everything was right where he'd left it, but the space seemed somehow different to him. Now that both of his adoptive parents were gone, everything seemed different. He was an orphan again.

But was he really an orphan? He relived the scene at his father's deathbed for the hundredth time. His biological mother and father weren't killed in a car crash. Or at least his mother wasn't. That's what his father had said.

Josh kicked the door shut behind him and carried his suitcase to the bed. His thoughts ricocheted from one unanswered question to another. If his adoptive father had lied to him about his mother's death, what else had he lied about? The tragic accident had been part of his story for as long as he could remember. Could his mother still be alive?

He checked his watch. It was almost three-thirty and Ms. Martin's daughter, Susan Scanlon, was expecting him to pick up Dan by four. She'd been so nice on the phone, insisting that they'd loved keeping Dan, and she wouldn't dream of charging him any sort of boarding fee. What was it she'd said? That Dan had a calming effect on their colicky baby? He wouldn't be a bit surprised. Dan had a calming effect on him, too. And right now, with thoughts about his biological parents swirling in his head, that was exactly what he needed.

Josh grabbed his keys off the dresser and headed to his car. He decided to put on some music and take the scenic route on this sunny autumn afternoon. Maybe the drive would help him clear his mind.

Josh took the winding road that flanked the Shawnee River, passing the venerable old restaurant and inn called The Mill. He had another ten minutes of open road ahead of him before he pulled back into Westbury. He rolled down the windows and cranked up his audio system. The crisp air

43

felt good—fresh and cleansing. By the time he pulled to the curb in front of Susan's home at five minutes before four, he'd made a decision.

Josh raced up the steps onto the front porch. He pressed the doorbell and quickly pulled his hand back. Hadn't she asked him to text when he got there so that he didn't wake the baby? A high-pitched wail arose from the other side of the door. He grimaced. Now he'd done it.

He waited, unsure if he should ring the bell again, now that the damage had been done, or text Susan as requested.

The front door finally opened and an attractive—if exhausted-looking—woman wearing sweats and no makeup opened the door. She bounced a sobbing infant on her hip.

"Josh?"

He nodded sheepishly. "I'm so very sorry," he said, pointing to Julia. "I forgot."

"It's okay," Susan replied without enthusiasm. "Come on in. Dan's in the backyard."

She led the way through the house to a set of double doors. "Julia was asleep and it's such a nice afternoon—I thought Dan would enjoy time outside." She opened one of the doors.

Josh stepped onto a covered patio and swung his gaze around the large yard. He spotted Dan at the same time that Dan spotted him.

Dan abandoned the squirrel he was chasing and bounded up to his master.

Josh dropped to one knee and embraced the dog that raced into his arms. "I've missed you." He roughed up Dan's ears. "I hear you've been a good boy? Taking care of Julia?"

At the mention of her name, Dan turned to the crying infant. He walked to Susan and touched Julia's foot with his muzzle, giving it a lick.

Julia's crying sputtered out. She drew a deep breath and yawned.

Susan patted the top of Dan's head. "That's a good boy," she said.

Josh stood and looked at Susan in astonishment. "Is that what happens? When Dan comforts her?"

"That's it. That's all it takes. I can rock and bounce her—and so can every other person in this town—but nothing comforts her—except Dan."

"Whoa," Josh said, eyeing his dog with admiration. "That's incredible."

Susan turned to Julia who was quietly looking at Dan.

"Would you mind staying for another ten minutes or so? Just until Dan gets Julia back down for her nap?"

"Of course. I woke her up with the doorbell, didn't I?"

"I'm afraid so," Susan said. "Wait until you see how Dan settles her down in her crib." Susan turned toward the nursery, with Dan and Josh following in her wake.

She placed Julia in her crib and the baby began to whimper.

Dan stepped to the slats of the crib and stuck his nose through the one closest to Julia's face.

The baby fixed her gaze on the dog until her lids drooped, then closed, and she was asleep.

Dan circled three times beneath the crib and lay down on the thick pink rug underneath. He put his head on his paws and closed his eyes.

Josh raised both eyebrows and grinned.

Susan motioned with her head for Josh to follow her out the door.

"Do you mind giving them a few more minutes before you leave? I figure this is my last chance for 'Nanny Dan' to work his magic."

They proceeded down the hallway and into Susan's large kitchen.

"Would you like something to drink? You must be tired after your flight."

"A cup of coffee would be great," he said, eyeing her cup-at-a-time dispenser.

Susan put a mug in place and inserted a pod of coffee in the machine. "Mom told me a bit about your—trip," she said. "I'm so very sorry for your loss." She handed him the coffee. "Cream or sugar?"

Josh shook his head. "I still can't believe Dad's dead."

"I know. We think our parents are invulnerable. It can take a while for it to sink in."

"It's not just his death," Josh said, taking a sip of his coffee and leaning against the counter. "You know that this was my adoptive father?"

Susan nodded.

"He told me—right before he died—that my birth mother was alive when I was adopted. Up until now, I'd always believed my biological parents were killed in a car accident. That it was the reason I was put up for adoption. And now I know it was a lie."

Susan swept a stray hair from her forehead. "That's a lot to take in," she said. "Did you find out more from your dad?"

Josh shook his head. "He passed almost as soon as the words were out of his mouth."

"So you're left with a bunch of unanswered questions." It was a statement rather than a question.

"I wonder what else my mom and dad were lying to me about?" he said quietly.

"I wouldn't go there." Susan laid her hand gently on his arm. "If there was anything else important that needed to be said, I think your dad would have said it."

"I'd like to believe that."

Susan tilted her head to one side and regarded him thoughtfully. "Do you want to find out about your birth parents?"

"I've been thinking about that nonstop since Dad died. Weighing the pros and cons." He swirled the coffee in his mug and stared into his cup. "I finally came to a decision on the drive here." He lifted his face to hers. "I need answers about them. Who they were—why they put me up for adoption."

"Makes sense to me. I'd want to know if I were in your shoes."

"My birth mother may still be alive."

"Your father, too, for that matter."

Josh inhaled slowly. "If I don't try to find them, I'll regret it for the rest on my life."

"Do you know how to go about it?"

"I did some internet research on the plane. The process varies state by state. Even if I find one or both of my parents, they may not want to see me." He looked down at the empty mug, rolling it in his hands.

"That's one of the risks," Susan said. "I helped clients find birth parents—and children—when I was in private practice in California."

Josh's brow furrowed.

"I'm an attorney," Susan added. "Several of my clients hired counselors who specialize in these issues."

"That's not a bad idea," Josh said. "I don't even know if they're still alive or if I can find them. And I'm so busy with school right now that I don't have time to work on it." He put his coffee cup on the counter and straightened. "Speaking of which, I'd better get home. I've got a lot of studying to do."

Susan lifted Dan's leash from a hook inside the pantry. "Let's get your boy for you. Thank you for letting us have him while you were away. He's a great dog. I'll miss him—and not just because of the effect he has on Julia."

"Why don't I leave him here until Julia doesn't need him any longer?"

Susan drew in a quick breath. "You don't want to do that; you'll want him with you." She wasn't able to keep the note of hope out of her voice.

"I'll be fine," he said. "I'll need to spend sixteen hours a day at the library until I catch up. It'll be easier for me if I don't have to go home to take him for a walk. Besides, Julia needs him, and I want to do something nice to thank you for taking care of him."

"If you're sure," Susan began, "if you're really sure, then I accept. With more gratitude than I can say."

Josh smiled at her.

"And if you're serious about finding your birth mother, I can help you with that."

"I am, but you've got your hands full."

Susan laughed. "With Dan here to make sure that Julia gets her sleep, I'll have time to do some digging."

"Now it's my turn to be grateful," Josh said.

"Then it's settled. Do you have any information that I can go on? Your birth certificate?"

"I have my adoption birth certificate," Josh said. "The one that shows your adopted parents in the spaces for mother and father."

"Perfect. That's all I'll need to get started." Susan quietly opened the front door and Josh stepped outside.

"I'll make a copy for you."

"That would be great. Give it to my mom tomorrow, if you can. She's stopping by after work."

"Will do."

"Good." Susan looked at him and held his gaze. "These things take time so don't get anxious. I'll keep you posted on my progress. And if you want to stop at any time, that's your prerogative."

"I won't want to stop. Something in my gut tells me that finding her will be wonderful, that she's just as anxious to meet me as I am to meet her."

Susan closed the door behind him and leaned against it. She hoped Josh was right; she hoped that he wasn't pursuing something that would break his heart. Time would tell.

Chapter 8

"That kid's got quite an arm on him." John made a throwing gesture as he and Maggie made their way up the long set of stairs to the VIP box at Highpointe College stadium. The stands were filled on this crisp autumn evening for the game with Highpointe's collegiate rival.

Maggie scanned the crowd and picked out Tim and Nancy Knudsen in a nearby section. She waved but they didn't see her. She thought about calling to them but decided against it. They'd never hear her above the din of excited fans.

Maggie loved college football—not so much the game itself but the emotionally charged atmosphere surrounding a match. There was nothing quite like it. The fact that John was consumed with the subject added to its attraction. He'd been talking about this game for weeks and spent the entire car ride analyzing Highpointe's defensive line and predicting today's outcome.

"These seats are incredible!" he said as they entered the box. "I can't believe we get to sit here."

"One of the perks of being college president," Maggie replied.

"I'm glad that this game was at night so I could go."

"Why don't you close early on the days when there's a Saturday afternoon home game?"

"I think I will. We're not busy when Highpointe's at home."

They were the first to arrive in the box.

"Where do you want to sit?" John asked.

"You pick."

"Can we claim these two—right in front? They're not earmarked for one of the trustees?"

She knew, from prior games, that a certain trustee of the college regarded those seats as his personal territory. Maggie looked at her husband. He could barely contain his excitement at being there. Kevin Baxter and his wife would just have to sit somewhere else for once. She wasn't going to

49

deny John. "Of course we can," she said, hanging her purse over the back of the chair.

Maggie checked her watch. The game was about to begin. Maybe the Baxters weren't planning to attend today's game.

The crowd roared as it got to its feet. The announcer said something on the broadcast system that Maggie couldn't understand and Highpointe's marching band played the national anthem. Maggie sang softly while John belted out the familiar words.

A smattering of applause welcomed the opposing team to the field. But when the home team ran out, the crowd went wild.

The referee tossed the coin, and Highpointe took the first possession. John sat forward in his seat as the other team's kicker sent the ball high into the air and the Highpointe receiver caught it and ran downfield.

John turned to Maggie to give her his commentary on the play she'd just watched. She smiled at him. She wasn't interested in the level of detail he was providing, but she loved him and his enthusiasm. She listened and nodded at appropriate intervals.

They continued in this fashion until the middle of the first quarter when Maggie noticed a tall man with a shock of white hair trailed by a petite woman in a track suit and sensible shoes making their way up the steps. It looked like Kevin and his wife would be in attendance after all.

Kevin leaned heavily on the iron railing as he pulled himself up to the box. He was winded when he finally stepped inside. His eyebrows shot up when he saw that Maggie and John were sitting in "his" seats.

Maggie rose. "You know my husband, John Allen, I believe?"

"We certainly do," Mrs. Baxter said. "Best vet in the state. You take care of all our animals."

John stood and shook Kevin's hand.

Kevin stared at the seats. He didn't move.

"Come on, dear. We can sit somewhere else for once," Mrs. Baxter said pleasantly. She took his elbow and began to steer him to the row behind Maggie and John.

Kevin stumbled and John reached out to steady him.

The Baxters took their seats. Kevin raised his arm to signal a vendor coming up the stairs. "Two beers," he said as he passed a twenty-dollar bill to the man.

"I don't want one," Mrs. Baxter said.

"They're not for you," Kevin replied curtly.

The game continued. The vendor made frequent visits to Kevin.

The score was tied at half time: 17 to 17. When the teams came out of the locker room for the second half, the opposing team immediately marched down the field and scored.

Kevin, now thoroughly inebriated, was on his feet, yelling obscenities.

Maggie turned in her chair. "Honestly, Kevin, you can't behave this way. We have to set an example."

Mrs. Baxter flushed and pulled her agitated husband back into his seat.

Highpointe fumbled the return kick and it was intercepted. The opposing team ran it back for another touchdown.

Kevin exploded out of his chair and lurched to the aisle.

"Where are you going?" his wife asked, grabbing his elbow. He jerked his arm free.

"I'm gonna talk to those idiots in the coaching booth." He gestured with his head toward the next box where members of Highpointe's coaching staff got a clear view of the action on the field.

Maggie grimaced. She turned to John. "Should I—?"

"No. Let me do it." John rose and followed Kevin. He caught up with him as Kevin was leaning into a man that John recognized as one of the defensive coaches. Kevin was nose to nose with the coach.

"What the hell's wrong with you?" Kevin's face was red, and spittle spewed from his mouth and landed on the coach's upper lip. "You gotta get that kid outta there."

The coach took a step back and put his hands on Kevin's chest.

"Don't touch me, you bastard!" Kevin swayed and swung his right fist at the coach.

John lunged and caught Kevin's arm before it made contact. Kevin stumbled and came down hard.

"I think you've had enough for one day," John said. "Let's get you home." John texted Maggie, and Mrs. Baxter came to the booth. Her reaction indicated she was embarrassed but not surprised.

"I'm so sorry," she said to the group gathered around her now docile husband. "Can you help me get him to the car? I can take it from there."

John took one of Kevin's arms and put it over his shoulder. The defensive coach did the same with Kevin's other arm. They assisted him down the stairs and into the VIP parking lot.

"Buckle him into the backseat, please," Mrs. Baxter said. "And thank you."

They did as directed.

"I hope she can handle him when she gets home," the coach said.

"It would serve him right if she let him sleep it off in the car," John said.

The two men returned to the stands.

"Thank you for coming to my aid," the coach said. "I wasn't going to take a punch, but I also didn't want to get into a fist fight with one of the trustees."

John laughed. "That might have been a problem. Glad I could help."

They began to climb the stairs. "Are you coming to the next home game?"

"I wouldn't miss it."

"Why don't you sit with us—in the coaching booth? I can get you onto the sidelines, too."

John's face broke into a grin. "I'm not going to say no to that offer!"

"Believe me—it's the least I can do. You saved me, man."

John nodded and they shook hands before they went their separate ways. John's mind was reeling. Wait until he told Maggie. The next home game couldn't get here soon enough.

Chapter 9

The man with gray hair, trimmed with architectural precision, sat in the cubicle with a worn leather book bag at his feet. He pretended to read one of the volumes stacked in front of him. The reference librarian should be taking her dinner break in the next half hour. If the nearby cubicles remained unoccupied, he'd make his move.

He'd been ready to spring into action the previous two nights, but other library patrons had wandered into the out-of-the-way section and he'd had to abort his mission. He hoped the third time would be the charm. Nigel had been most insistent.

The librarian turned off the small lamp at her workstation, logged off her computer, and placed a "Will Return in 30 Minutes" sign at the front of her desk. She removed an insulated lunch sack from her desk drawer and headed toward the staff break room.

He watched as she turned the corner and disappeared from view. He stretched himself taller in his seat and looked around. He was alone in this section of the library. If he was going to do this, he had to do it now.

The man reached into his bag and withdrew a heavy manila envelope, then walked to the librarian's desk and let it slip from his hands. When he bent to pick it up, he deftly opened the bottom desk drawer.

A curse froze on his lips. The keys to the rare book room were gone. He hadn't even considered the possibility that the keys wouldn't be there.

Worming his hand farther into the drawer, he felt around for the keys but stopped abruptly. The precise and tidy librarian would certainly notice if the drawer were amiss. He had to be more cautious.

He cast his eyes over the desktop in search of the keys, but movement out of the corner of his eye urged him to duck his head back down, and fast. He picked up the envelope, silently shut the drawer, and returned to his cubicle.

A woman in her thirties—undoubtedly a graduate student—loped through the space.

What was he going to do now? He dropped his head into his hands and rubbed his temples while staring at the envelope that lay on the desk before him. How would he get the book back into the room? Nigel had given him explicit instructions over the phone when he overnighted it three days ago. And he'd been calling him every day since. Was it really that important? Nigel insisted that it was.

He startled when someone touched the back of his shoulder.

"I'm sorry to disturb you," the librarian said softly, looking a little startled herself at his reaction. "I'd like to ask a favor."

He cleared his throat, recovering himself. "Sure."

"Would you mind watching the rare book room for me? My daughter's just gone into labor, and I need to leave right now. I'm staying with my grandchildren, and she and her husband can't head to the hospital until I get there."

Relief washed over him. "Of course I will."

"Thank you so much," she whispered. "I didn't want to ask those kids that work the checkout desk." She shook her head in disapproval of the students who found work-study employment at the library. "I don't have time to explain the sign-in procedure to them, but you already know it."

She moved to her desk, and he followed her. "My daughter's four weeks early so I hadn't made plans for my backup yet." She pulled the keys he'd been searching for from her purse and handed them to him. "You'll have to stay until the library closes. Is that okay?"

"I was planning to be here that late anyway."

"I can't tell you how much I appreciate it. When you leave, just give the keys to whoever's working at the front desk. Tell them to lock them up in the main circulation drawer."

"Main circulation drawer." He nodded at her. "Got it. Don't worry about a thing."

The librarian turned to the exit.

"Good luck to your daughter," he called to her, fingering the keys. He retraced his steps to the cubicle and picked up the manila envelope. He once again checked to make sure that he was alone in this part of the library, then unlocked the Hazel Harrington Rare Book Room.

He found the bookcase where he thought the Tennyson should be shelved. The adjoining volumes were tightly packed. He pulled *The Princess* from the padded envelope and tried to squeeze it into place but couldn't do so without damaging the ornate leather binding. He moaned softly. He'd have to rearrange the shelves to make room.

He stepped to the door and swept his eyes around the room beyond. He was still alone.

As he shifted and slid books on the shelves above and below, he reminded himself frequently to slow down. He wasn't rummaging through a used bookstore; he was handling priceless artifacts. After another fifteen minutes, the Tennyson volume was in its rightful place. He stepped back and observed the bookcase; the books on all six shelves were evenly spaced and orderly.

He released the breath he'd been holding and smiled for the first time since he'd received the most recent call from Blythe Rare Books. He checked his watch. Nigel would still be asleep. He'd return to his cubicle and send a text message: *Mission accomplished.* All was well.

He exited the rare book room and locked it. After he sent the text, all he had to do was kill time until the library closed, and he could hand off the keys as he'd been instructed.

———

The familiar ring tone of an incoming call emanated from his jacket pocket, disturbing the silence of the library parking lot. He brought the phone to his ear as he walked to his car.

More than an hour ago, he'd told his wife he'd be home. She was still checking up on him, even though he hadn't pulled a late night at the casinos in over a decade. He swallowed his irritation and answered through gritted teeth.

"I'M ON MY WAY."

"Not to me, you're not," a clipped British accent snapped back.

The man stopped, his free hand running over his neat hair. "Oh—I thought it would be someone else." He opened his door and slid into the driver's seat. "What are you doing up this early? Did you get my text?"

"I got it. That's why I'm calling."

"Everything went fine. Tennyson is safely tucked away on the shelf."

"Did anyone see you?"

"No. Not a soul in sight. You can consider this one all wrapped up."

"Not quite," Nigel said. "There's still the matter of the money."

"What do you mean?" The man pulled his car door shut.

"The money I paid you for that book. Twenty-five hundred—U.S. I looked it up."

"So?"

"So," Nigel raised his voice. "I need the money back. I paid you for that book, and I don't have it any longer. I had to return it to cover our tracks."

"After all the deals we've done together over the last dozen years? You've made more than a million dollars off the books I've sent you. And now you're worried about a measly twenty-five hundred?" The vein in the man's temple throbbed.

"That's exactly what I'm saying."

"You didn't have to send the Tennyson back, you know. I can't believe that librarian actually believed it was the copy from Highpointe. There's no way she could positively identify it."

"Maybe not, but better safe than sorry. As you say, we've made a lot of money off Hector Martin's gift to Highpointe. We don't want anyone to start poking around."

The man remained silent.

"Just the twenty-five hundred you owe me."

"I don't have twenty-five hundred—at the moment," the man said. Even though the interior of the car was still cold, a bead of perspiration formed at his scalp line. "I can't pay you."

He could hear Nigel suck in his breath. "That would be very unfortunate—for you. I've never had to—turn to more 'robust' methods with you."

A shiver ran down the man's spine.

"You don't want me to go there. You've got until Christmas"—Nigel snickered—"in recognition of our long association, as you so deftly pointed out. Get me the cash. Before Christmas. Or it won't be 'merry,' as you Americans say, for you and yours."

The line went dead, and the man threw his phone into the passenger seat, then rested his forehead against the steering wheel and stared blankly at the odometer. What in the world was he going to do? How would he get his hands on that money?

Chapter 10

Josh set his paintbrush on the tray of his easel and turned toward the sound. His classmate, Lyla Kershaw, was crunching her way across the lawn hardened by the early morning frost, wrangling her canvas, easel, a folding chair, and a tote with her paints.

He jumped to his feet and raced to meet her. Lyla was old enough to be his mother. He'd learned from their casual conversations in class that she worked as an accountant in the college library and had always wanted to paint. She was an intelligent, cheerful woman with kind brown eyes. He liked Lyla Kershaw. "Let me help you with that," he said, reaching for her canvas and the chair.

"Thank you," she said, her breath crystalizing into a small cloud of ice. "I should have made two trips. You're very thoughtful to help me."

"My father would have skinned me alive if I hadn't." The words caught in his throat.

Lyla noticed the change in his expression. "You haven't been in class for a while. Is everything okay?"

"I lost my dad two weeks ago," Josh said as they crossed the lawn to the place where he'd set up his easel.

"Oh—I'm so sorry to hear that, Josh. Had he been sick?"

"No. Sudden heart attack."

"That's very hard." She drew her lips into a thin line. "How's your mother doing?"

"She—she died earlier this year."

Lyla stopped abruptly and looked at the young man in front of her. "I'm terribly sorry. What a horrible shock to lose them both—so close together."

Josh nodded in acknowledgement. He inclined his head to the mature maple tree in front of him, its leaves at the peak of their color. The rising sun streamed through its branches and carpeted the frosty lawn in a sea of diamonds. "Where would you like to set up?"

"How about right here, next to you? Would that be all right, or would you like me to approach this from a different perspective? You got here first, after all."

Josh set up her easel and chair next to his. "That'd be fine. I don't own this view, you know." He gave her a small smile. "The professor might be interested in the different ways we painted the same scene at the same time."

"Good point. Your work is better than mine, anyway." She settled into her chair as Josh returned to his seat and poured the last of the coffee from his thermos into the cap that served as a cup.

"I don't think so," he protested.

She sat and turned to him. "I know so. Your use of color is brilliant." She leaned toward his canvas. "Look at what you've done already."

"Thanks. I needed to paint this morning," he said. "I've been out here since it began to get light."

"Painting is therapeutic," Lyla said.

"It sure is. It forces you to turn your attention away from what's bothering you and onto the subject that you're painting." He leaned back and looked from his canvas to the tree. "I told myself that I should drop this class. It doesn't count toward my degree."

"What program are you in?"

"I'm going for my master's in educational administration," he said. "And I'm behind in all my classes after being away for two weeks."

"Sometimes you have to do things that feed your soul, too," Lyla said. "That's why I'm taking this class." She unpacked her brushes and paints. "You'll get caught up." She selected a brush. "Was your father local?"

"No. He lives—lived—in Atlanta. I got called away when he was in the hospital."

"Did you get to see him before he passed?"

"Yes. I got there just in time. The nurse said that he waited for me."

"People do that. My mom did." Lyla began to paint. "My parents are both dead. I feel like an orphan, but I'm in my fifties, so that's a natural part of life. You're too young."

They painted companionably as the sun rose in the sky.

"I'm an orphan for the second time," he broke the silence.

She turned to him and raised an eyebrow.

"I was adopted. My adopted father is the one who just died. He and my mom always told me that my birth parents had been killed in a car accident. I grew up believing that."

Lyla nodded and remained silent.

"My dad waited for me to get to the hospital to tell me that my birth mother was alive when I was adopted."

"I see. Did he say anything else about her?"

Josh shook his head. "That was it. He closed his eyes and was gone." Josh drained the coffee from his cup.

Lyla reached into her bag and withdrew her thermos. She gestured to him with it. "Refill?"

Josh held out his empty cup and she poured.

"Thank you." He leaned back into his chair, contemplating the steaming liquid. "I don't know what to think about it all."

"I'm sure that your adoptive parents were trying to do the best for you," she said.

"I wish they'd told me sooner. Now I've got all of these unanswered questions."

"Understandable. What do you want to do about it? Have you ever wanted to find out about your birth parents?"

"When I thought that they were both dead, I didn't. I've never been interested in genealogy."

"And now?"

"Since my mother was alive when I was adopted, she might be alive now." He met Lyla's gaze and his eyes were filled with pain. "I'd like to find her. I'd like to know why she gave me up. How do you give up a child?"

Lyla shifted in her chair. "There's—there's lots of good reasons. It doesn't mean that your birth mother was a bad person or that she didn't love you."

"You think so?"

"She may have felt that she couldn't give you the life you deserved. And now, all these years later, she may be longing to find you, too."

Josh stopped his brush mid-stroke and stared at the tree.

Lyla took a deep breath. "Are you going to look for your birth mother?"

Josh sat in silence. He finally turned back to her. "I am. No matter what happens, I have to know."

"How will you go about it?"

"A lawyer friend is going to help me."

"That's wise."

"I guess there are counselors that specialize in this sort of thing—that help with reunions. I hope I can find her; I hope she's still alive."

Lyla reached over and touched his elbow.

Josh smiled at her ruefully. "I didn't mean to monopolize you with my troubles. You came out here to paint in peace."

"You did nothing of the kind. I was glad to listen. I hope it helped."

"It did. Thank you."

"I'm here—anytime you want to talk." She fished a business card out of her satchel. "You know I work in the library at Highpointe?" She took a pen from her pocket and scribbled a number on the back of the card before handing it to him. "That's my cell and it's always on. You can call me anytime."

He took the card and placed it in his wallet.

"I mean it," she held his gaze. "Anytime. This might be a difficult journey for you. I'd be happy to listen whenever you want to talk."

"That's kind of you." The lines around his eyes relaxed. "I don't know why, but I feel incredibly comfortable with you."

Lyla felt a flush rise from her collar.

Josh looked at his watch and jumped from his chair. "I have to get to class. I can't afford any more absences. You've got the tree to yourself now. Can't wait to see what you do with it." He bundled up his supplies and began walking briskly to his car.

"Don't forget what I said," she called to his retreating figure. Then, in a lower voice, she added, "I'll be praying for you, Josh."

Chapter 11

Sunday rolled over and looked at the bedside clock. Three twenty—five minutes later than the last time she'd checked. She stared at the ceiling.

Her internal clock was askew after the long flight home from London. She'd forced herself to stay awake through an early dinner, tumbled into bed at six thirty, and was asleep the moment her head hit the pillow.

Once again, her dreams had led her to a dusty bookshop with cavernous aisles that drew her deeper and deeper into a fetid, spiderweb-filled chamber. A heavy metal door slammed behind her, entombing her in the space. When she'd woken, clammy with perspiration, she'd been flailing her arms and legs, trying to escape.

Sunday threw the covers back and flung herself out of bed. The disturbing dream was a recurring one. Even in London. In fact, every night since she'd found the eerily familiar-looking Tennyson volume in that balding man's bookshop, the dream had been scaring her awake.

She padded to the bathroom and flipped on the light. Dark half-moons underscored the eyes staring back at her from the vanity mirror, and she sighed. "Might as well get dressed and go to work," she said to the sallow-looking reflection. She knew she was never going to get back to sleep, and she didn't want to face that dream again. It was time to find out if she was right about that book.

She turned the shower on before leaning toward the mirror and combing fingers through her hair. It really needed a wash, but she was too exhausted and too anxious to spend the extra half hour on it. She plucked the shower cap off its hook and jammed the hair underneath. Dry shampoo and a ponytail would have to do.

Sunday started her car at five minutes after four. The only car on the road, it took just fifteen minutes to get to the college. As she drove through the deserted campus, the imposing red-brick structures that usually charmed her looked cold and forbidding in the twilight.

She pulled into her assigned parking spot in the employee lot behind the library and cut the engine. The back lot was empty and dark, except for a streetlamp spotlighting the window of her second-story office. An involuntary shiver ran down her spine.

Did she really want to be in the building alone? Looking down, she realized her fingers were still clutched around the keys in the ignition and her foot was pressed hard against the brake. Her body was giving her all the signs to flee. She let go of the keys and released her foot. What in the world was wrong with her? She'd been to work this early before. With the door locked behind her, she'd be perfectly safe.

She hoisted herself out of her car and hurried around the side of the building to the front door, her heeled boots clicking loudly in the still air and the keys to the library jutting out of her fist like claws.

She told herself that she was being silly, that she should slow down, but she ran the last ten feet to the entrance and sprinted up the stone steps to the double doors. She hastily glanced over her shoulder, then shoved her key into the lock and turned it.

Sunday pushed through the large door, and the alarm system blasted at her eardrums. She shut the door and the keys skittered out of her hand to the floor. The alarm continued to beep, the frequency of the bursts increasing to alert her that she had fifteen seconds remaining to disarm the system. She hurried to the keypad and entered the code to silence the alarm. She returned to the door, picked up her keys, and inserted the key in the lock, throwing the deadbolt from the inside with one swift motion.

She slumped against the door, breathing heavily. She was safe now. Across the dark hall, she switched on a row of lights that led to the Hazel Harrington Rare Book Room and set off in that direction.

Sunday quickened her pace as the door to the room came into view. She reached for the handle to insert her key into the lock and cursed as the door swung open. Who had forgotten to lock the door? Hadn't she made it clear to the library staff and cleaning crew that it was to remain locked at all times?

She'd have time to deal with all of that later. She needed to check on the Tennyson. Fiction authors were shelved alphabetically. She rushed through the rows, past Browning and Hardy, through Mitchell and Salinger. She stopped abruptly when she came to the T's. Her eyes moved across the volumes until they found Tennyson. There on the shelf, sandwiched between a second edition of *The Lady of Shalott* and *The Life and Works of Alfred, Lord Tennyson*, sat the beautifully embossed copy of *The Princess*.

Sunday rubbed her hand across her tired eyes. When she looked at the shelf again, the volume was still there.

She grabbed it and carried it to the desk positioned at the back of the room. She flipped on the desk lamp, snatched the magnifying glass that resided in the top drawer, and sat down. When she opened the book to its copyright page, there could be no mistake: It was a first edition.

Sunday turned to page [ix]-8 as quickly as she dared without damaging the pages. As she expected, the upper-right corner of the page was torn from the top, a distance of six millimeters, at a thirty-degree angle. Exactly like the tear on page [ix]-8 in the copy of the book in London.

She removed her glasses and set them on the desktop, cradling her head in her hands. How was this possible? There couldn't be two first editions with the same manually made defect. The library's volume lay on the table in front of her, and she'd seen an identical volume less than a week ago in London.

She had to have been mistaken. The volume in London could not have had the same tear on page [ix]-8. She wished she'd taken a picture of it. The tear must have been on another page, and in her excitement, she'd made a mistake. Gotten it wrong.

Even as Sunday thought this, she felt almost certain that she hadn't been wrong. But what other explanation could there be?

She rose stiffly and reshelved the Tennyson volume. Fatigue washed over her, and she headed to the employee break room to brew a cup of coffee. She checked the large clock in the main reading room as she passed through it. It was still far too early to text President Martin. The last thing she wanted to do was wake the woman with a text that said she'd been wrong; Highpointe's precious Tennyson volume was securely in place.

Sunday put her cup under the brewer, inserted a coffee pod, and pushed start. President Martin's first impression of Sunday Sloan would be of a hysterical young woman with an overactive imagination.

She groaned and took her coffee to an old sofa that ran along the wall. She sank into the soft leather, sipped her coffee, and waited for the sun to rise.

Lyla Kershaw entered the employee breakroom shortly before eleven to find Sunday snoring softly, slouched in the same position on a corner of the sofa. The morning commotion of employees making cups of coffee, opening and shutting the fridge to stash lunches, and chit-chatting away hadn't had any effect on her.

Lyla knew that Sunday had made the long flight home from London yesterday, and she wasn't scheduled to return to work until tomorrow. She had been sound asleep on the sofa when Lyla arrived at six-thirty that morning. What had compelled Sunday to come to the library so early? She'd admonished the other staff members to let her sleep, but it was almost time for lunch breaks to begin. Sunday would have to be woken up.

Lyla approached her sleeping colleague and took a deep breath. She leaned over and rested her fingertips on Sunday's shoulder, pressing gently. "Sunday," she said softly.

Sunday's brow furrowed but her eyes remained shut.

Lyla gently pushed her again, calling Sunday's name louder.

Sunday started and her eyes flew open. She glanced around the room, then settled her gaze on Lyla.

"Oh, my gosh," Sunday said. "Was I asleep?"

Lyla smiled at the young woman she considered to be one of her best friends. "You most certainly were."

Sunday leaned forward and scrambled to her feet. "What time is it?" Her eyes found the breakroom clock. "It's almost eleven!"

"You were really zonked out. When did you come in this morning?"

"Early," Sunday tucked her shirt into her slacks and straightened her sweater. "Why didn't you wake me?"

"I knew you just got home and must be exhausted. I figured you needed the sleep." She caught Sunday's eye. "You weren't supposed to be at work until tomorrow. Why are you here?"

"It's a long story," Sunday said.

The clock clicked to eleven and a student staffer entered the room.

"I'll tell you later. In private," Sunday said. "Right now, I need to get to my desk. I've got a ton of emails to catch up on."

"Why don't you go home and relax? Get yourself back on local time. Start fresh tomorrow."

Sunday shook her head. "I'll be fine. I've got stuff to do." *Like text President Martin the news that I'm a paranoid idiot,* she thought.

Sunday headed toward the door. "Let's have lunch later this week. We'll talk then."

Chapter 12

John knocked on the door of Celebrations. The sign on the door to Westbury's favorite gift shop said Closed, but John had called ahead to ask its proprietor, Judy Young, if she'd stay late for him if he couldn't get away from Westbury Animal Hospital before she closed for the day.

Judy had readily agreed. John didn't come into her shop very often, but when he did, he always spent a lot of money. He wasn't a bargain hunter and never appeared to have a budget in mind. In short, he was her favorite kind of customer.

Judy pulled her reading glasses off her nose and let them dangle from the chain that was a permanent fixture around her neck. She left her position behind the register where she was totaling up the day's receipts and unlocked the door, welcoming John with a smile and a hug.

"What brings Westbury's beloved veterinarian to my shop on such a rushed basis? Maggie's birthday isn't for months yet."

"You know me so well, don't you? I'm not good with remembering dates so I'm always grateful when you remind me of her birthday and our anniversary."

She looked at him quizzically. "What do you need?"

John cleared his throat. "I'm babysitting Julia tonight," he said. His voice held equal parts pride and panic. "All by myself. For the first time."

Judy cocked her head to one side. "I thought it was Maggie's night with her."

"It is, but Maggie has a meeting, so I volunteered to take care of Julia. No problem. I didn't want Maggie to call one of you to take over for her." He shifted from foot to foot.

"I'm sure you'll do fine," Judy said. "And Susan will be there if you need anything."

"That's just it," John said. "Aaron has the night off, and he and Susan are going out. Dinner and a movie."

"That's wonderful! This is their first date night since the baby came. We've all been telling them that they need to go out. Nothing will happen to Julia."

"Exactly," John said. "Maggie says that the first time you leave your baby with a sitter is a big step. I don't want them to cancel just because I'm the one with Julia. I thought I should come prepared with some stuff to occupy her."

"She's not even six months old, John," Judy said. "And she's got every toy imaginable. You'll be fine."

John rubbed his hands together. "I know, but I thought I'd like to bring her something for her first time with just her grandpa. Maybe a stuffed animal. Or a book?" He cast his eyes in the direction of the children's section of the shop. "I won't keep you long, I promise."

Judy placed her hand on top of his and squeezed. "It's fun to pick out gifts for a child that you love. This is your first grandchild," she said. "Take as much time as you need."

John nodded and set off to make his selections.

John pulled to the curb in front of Susan's and wrestled the enormous bag bearing the Celebrations logo from the backseat. He walked up the steps to the front door, the bag bumping against his thigh. Maybe he had gone a bit overboard, but he really felt Julia needed one of those enormous stuffed giraffes—and the elephant that went with it. He should have bought the zebra, too. He'd call Judy in the morning and ask her to put it aside for him.

He paused at the door and listened. The house was quiet. He pulled out his phone and texted Susan that he was there.

"Thanks for doing this without Maggie," Aaron said as he held the front door open for John. "I can't wait to take my wife out for a night on the town."

John moved the giant Celebrations bag in front of him and stepped across the threshold. The two men shook hands. "Is Susan okay with it just being me?"

Aaron hesitated.

"She's worried, isn't she?" John asked. His shoulders sagged.

"She'd be nervous about leaving Julia with anyone."

"She's run errands while the others stay with Julia." John bit his lip. "It's because I've never had children. She thinks I don't know what I'm doing."

Aaron opened his mouth to speak, then shut it.

"It's not like you're going to Siberia. You'll be within five miles of the house."

"That's exactly what I told her."

"You can call as often as you want." John held up his cell phone.

"It'll be fine," Aaron agreed. "Susan's checking on Julia. She'll be right out."

As if on cue, Susan stepped into the entryway. She looked at John and her eyebrows shot up. "What in the world?"

John smiled sheepishly. "Since it was my first time with her on my own, I thought it might be good to have some new things to distract her. If she got fussy."

Susan put her arm around John's shoulders and hugged him to her. "You are the dearest man. You know that she's asleep, don't you? Now that Dan is here, Julia is on a regular nap and bedtime schedule."

"Maggie mentioned it." John shrugged. "I just thought—"

"You're disappointed, aren't you?" Susan ran her eyes over his face. "You wanted to spend some time with her while she's awake, didn't you?"

"Well—yes. Whenever I come over, Maggie's always here—or Judy or Gloria or Joan. They're holding her."

"Why didn't you say something?" Susan swallowed the lump in her throat. "You're Julia's grandpa, you know. I'm not going to let them hog her."

"It's not a competition. I feel silly even bringing it up."

"You're absolutely right to bring it up. Julia's asleep so I don't want to wake her now. Why don't we leave all of your gifts right over here," she pointed to a table in the entryway, "and you can come over Sunday afternoon after Julia's nap to give them to her. I'll make sure that you get as much time as you want with her."

John beamed. "That'd be great. Thanks for understanding."

"Of course!" Susan cleared her throat and looked at Aaron. He raised a brow and she nodded imperceptibly.

"We'd better make tracks. We've got reservations at Pete's before the movie."

Aaron beamed at her.

"Have fun and don't worry about a thing. We'll be fine here," John said.

"I know you will be." Susan headed for her garage. "Oh—and Mom called. Her meeting canceled so she's on her way over."

"That's great. Since Julia's asleep, it'll be nice to have an evening with your mother."

"She still working herself to death?"

"Not to death, but more than she'd like."

"Feel free to order a movie, if you guys want. We've got subscriptions to all the channels."

"We may do that."

Susan and Aaron made their exit. Aaron's taillights disappeared at the end of the street as Maggie pulled into the driveway.

John opened the door and watched her walk to him. A surge of warmth, pride, admiration, and desire, in equal measure, cascaded through him.

"What a wonderful surprise," John said. "I'm so glad to see my best girl."

Maggie leaned in to kiss him squarely on the mouth. She stepped around the enormous Celebrations bag. "What in the world is in there?" She eyed him curiously.

John flushed.

"Is this your doing?"

"You'll see on Sunday," he said, taking her elbow and steering her to the family room. "What happened to your meeting?"

Maggie sank into the sofa and kicked off her heels. "You remember that young librarian I told you about? The one that thought one of our rare books was stolen?"

"She called you from London?"

"That's the one." Maggie drew her knees up and wrapped her arms around them. "She texted me this afternoon. Apparently, our volume is safely in place in the library."

"So it wasn't stolen?"

"Nope."

"If I remember rightly, wasn't she pretty certain it had been?"

"Yes. Based on a manmade tear on one of the pages."

"The same book has the same tear—on both sides of the Atlantic?"

"It seems so," Maggie replied.

They regarded each other silently.

"That doesn't seem likely," John said.

"I agree." Maggie shook her head. "She must have been wrong about the book in London. Maybe it was torn on a different page."

"That would explain it."

"We've got our volume, that's all I care about," Maggie said. "I'm so glad I don't have another criminal matter to deal with."

"Amen to that," John said. "Want to veg out and watch a movie?"

"You read my mind. I'd love to. Let's check on Julia and Dan, then weld ourselves to this sofa and relax."

Chapter 13

Grace Acosta brought her arm over her head to wave at David, flanked by two dogs, loping across the dormant lawn of the dog park. She moved toward him, her hair bouncing around her shoulders. The park was deserted on the overcast afternoon that held the promise of freezing rain.

"Thanks for coming," David said as he drew near her.

"Sure," Grace said, twining her fingers over her head and stretching. "I needed a break from that essay for English class."

David turned his head aside.

"You are working on it, aren't you?" Grace asked. "If you want to get into Highpointe next fall, you've got to get a good grade on it."

"It's extra credit, and I really don't have time right now."

"What do you mean?" Grace took a step back. "You'd better make time."

They stared at each other as Dodger sat quietly at his master's side and Cooper sniffed at Grace.

"You know how busy I am at Forever Friends." David broke the silence.

"Running Forever Friends isn't your future, David. I thought you wanted to be a vet. You need to go to college for that."

"Don't you think I know that? I still plan to be a vet, but I've got other things I want to do first."

"Like what?"

"I'm checking out service dog schools for after graduation."

"Like guide dogs for the blind?"

"Yes."

She sighed heavily. "That's nice, David. I just thought that both of us were going to Highpointe together. It's selfish of me, I know. To be honest, I'm nervous about college."

"You're nervous? Are you serious?"

Grace shrugged.

"You're going to be the valedictorian of our class. College will be a breeze for you."

"Not the making friends part. I was counting on you being there." Cooper shoved his muzzle against her side, and she bent to pat his head. "Who's this guy?"

"His name is Cooper."

Grace raised an eyebrow at David. "Is he from Forever Friends?"

"He was. Frank let me adopt him." David continued.

Cooper gave her hand a slobbery lick.

"Will you stay on at Forever Friends while you're in training?"

"No." David shifted his weight from foot to foot.

"That's good. Maybe I'll get to spend more time with you than I do now." She smiled at him and his heart did a flip-flop.

"About that"—David took a deep breath and continued in a rush—"the school isn't near here."

"What do you mean?"

"The one I want to go to is in California."

Grace's back stiffened. "That's a long way away. It's too far to come home on weekends."

"I know. I'm sorry."

"How long will you be gone?"

David coughed into his elbow. "It's a three-year program."

"WHAT?"

"I want to get trained so I can start a service dog school at Forever Friends."

Grace wrapped her arms around herself and took a deep breath. "That's a terrific thing to do, David. It really is. I'm happy for you."

"I'm so glad you understand," David began.

Grace put her hand up to stop him. "There's no place in this plan for me, David. We won't see each other for months at a time."

"We can text and talk on the phone."

Grace shook her head. "You don't like to do that now. Why would it be different when you're away?"

"I'll be better. I promise I will."

Grace gave Cooper one last pat on the head. "I've got to get back to my essay."

"Okay," David said. "I'll walk you to your car."

"No," Grace replied. "I'd rather go alone." She turned and began to walk.

"Are we still—?" David called after her.

She turned her head over her shoulder. "I don't know, David. I need time to think."

David's mouth went dry as he watched the girl who had become his best friend, and held his heart, retreat into the gray mist.

Maggie glanced into the backseat of John's Suburban as she buckled her seat belt. She shifted to get a better look at the enormous shopping bag imprinted with the Celebrations logo.

"What in the world?" She swiveled to look at him.

John kept his eyes locked on the rearview mirror as he backed out of the garage. "It's just—something I forgot to pick up when I was there the other day."

"You mean when you went in and bought out the children's section? I ran into Judy at the grocery and she couldn't stop talking about what a generous grandfather you are."

John shrugged. "It's part of a set."

Maggie chuckled. "Julia's got more toys than she'll ever have time to play with."

"I know that," John glanced over at Maggie. "But they're not toys from me. Not from her grandpa."

"That's true enough." She reached over and squeezed his elbow. "It's fun to spoil a grandchild. You deserve it."

"I promise I won't make a habit of it." He turned onto Susan's street and started his windshield wipers. "Looks like the storm they've been predicting is here."

Maggie checked the thermometer on the dashboard. "Thirty-four degrees. We'll have freezing rain soon."

John pulled into Susan's driveway. "We won't stay long."

Maggie hurried to the front door while John wrestled the huge bag out of the backseat.

Aaron flung the door open as Maggie was reaching for the doorbell. "I saw you pull up. Go on in. I'll help John." Aaron stepped around Maggie and hurried down the steps to John.

"There's a casserole dish on the floor behind the driver's seat," John said. "Maggie whipped up something for your dinner."

"Got it," Aaron said. "It's really starting to come down. I'll lock your car and bring in the casserole."

John nodded and bent his head against the rain that was turning to sleet.

Susan took their wet coats and ushered them into the family room. A fire danced behind the grate and candles lined the mantelpiece, reflecting in the mirror and casting a warm glow into the room.

Julia was rocking happily in her swing, her eyes bright and attentive.

John made a beeline for her, clutching the large Celebrations bag. A furry, black-and-white-striped face peeked out of the tissue paper. He set the bag next to the swing.

Julia held out her arms to John and waved her feet.

John picked her up. "How's the best girl in Westbury today?"

Julia cooed.

John turned to the others. "She knows me!"

Susan laughed. "Of course, she knows you." She raised her eyebrows at Aaron. "Her father and you are the two people she has completely wrapped around her little finger."

The two men exchanged a sheepish glance.

"I'll neither admit nor deny," John said. "Isn't that what criminals on television say?"

"Something like that," Susan said. "And it's fine. Every girl should be the apple of her father's and grandfather's eyes."

"Let's see what we've got here," John said, sinking to the floor with Julia on his knee. He slid the bag over to them and removed the tissue paper.

Julia squealed.

John pulled the stuffed zebra out of the bag and moved Julia close to it.

Her eyes grew wide. She regarded the animal, twice her size, silently.

John took her hand in his and, together, they gently patted the stuffed animal's back.

Julia chuckled and reached for the zebra's thick mane.

John beamed. "This is the one I didn't buy the other day," he said as Maggie, Susan, and Aaron looked on. "I knew she'd like it. That's why I went back. She needs the complete set."

"The rest of what you bought is over here," Aaron said, walking to the far corner of the room. "I'll bring them over to you."

"Thanks," John said. "Given the weather, I think she should open these and then Maggie and I had better head home before the roads get icy." He unwrapped the giraffe he'd purchased from Celebrations earlier and showed it to Julia.

No longer unsure of these stuffed creatures that dwarfed her, Julia laughed and waved her hands in front of her face.

John set her on the floor and, together, they inspected a huge stuffed elephant. He lined up all of the animals in front of his delighted granddaughter. She wiggled and grinned.

The delighted pair worked their way through the remaining toys, puzzles, and books that John had bought for her.

John looked at the toys and wrappings strewn around them. "I guess I did get carried away," he said, making a show of grimacing. "It snuck up on me."

Susan joined them on the floor. "You had a blast doing this, didn't you?"

John nodded.

She leaned toward him and pulled him in for a hug. "Then that's all that matters. You are a dear, you know that?" she whispered in his ear.

Susan began to stack the puzzles and books. "She's not quite ready for these yet. We'll save them until she is, and you can give them to her all over again."

"That'd be great," John replied. He rose from the floor, stretching.

Maggie picked up Julia and bounced her granddaughter on her hip.

John caught one of Julia's hands in his. "We'll be on our way. Thanks for spending time with grandpa. I'm glad you liked your animals." He kissed her hand. "We're going to have a lot of fun with them when you get a little older."

Maggie transferred Julia to Aaron, and they all walked to the door. The sleet had already turned to ice on the steps.

John took Maggie's elbow and they made their way slowly to his car.

"Text me to let me know you got home safely, okay?" Susan called after them.

Maggie raised her hand over her head to indicate her agreement as she got into John's car.

John backed out of the driveway and they headed for Rosemont. The inclement weather did nothing to dampen the warmth of happiness in his heart.

Chapter 14

Josh was thrown back on his heels as he knelt in Susan's entryway and absorbed the shock of the big black dog that raced into his open arms. He buried his face in the fur of the dog's neck. Dan squirmed free of Josh's grasp and covered his master's face and neck with wet kisses.

"I was afraid you'd forgotten me," he said softly to the dog.

Susan smiled at the scene in front of her. "I think Dan is the smartest dog I've ever seen," she said. "He was devoted to Julia, for sure, but I always felt like he knew he was working."

Josh rolled onto his back and wrestled with Dan.

"Like a Seeing Eye dog," she continued. "Dan was on duty the whole time he was here. He never played like he's doing with you, now."

Josh moved Dan aside and got to his feet.

"Not that we didn't walk him or play with him in the yard," she added hastily. "But he never let loose with such joyous abandon. It's clear from all this," she drew a circle in front of her with her finger, "that he missed you and he's glad you're back."

"You're sure that you're okay with me taking him home now? Julia doesn't need him?"

"I'm positive. The doctor says that she's grown out of her colic."

"I'm glad that she's better. And that Dan helped."

"Me, too. It was really rough. She had a very bad case of it." Susan looked into Josh's eyes. "Aaron and I want you to know how grateful we are that you let us keep him for so long."

"No big deal."

"I think it was a big deal. Especially since you just lost your dad. Having Dan to come home to would have been comforting. It was very kind of you to leave him with us."

Josh flushed and cleared his throat. "You said that you had some news about my mother?"

"I do. Can you talk for a minute?"

Josh followed Susan into her kitchen. "I was able to get a copy of your original birth certificate." She picked up an envelope from the kitchen island and held it out to him.

He hesitated, then took the envelope.

"It contains the name of your birth mother."

Josh's pulse quickened. "What about my birth father?"

"It says that he was deceased at the time of your birth," Susan said.

"Why wouldn't they still put his name on the certificate?"

"If the parents aren't married, the birth father has to agree to be listed on the certificate."

Josh stared at her.

"If he was deceased, that couldn't have happened." Susan stood silently and allowed him to process this information.

"So maybe my adoptive parents didn't lie to me about my birth parents. Not really." He raked both hands through his hair. "Maybe there really was this terrible accident that they told me about, and my father was killed instantly. My mother lived long enough to give birth to me and then died right after that. Maybe that's what my father was trying to tell me."

"That's quite possible," Susan replied.

They stood in silence. "Do you want to find out about your birth mother?"

Josh nodded firmly.

"Her name is on that certificate."

Josh didn't move.

"Would you like me to take the next step? Find your birth mother—or find out about her?"

"I should do it myself. I shouldn't waste your time."

"It's not a waste of my time. People engage what are called Search Angels to help them find their birth parents all the time." Susan touched Josh's elbow. "You and Dan were our 'Colic Angel' so I'd be honored to be your Search Angel. I haven't started yet because I wanted to make sure that you wanted to continue."

"I do." He hesitated, then handed the envelope back to her. "I don't think I want to know her name until you find out more. Will you keep this for me? For now?"

"Of course."

Dan pushed against his master's leg.

"I think this guy needs to go out. I'm planning to take him to the dog park."

"Then you'd better get moving—it looks like it's about to start raining again." Susan saw them to the door. "And if you ever need a dog sitter, you don't even need to ask. Just bring him over to our house." She bent and circled Dan's neck with her arms. "I love you. You're the best boy, and I'll never forget what you did for us."

She stood with tears in her eyes.

Dan gave her hand one last lick and followed his master out the door.

Chapter 15

Sunday entered Pete's Bistro by the back door, closing her umbrella as she stepped inside. She stowed it in the bin provided and stamped her feet on the doormat. The aroma of chicken soup and something spicy that she couldn't identify permeated the air. She set out for a booth by the front window that was occupied by her closest friend.

Lyla turned abruptly when Sunday called her name.

"Don't get up to hug me," Sunday said. "I'm drenched." She removed her trench coat, folded it, and set it on the bench as she slid into the booth opposite Lyla. "You look like you were miles away."

Lyla pursed her lips into a thin smile and shrugged. "I guess I was."

"What's up?" Sunday asked. Lyla wasn't her usual chipper self.

"Nothing important," Lyla said. "At least nothing I can do anything about now." She reached across the table and patted Sunday's hand. "So— tell me about you. How was your trip?"

"It was a mixed bag."

Lyla lifted an eyebrow. "Do tell."

"The conference was fabulous. Better than I expected. I learned a ton and made some really great contacts."

"I'm glad to hear that."

"One man in particular is becoming a very good friend. He has expertise in rare books. We've been emailing back and forth since I got home."

"Ohhhh—" Lyla drew out the word. "A good friend, huh?"

Sunday laughed. "Yes—a good friend. He's a librarian at Oxford. Very interesting and distinguished. We attended most of the same sessions at the conference and ended up sitting together."

Pete Fitzpatrick stepped to their table, menus in hand. "Would you ladies like to look at menus or will it be the usual?"

"The usual," they both said in unison.

"Two Greek salads with chicken coming right up," Pete said.

"You can't beat perfection," Lyla said.

"Hot tea to drink?"

Both women nodded, and Pete retreated to the kitchen to place their order.

"One of these days we ought to order something different. Surprise him," Lyla said. "So—sounds to me like this guy was interested in you."

Sunday shook her head. "It wasn't like that. He was just very nice and good company." She smiled at her friend. "He's closer to your age than mine. I think the two of you would hit it off, actually."

"Isn't that my luck," Lyla said. "Someone finally finds the man for me—and he lives in England!"

A waiter arrived at their table and set a pot of tea and two mugs in front of them.

Sunday poured the steaming liquid into a mug and slid it to her friend. "You've never been married, have you?"

Lyla curled her fingers around the mug and brought it toward her, inhaling the fragrant notes of chamomile. She shook her head no.

"Did you ever want to marry? Sometimes I'm not sure that I do. I certainly don't want to tie myself to the wrong man."

"That's why I've never married. I met my Mr. Right when I was in college but—" The words caught in Lyla's throat and she couldn't continue. She dropped her gaze to her hands. How could this still be so painful, almost thirty years later?

"Here you go, ladies," Pete said. He set their salads in front of them and placed a plate of freshly baked pita bread on the table between them. "Anything else I can get you?"

Both women shook their heads.

Lyla put her napkin on her lap. "You said that the trip was a mixed bag. What you've told me sounds great. What went wrong?"

Sunday looked across at her friend, her fork halfway to her mouth. Should she tell Lyla about the Tennyson volume—about how she'd humiliated herself in front of President Martin with her suspicions?

"I visited a rare bookstore in London," Sunday began and paused.

"You love those shops," Lyla replied. "That must have been fun."

"It was," Sunday stammered. "It just—"

"Just what?"

Sunday took a deep breath. "It just reminded me that we have no idea of the exact value of the rare book collection at our library," she finished.

Lyla leaned back into the booth. "Is that what bothered you about your trip? That we don't have a value on our collection?"

Sunday nodded vigorously. She didn't want to confess to Lyla what had really happened at the London bookshop.

"There must be some way you can establish a ballpark value of our collection."

"It'll be a huge job. Someone has to go through each volume and determine which edition we've got and its condition. Each book—each publisher—has its own standards and conventions. I don't know how I'll ever get through it all. I've made a start but it's going to take years." Sunday resumed eating her salad. She wasn't lying to her friend. Establishing the value of Highpointe's rare books was one of her goals.

"Why don't you enlist the help of the Friends of the Library? They're all retired librarians and retired bookstore owners, aren't they?"

"Yes, they are."

"Surely they can do the analysis correctly."

"I would think so."

"And you could trust them."

Could she trust them? Sunday wasn't so sure. Her gut still told her that something funny had gone on with the Tennyson volume.

"I'll think about it," Sunday said.

Lyla picked up the teapot and freshened both of their cups. "You could use Hector Martin's collection notes as a starting point."

Sunday's head snapped up. "What are you talking about?"

"His notes. The ones he gave us when he donated his items."

"I haven't seen them." Sunday put her fork on her plate and pushed it away. "I never heard of them—until now."

"What? Didn't you find Hazel's copy?"

Sunday shook her head. "The only records I have were the initial estimates she gave the college to get that room built. A few books and their values were given as examples, but that was it. What was in the notes?"

"All sorts of information. Where he purchased each book; how much he paid; whether it was a first edition. That sort of thing. He was a meticulous recordkeeper."

Sunday's pulse raced and she could feel her face flush. "That would be incredibly helpful. I went through everything I could find on the collection when I did my inventory last year—right before we moved the books to the secure room. I didn't find any notes. Were they handwritten or typed?"

"Handwritten by Hector himself."

"Gosh—what a shame to have lost them."

Lyla tilted her head to one side and her eyes gleamed. "We haven't lost them. I kept the original list in the accounting files."

"You didn't! That's wonderful."

"I made a copy for Hazel, but I kept the original. I may not be a rare book expert, but even I know he gave us some very valuable volumes. I figured that information should be part of our accounting records."

Sunday leaned across the table toward Lyla. "You're brilliant. Will you make me a copy?"

"You bet. I'll do it this afternoon." Lyla's brows furrowed. "I'm surprised that you never found Hazel's copy of Hector's notes. She understood how important those notes were and kept them in her desk, under lock and key."

"Maybe she forgot about them or they got misfiled," Sunday said.

"That would have been very unlike Hazel," Lyla said.

Or maybe someone stole the list after Hazel died, Sunday thought. Hector Martin's notes sounded like a roadmap to what was most valuable in his collection.

"His notes will give me a good place to start. I can focus on the most valuable items to begin with."

Pete brought the check and placed it on the edge of the table. "Whenever you're ready," he said.

Sunday snatched the check and handed it and her credit card back to Pete.

"You don't have to do that," Lyla said. "We always go Dutch."

"Not today we don't," Sunday said. "You're a lifesaver, Lyla."

"For heaven's sake," Lyla began.

Sunday held up a hand. "You have no idea how helpful you've been."

Lyla smiled broadly. "I'm thrilled I could help. You'll get a value on that collection in no time."

And I'll also cross-check Hector's notes with my inventory, Sunday thought, *and find out if any of those rare volumes are missing.* She couldn't shake her unease over the Tennyson volume. If she found that other volumes were missing, it would prove that someone had been stealing from Highpointe's rare book collection.

Pete returned with her credit card receipt. She quickly calculated the tip and signed it. The sooner they returned to the library and she got her hands on Hector's notes, the better.

Chapter 16

Susan pulled the blanket over her daughter's feet and tiptoed out of Julia's room. She made a beeline for her desk in the spare bedroom. Now that she was working from home four days a week, they'd converted the bedroom into an office.

The morning was clear and bright. She opened the shutters and let sunlight fill the room. This would be the perfect home office when she returned to Scanlon and Associates in a few weeks, after her maternity leave was over. She had been surprised that her brother-in-law Alex Scanlon had suggested the arrangement after being elected mayor of Westbury in the special election.

"I've got to leave my law practice in hands I can trust," he'd said to her. "I need someone capable and experienced. That's you, Susan."

She'd asked if any of the associates wanted to step up and run the firm. He'd told her that they were a very talented bunch, but that no one had the requisite experience. If Susan didn't accept his offer, he'd be forced to merge with Stetson and Graham. His entire team would hate that. They'd be happier working for her.

Susan knew how much Alex disliked Bill Stetson. She'd told him she'd think about his offer. He'd sweetened the deal by suggesting that she work from home unless she had to attend a client meeting or go to court. They'd settled on four days a week, and she'd accepted his offer.

Susan sat in her desk chair and spun around to survey her domain. Alex had supplied the highest quality computer monitors and printers. Her new desk was ergonomic, and her chair was the latest word in functional design. Her office phone contained features she had never heard of.

Susan sighed when her eyes fell on the dog bed along the side of the room. A shaft of sunshine traced over its empty surface. She'd purchased it for Dan when he'd been staying with them, helping with Julia. It had been time for Dan to go back home—Josh needed him more than Julia did—but Susan missed him terribly. She'd have to talk to Aaron again about getting a dog to keep her company.

Susan swung back to her desk and ran her hand over the smooth wood. She loved being a mother and taking care of Julia, but she was looking forward to returning to the practice of law.

She pulled a stack of unopened mail and computer printouts toward her. Everything pertained to the inquiries she'd made to find Josh's birth mother. So far, she'd come up empty-handed. She could understand how difficult this process must be for anyone trying to find their birth parents. She felt like she was on an emotional roller coaster, and she wasn't even dealing with a search for her own parents.

Finding Josh's original birth certificate had been encouraging. She contacted the adoption agency and found out that his birth mother had signed the papers giving Josh permission to collect her name and address if he ever came searching for her. She'd even updated her address four times during the three years following his birth. After that, the trail had grown cold.

Josh's mother had a fairly common name, which didn't help. The woman could have married after she'd had Josh and taken her husband's name, which also complicated the search.

Why had she been so conscientious in updating her information after the birth, then suddenly stopped? Four new addresses in three years told Susan that this woman's life was in a state of flux. Perhaps she was nomadic and had started a new life, far away from where Josh was born.

Susan had tackled social media sources with gusto, posting on every relevant Facebook page or group, Instagram account, or Twitter feed. She'd received lots of encouragement and helpful advice, but nothing that led to Josh's mother.

She picked up her letter opener and began slitting the envelopes in the pile of mail in front of her. All were responses from reunion registries. She skimmed the first letter until her eyes fell on the familiar words "regret to inform you," then slid it into a fat manila folder labeled "Registries—NO."

She worked her way through the letters until all were filed in the "NO" folder. She updated the spreadsheet listing the registries she'd contacted. Only two of them had not responded.

Susan squeezed her eyes shut and sent up a prayer that one of them would have the answer she was seeking. For Josh's sake, she hoped she would hear something soon.

Aaron followed Susan to the front door of Rosemont, Julia nestled in his arms. Roman and Eve trotted at his heels.

"Thanks for keeping her for us," Susan said.

"She was a perfect angel," Maggie said. "She can spend time with her grandma and grandpa anytime she wants."

"We love having Julia," John chimed in.

"It was nice to go out for breakfast, just the two of us," Susan said, smiling at her husband. "Aaron now gets one weekend a month where he's not on call at the hospital."

Julia began squirming in her father's arms, focused on the two dogs that were sitting dutifully at his feet.

Aaron squatted, holding Julia on his knee. She reached for the dogs and both responded by moving in to allow her to thrust her tiny fingers into their fur. She giggled continuously as she gently stroked first Roman and then Eve.

"She certainly loves these guys," Susan said.

"I think we may have another vet in the making." Aaron raised an eyebrow at John who was grinning widely.

"Seems like she's a natural," John replied.

"I'm sure she was depressed when Dan went home," Susan said. She turned to John. "Is she too young? Can children this age form attachments to pets?"

"Absolutely. I've seen it in my practice. It can be very special for both the child and the animal." John glanced between Aaron and Susan. "I advise parents of young children to monitor them closely with their pets to make sure that the child doesn't hurt the animal and the animal tolerates the child. Kids have jerky motions that can spook a dog. It's wise to have a crate or separate space where the dog can go to get away from the child."

"My office would be perfect for that," Susan said. She knelt next to her husband, and they both watched as Eve licked Julia's fingers. "What do you think?"

Aaron got to his feet. "I think Julia might have an affinity for dogs, but I think you're the one who really wants one."

Susan shrugged. "I won't deny that—I'd love to have a dog to keep me company. We never had one growing up, but after Dan, I don't ever want to live without one."

"Why don't you go to Forever Friends? It's early enough that it might not be too busy yet," John said. "All three of you. Just to look. Decide before you get there that you won't adopt an animal. You can see how Julia reacts to the dogs there. If she seems afraid, that'll give you your answer."

Aaron and Susan looked at each other.

Susan's eyes glistened with hope.

"I guess we could do that," Aaron said. He looked into Susan's eyes. "Can you promise me that we'd just be going to see how Julia does? We won't come home with a dog?"

Susan made an "X" across her chest. "Cross my heart and hope to die."

Julia cooed happily.

"There—you see? Julia wants to go to Forever Friends, too."

"We don't have anything else to do this morning and we've got a couple of hours before nap time, so we could stop on the way home," Aaron said.

Susan pulled the front door open and stepped out into the mid-morning sun.

Aaron and Julia proceeded down the steps to the car. Aaron began buckling Julia into her car seat. Susan turned back to John and Maggie and gave them a silent thumbs-up.

"Have fun," Maggie called.

Susan mouthed the words "I'll let you know" and raced down the steps to join her family.

Chapter 17

Aaron turned to Susan as they pulled into the lot of Forever Friends. "We're not coming home with a dog today, agreed?"

"Of course not. We're just here to see how Julia reacts." She pointed to the clock on the dashboard. "We've only got an hour before she needs to go down for her nap. Now that I've finally gotten her onto a schedule, I'm not going to jeopardize that. We'll be in and out of here in no time."

Aaron parked the car and leaned over to kiss her. "Got any plans for us for nap time?"

Susan's eyes twinkled. "I just might."

They unhooked Julia from her car seat and debated strapping her into her stroller. In the end, Aaron decided to carry her. They entered the lobby of Forever Friends and followed the sign that directed them toward the dog pens.

The shelter was already bustling on this clear Saturday morning. Dogs were barking and pacing at the front of their cages, reacting to visitors on the other side of their enclosures.

Julia turned wide eyes on the animals and people around her but didn't fuss.

They walked up and down the rows, looking at the dogs. Aaron stopped in front of the cage of a golden retriever. The posted information reported that the dog had been found wandering the streets. He was good with other animals and was thought to be two years old. The dog sat patiently, wagging his tail slowly along the concrete floor and keeping his eyes locked on Aaron.

Susan checked her watch. "We really should get going. It's almost time for Julia's nap. We'll be late putting her down as it is."

Aaron turned his eyes to hers.

"We've accomplished what we wanted to," Susan gestured to Julia. "She's not scared of dogs. She'll be fine when we do get one."

He cleared his throat. "Maybe we should take this boy to the get-acquainted area."

"Oh, my gosh, Mr. We're-Not-Getting-a-Dog-Today." She leaned over and hugged him. "You're a complete softie."

"What do you think?" Aaron pointed to the pen.

"He's very sweet. And gorgeous. He won't be up for adoption long."

"That's what I think," Aaron said. "If we want him, we have to decide now."

Susan looked into her husband's eyes. "You really like him, don't you?" Aaron nodded.

Julia began to whimper.

"We'd better go, before she starts to wail," Susan said.

"What do you think of the doggy, Julia?" Aaron held her out to the pen.

Julia stuck a finger through the wire grid, and Cooper licked it. Julia chuckled.

"You see," Aaron said. "It's like it was with Dan. This dog has special powers."

Susan regarded her daughter. The dog had a calming effect on Julia. There was no denying it.

"Why not?" Susan said. "We're here. We may as well see about"—she bent to read his information card—"Cooper. Julia can take a later nap for one day."

Aaron signaled to the technician coming down the hallway. "Can we take this boy to the get-acquainted pen?"

"Sure," the young man said. He pulled a key from the ring on his belt and unlocked the cage. He slipped a leash on Cooper and led them to a private room with a window in the door.

"Take all the time you need," he said. "When you're ready, signal to me from this window. If you want to take this guy home," he said, ruffling the fur by Cooper's ears, "I'll take you to the adoption area. If not, I'll take him back to his pen."

"Thank you," Susan said as the technician closed the door.

Julia beamed at the dog with the fluffy tail that seemed to wag perpetually. She waved her arms with happy abandon, trying to reach Cooper.

Aaron leaned toward him, and Julia grasped a handful of Cooper's fur at the back of his neck.

"Careful—" Susan began. "We have to be gentle with the doggy."

Cooper turned his head and licked Julia's arm.

Julia let out peals of laughter.

Susan shot Aaron a glance as Julia continued to tug at Cooper's fur and he good-naturedly wagged his tail. "What do you think?"

Aaron gave her thumbs-up.

Julia released Cooper and snuggled into Aaron's shoulder.

Cooper circled three times and lay down at Aaron's feet.

Susan and Aaron looked at each other in surprise.

"He's the one," Susan said. "We're meant to have him."

Aaron nodded his agreement. "Are we prepared to take him with us, right now?"

"I've still got Dan's bed and water bowl. All we'll need is a collar, leash, and food."

"Plus, toys and treats," Aaron said. "I can go to the store to get those."

"I'll bet we can get a certain veterinarian to make a house call to check him out." Susan grinned at Aaron. "Let's do this!"

Aaron stepped to the door as the technician pulled it open. David Wheeler was on his heels.

"We'll take him," Aaron said.

David cut him off. "I'm sorry," he said, "but Cooper's already been adopted. His pen was supposed to have been posted with an 'Already Found My Forever Home' sign." David glared at the technician.

"We've got other dogs this size," the technician said. "A couple of Labs and a German shepherd. Would you like me to bring those in to you? One at a time?"

Julia began to whimper.

Susan turned to her husband.

"No." He stated curtly, shifting Julia to the other shoulder. "We'd better get her home."

"I'm really sorry," David said. "Why don't you come back tomorrow? We get new dogs in all the time."

Aaron strode past him, then turned back. He forced himself to take a deep breath. "It's not your fault," he said. "We really weren't in the market to get a dog today, anyway."

Julia began to cry.

"This guy had a special calming influence on Julia, but we'll find another dog. Don't worry about it." Susan tilted her head to one side. "You're David Wheeler, aren't you? You have a therapy dog that you take to the hospitals?"

"Yes. Dodger."

"We met when Nicole had her kidney transplant. I'm her half-sister."

"I thought you looked familiar." David swallowed hard. "You're Maggie's daughter, aren't you?"

"I am. Susan Scanlon." She held out her hand and they shook.

"Let me know when you come back to find another dog. I'll help you pick out a good one."

"Thank you, David," Susan said. "Don't worry about us. I'm glad that this guy," she pointed to Cooper, "is going to a good home, even if it isn't ours."

Chapter 18

Maggie pulled into the cold garage shortly after noon and was surprised to find John's car still there. He had Saturday afternoon appointments at Westbury Animal Hospital. She gathered her grocery sacks from the back of her car and hurried into the kitchen, depositing them on the counter.

Eve and Roman didn't greet her at the door. Something was definitely amiss. Putting her purchases away could wait. Maggie pushed through the kitchen door. John had looked flushed after Susan and Aaron left this morning. What if he was sick?

She passed the dining room and rounded the corner to the living room. She halted in her tracks at the sight in front of her. Four rows of red and green totes were stacked to the nine-foot ceiling.

She walked over to the totes, peering at the neat labels she had made the year before with her label maker. Her family teased her about her organizational proclivities but looking at this towering array of totes proved the usefulness of her habit. Thanks to these labels, she knew what was in each one: garlands, Santas, angels, ornaments, and lights—tote after tote of lights.

"John?" she called as she raced up the stairs to the second floor.

He didn't answer.

"JOHN!" she called again from the second-floor hallway.

Eve and Roman began to bark in response.

All three of them were in the attic.

Maggie climbed the steep steps to the third floor where she found her husband moving additional red and green totes to an area at the top of the stairs. Eve and Roman pranced at his feet. Even they sensed that John was up to something unusual.

"What in the world?" Maggie exclaimed as she stepped off the top step into the attic.

John spun around, startled by the sound of her voice. He put a hand on his chest. "I didn't hear you come in," he said.

Maggie picked her way carefully through the decades of dusty and discarded treasures stored in Rosemont's attic to come to his side. She slipped her arms around his waist and kissed him. "What's gotten into you? Why in the world did you drag all of those Christmas decorations downstairs? We're not hosting anything this year. Mike and Amy and the girls aren't coming from California. I thought we decided to hang a wreath on the front door and call it good."

"That was my idea and you agreed to it, but I think you've been a bit blue after the quiet Thanksgiving we spent with Susan and Aaron."

Maggie shrugged. "I love entertaining, having my friends and family in my home. I won't deny it. But there's no point in going to all the effort to decorate just for us."

He drew her close to him. "I heard you whispering to the house that you were sorry she wouldn't be getting dressed up this year."

Maggie turned her face into his shoulder. "I didn't know you heard."

"I'm aware that you talk to Rosemont from time to time." He rocked back on his heels to look at her. "It's like this house has feelings. When my afternoon appointments canceled, I decided to come home and bring down all of the decorations. To surprise you."

Maggie raised an eyebrow.

"You said yourself that we don't have anything else on the schedule this weekend, other than church tomorrow morning. Why don't we go out now and get ourselves the biggest Christmas tree we can find? We can pick up a pizza at Tomascino's on the way home. I'll light a fire and we'll eat pizza and decorate the tree."

"I can only think of one thing I'd like more." Maggie slid her arms around his neck. "This is a very romantic idea."

"I'll put lights up outside tomorrow." He pressed his cheek against hers.

"I'll decorate the inside while you do that." She trailed kisses along his neck.

"We'll work until dinnertime tomorrow. Whatever we get done before then will be it. I'll put the totes back in the attic before we eat."

"Brilliant," she said, making her way to his earlobe. "Let's get going. I've got one stop in mind—on the second floor—before we leave here."

"I love the sound of that," John said, ushering her down the stairs and across the hallway to their bedroom.

Later that night, as the last embers of the fading fire glowed in the grate, John climbed the ladder and placed the star on top of the tree.

"It's perfect." Maggie clasped her hands as she stepped back to admire their handiwork. "Just perfect. I can't believe we got it all done in one evening."

John descended the ladder as the grandfather clock struck one. He and Maggie looked at each other.

"I didn't realize it had gotten so late," Maggie said. "You got up at four. You must be exhausted."

John put his arm across her shoulder as they stood and looked at the tree. "I'm beat, but this was a lot of fun. I like doing this—just the two of us."

"Me, too." She turned to him and her eyes were moist. "I feel so much happier now that we have a tree. It feels like Christmas. Thank you so much for making this happen, John."

"If you're happy with it, I'm thrilled." He whistled to wake the dogs, who were sleeping in front of the fire. "I think it's time we all headed to bed."

She pulled his face to hers and kissed him, deeply, before all four of them went upstairs.

Chapter 19

Sunday tore her eyes from the papers spread in front of her and looked at Lyla, standing in the open door to her office.

Lyla pointed to Sunday's desk. "You're staying late again? What're you working on?"

"I've been going over Hector Martin's notes."

"They're that interesting?"

Sunday shrugged one shoulder. "They are to me."

"But every night this week? You need to get a life. You'll never meet Mr. Right if you're holed up in this office all the time."

Sunday swallowed the retort on her lips. She loved her friend and wasn't going to point out that Lyla—a spinster in her early fifties—had no room to talk on the subject of relationships.

"I know. It's just that I never have time during the day to work on this. I'm almost done."

Lyla approached Sunday's desk. "What exactly are you doing?"

Sunday stood abruptly and came around the desk to meet her friend. "Making notes—comparing his list to the inventory I prepared before we transferred the books to the secure room."

"And that has to be done in such a hurry?"

Sunday looked into the hallway to make sure that no one could overhear. "I don't know yet."

"What do you mean?"

Sunday took a deep breath and lowered her voice. "I'm finding some— irregularities."

"Irregularities? Care to fill me in?"

"Not yet. I need to get through all of this first." Sunday swept her hand back toward her desk.

"Do you need help?"

"No, but thank you." She took Lyla's elbow. "Don't say anything about what I'm doing, okay?"

"All right."

"Does anyone else know that you gave me a copy of Hector's notes?"

"No."

"Good. Let's keep it our secret."

"Should I be worried about something?"

"Maybe. I don't know yet. Let me finish up. I should be done in the next couple of weeks."

Lyla nodded and headed toward the door, then turned back. "You're working on this after hours so that no one knows what you're doing, aren't you?"

Sunday pursed her lips.

Lyla shivered involuntarily. "Gosh—now you've got me spooked. The last time we had any drama around here was when one of the student staff members ate the head librarian's leftovers."

Sunday laughed. "I remember. The poor kid thought someone had abandoned them."

"Or so he said."

"He was hungry. And probably broke," Sunday said. "I remember my student days. I didn't think the head should have made such a stink about it."

"I guess leftovers from Stuart's Steakhouse were a big deal to him."

Sunday smiled at Lyla. "Don't you have choir rehearsal tonight?"

Lyla nodded. "We're working on our Christmas Eve music. It's going to be spectacular."

"You'd better get going. See you tomorrow."

Lyla continued to the door. "Don't stay too late," she admonished.

Sunday placed her hands on her hips and stretched her back. She was tired but needed to press on. Hector's notes about his collection were a fascinating historical record, and she was enjoying reading them. Later, when time permitted, she would scan his notes into the computer and index them.

Lyla had run a total of what Hector had paid to acquire his collection over a period of forty years. It had come to just over $800,000. Sunday could only guess what it would be worth today: millions and probably tens of millions. Enough to tempt someone with criminal intent. Finding the thief—or thieves—would be a challenge. Her focus at the moment, however, was on comparing Hector's notes to her recent inventory.

Sunday sat back down at her desk. She'd already found six volumes listed in Hector's notes that she had not cataloged in her inventory. They were among the most expensive books that Hector had acquired, and a quick Google search told her that all of them would be extremely valuable in today's market.

She'd checked the secure room, just in case she'd missed them somehow when she was taking inventory. None of the six were in place on the shelves. If they had been included in the books that Hector had donated, they weren't part of the collection now.

Sunday slid her ruler to the next line on Hector's notes, then searched for the corresponding item on her inventory. She found the volume on her computer, made a checkmark on her copy of Hector's notes, and moved the ruler down the page.

Sunday didn't know what she was going to do with this information when she was done with her analysis, but identifying any missing volumes was the place to start.

※

Sunday looked at the older man with the precise haircut who stood in her doorway. "Thank you for making time to attend tonight's meeting, Professor Plume," she said. "I know it's finals, and you must be up to your eyeballs in grading."

Anthony nodded in agreement. "I am up to my eyeballs, as you say, but I'm also happy to be here," he said. "My doctoral dissertation was on nineteenth- and early-twentieth-century authors and poets. Highpointe's got significant holdings in those categories."

Sunday nodded.

"I've used some of our volumes in my research for an article I just published."

She came around the side of her desk and motioned for him to follow her down the corridor. "I'd love to read it."

"I'll get you a copy." He matched her brisk pace. "I think Maggie wants you to have someone on your committee with the specialized expertise that

Hector Martin's gift requires. She knows that you're stretched very thin over here and you could use some help evaluating and managing the collection."

Sunday stopped short outside of a meeting room at the end of the hall. The aroma of strong coffee and the sound of jovial conversation spilled out into the hallway.

She turned to Anthony. "I'll be glad for any assistance you can provide. If you're in town over the holiday break, I'd love to give you an in-depth tour of the collection."

"I'll be going to my sister's home outside of London," Anthony said. "May I have a raincheck?"

"Of course. Any time that's convenient for you." She followed Anthony into the room and stepped to the whiteboard. She tapped it with the cap of a marking pen. "All right, everyone. It's time to get started."

She moved to her chair at one of the rectangular tables set up in a large square. "Please take your seats."

The group of people at the back of the room milling around a table laden with Christmas cookies and a large urn of coffee reluctantly ended their conversations and took seats at the tables.

"Thank you for coming to this meeting of the Friends of the Library," Sunday said. "I know this time of year is very busy for everyone, and I appreciate your continuing support."

She looked at the polite faces turned to hers. "First, I'd like to introduce all of you to our newest member of the committee." She pointed to Anthony and gestured for him to stand. "Professor Anthony Plume is the academic dean of English and Literature. He's an expert on a large portion of the holdings in our rare book collection. His input will be invaluable to us in our management of the collection."

A polite smattering of applause skittered around the room.

"Would you like to say a few words?" Sunday asked Anthony.

He rose from his chair. "I'm delighted to be here," he said. "Ms. Sloan—and all of you—have done a wonderful thing by making the rare book room a reality. I'm looking forward to working with you in the future."

He took his seat and Sunday continued. "As you know, we finished moving our collection into the secure rare book room in March. I've been working—as time permits—on inventorying our holdings and cataloging everything."

"Are you still at it?" asked a retired librarian from the Westbury Public Library. "I would have thought you'd be done by now." He removed his glasses and polished them with his handkerchief.

"I'm afraid I am," Sunday said, swallowing hard to hide her irritation. "It takes a lot of painstaking research to figure out what we have, which edition of a book is on our shelves. Each publisher followed different conventions, and there are often minuscule differences between printings. Other factors come into play, too. The analysis can't be rushed. And once I've ascertained which edition we have, I have to do more research to find today's market value of the item."

"I had no idea it was so complicated," said a woman who had been named fourth-grade teacher of the year for two years running. "This is fascinating. Can you give us some examples?"

"If you're really interested, I'll make a presentation on the topic at our first quarterly meeting next year."

Every head in front of her nodded in agreement.

"I'd be delighted to do that," she said. "For now, I'll give you this to think about—our collection has a copy of the first printing of *Gone with the Wind*. It's in a special display case in the Hazel Harrington room. Our copy is in very good condition and is probably worth at least five thousand dollars."

There was a collective intake of breath from those seated around the table.

"As you know, the book was a bestseller right away. Additional printings and Book-of-the-Month-Club editions were turned out immediately. They look almost identical to the first edition, but they're only worth a few hundred dollars. There are thousands of them out there in used bookstores. You may think you've made a real find by checking the copyright page and seeing the date of printing as 1936. If it's in May of 1936, you've got a valuable first edition. If it's June of 1936, you don't."

"We also have a first edition of *On the Origin of Species*. There's a group at Cambridge University in England that authenticates all first editions. I'll talk about that process, too."

The room was quiet as all eyes were on her. Sunday felt her pulse race. She loved talking about books to fellow bibliophiles.

"We've got lots to look forward to in the New Year," she said. "For now, I'd like to thank you for everything you've done for the library and for the support and friendship you've extended to me." She drew a deep breath. "And now, I'd like to read you a story. We all love being read to, don't we?"

Heads bobbed in unison.

"We have a signed original of *How the Grinch Stole Christmas!* in our collection." She picked up the volume, turned carefully to the first page, and began. "Every Who down in Who-ville liked Christmas a lot—"

Chapter 20

Lyla threaded her way through the students piling out of class until she caught up to the tall young man loping toward the exit to the building.

"Josh," she called.

He turned around and smiled when he spotted her.

"Hi," he said, stepping out of the sea of students.

"I missed class last week. Bad cold," Lyla said.

"I wondered why you weren't there. Feeling better?"

Lyla nodded. "I wanted to see how you're doing before everyone scatters for winter break."

"Okay," Josh replied. "I got caught up in all my classes and managed to pass everything—without destroying my GPA."

"That's terrific. You should be proud of that," Lyla said. "What are your plans for the holidays?"

"I'm headed to Atlanta to go through my parents' house and put it on the market."

"That's a big step. Was it your childhood home?"

"Yes. I grew up in that house."

"Are you sure you want to sell it? Maybe you'd like to return home when you graduate?"

He shook his head. "I'm not living in Atlanta."

"Do you know where you want to go when you graduate?"

"Actually, I'd like to stay right here. In Westbury."

Lyla's pulse quickened. That would figure nicely into her plans. "That would be ideal!"

He raised an eyebrow at her.

"I've got someone I'd like you to meet."

"Oh?"

"She—she's a colleague of mine. I think the two of you would hit it off."

"I don't know about that." Josh held up his hand. "I'm not looking for anybody right now."

Lyla tilted her head to one side. "What's the harm in meeting her? What've you got to lose?"

Josh paused.

Lyla jumped in. "I'll set up an introduction. Coffee? When do you leave?"

"First thing in the morning."

"When do you get back?" Lyla pressed on.

"Right after the New Year."

"That'll be perfect. I think the two of you are really going to like each other." Her eyes twinkled. "What a lovely way to start the New Year."

Josh rolled his eyes and grinned in spite of himself. "You're quite a salesperson."

"Pull out your phone and send me a text. That way I'll have your number, and I can get this set up."

Josh did as she requested. "I'd better get going. I've got a lot to do before I leave."

"Have a nice holiday." Lyla's voice became soft. "This will be the first Christmas without your parents. That'll be hard."

Josh studied his shoes and nodded.

"Any luck finding your birth mother?"

He shook his head. "Not yet, but we're still looking."

"Good." Lyla reached out her hand and squeezed his elbow. "I hope you find her soon."

Josh swallowed hard. "Thank you. And thanks for being concerned about me. Have a Merry Christmas."

"I will," Lyla said. "Next year will be a good year for you. Just wait and see."

"Are you feeling better?" Sunday approached her friend in the library break room.

Lyla nodded. "The antibiotics kicked in over the weekend. I even went to my painting class this morning." She pointed to the empty chair on the other side of the table. "Do you have time to sit and talk for a minute?"

Sunday pulled out the chair. "I guess. I'm so far behind on everything that a few minutes won't make a difference."

"Are you still working on"—Lyla bent across the table and lowered her voice so that the other staff members taking their lunch breaks couldn't overhear their conversation—"that comparison?"

Sunday pursed her lips and nodded imperceptibly.

"When will you be done?"

"Soon. Now that the students will be gone on break, I'll have more time. I'll finish by the end of the year."

"Are you going anywhere for the holidays?"

A shadow passed across Sunday's face. Where would she go?

"I'm staying right here. I'm looking forward to getting caught up."

Lyla leaned back in her chair. "What about Christmas?"

Sunday shrugged. "I'm not big on Christmas."

"I understand. I feel the same way."

"It can be a pretty lonely day, if you don't have family."

"I usually stay at home and do something productive. Clean out a closet or organize my spices." Lyla heaved a sigh. "Pathetic, actually."

"Don't you have friends who invite you over?"

"I do, but it makes it worse for me—to be with these close-knit families. I'm a third wheel." She looked at Sunday. "Do you know what I mean?"

"Yes. I go to a matinee movie on Christmas," Sunday said. "I hardly ever go to the movies and good ones come out at Christmas, so that makes it special."

"What a stellar idea," Lyla said. "Much more fun than organizing my broom closet."

Sunday smiled at her friend. "Why don't we go together this year? Would you be interested?"

A smile played at the corners of Lyla's lips. "Sounds fun. Let's get something to eat after. I'll call around to find out who's open. My treat."

"Deal," Sunday said. "I'll pay for the movie tickets."

"This'll be great." Lyla sat up straighter. "What about Christmas Eve? What will you do?"

Sunday's eyes telegraphed sadness. "I treat it like any other night."

"I sing at two services on Christmas Eve. They're beautiful. I'd love for you to come to one or both."

Sunday's eyes grew moist. She hadn't been to church since that fateful Christmas Eve during her college years when she'd lost both of her parents in a car wreck on an icy road. She'd tried to go to church last Christmas Eve and had sat in her car in the church parking lot, her mind full of angry recriminations against God for taking such wonderful people from her—from the world. She'd wanted to move past her anger and grief; she'd wanted to partake in the joyous service with an open heart. Instead, she'd restarted her engine and driven home.

"Or none. Whatever you want," Lyla stammered. "I thought you might enjoy—"

"I'll—I'll go to both services," Sunday was surprised to hear herself say.

Lyla rocked back in her chair and beamed. "Then it's settled." She looked at her friend. "Since you're here, I've got something else to talk to you about."

Sunday brushed her hand across her eyes. "What's that?"

"You're not seeing anyone, are you?"

"No. Why?" Sunday cocked her head to one side. "What are you up to?"

"I'm not up to anything," Lyla smiled sheepishly. "I just have someone I think you should meet."

"I'm not in the market—"

"Oh, for Pete's sake. You'd love to meet someone, and you know it."

Sunday couldn't suppress a smile. "So who is this guy? How do you know him?"

"He was a student in that painting class I took."

"A student? I'm too old for a student."

"A graduate student, and I think you're about the same age. I can't tell. He may be a year or two younger, but who cares?"

"That's true. So, what makes you think we'd be interested in each other?"

"I don't know, exactly. He's a very nice young man, and I sense that the two of you have a lot in common." Lyla paused and chose her words. "From the first time I talked to him, I thought, 'Here's the guy for Sunday.'"

Sunday became serious. "When do you want us to meet?"

"He's gone home for the holiday. To Atlanta. Both of his parents died this year, and he's closing up his family home."

A shiver ran down Sunday's spine. They did have something in common.

"He'll be back after the New Year. I thought I'd set up a meeting at a coffee shop before the next semester starts."

Sunday cleared her throat. "That'd be fine."

"Terrific!" Lyla's grin spread. "Mark my words, Sunday Sloan, next year will be a good year for you!"

Dan bounded up the steps as Susan opened the front door. Julia squirmed against her hip, trying to get down to play with her canine friend.

"She remembers him," Josh said as he followed Dan through the door.

"She certainly does." Susan smiled as she shut the door and squatted to let Julia and Dan say hello to each other.

"Thank you for agreeing to take him," Josh said. "Three weeks is a long time to leave him at a kennel."

"I wouldn't hear of it," Susan said, ruffling the fur in back of Dan's ears. "This guy is always welcome here."

"I thought you were going to get a new dog."

"We almost did," Susan replied. "We picked one out at Forever Friends, but they'd messed up his paperwork and he'd already been adopted."

"That's a shame," Josh said.

"We'll find another one." Susan stood. "After the holidays."

"I'm glad," Josh said. "Any more word on—my mom?"

Susan shook her head. "I'm still waiting to hear from some of the registries. Most of them are staffed by volunteers, so I don't expect to hear anything more until after the holidays."

Josh dipped his head.

"We've still got a lot of avenues to pursue," Susan touched his arm. "Don't get discouraged."

"Do you think we'll find her?"

Susan swallowed hard. "I do." *I hope we do*, she thought. "Keep the faith."

"I will."

"You're wrapping up your dad's estate while you're home, aren't you?"

"That's my plan."

"Do you have a lawyer helping you?"

"Yes. My dad's attorney."

"Good. And if you have any questions about anything that the lawyer recommends—if there's anything you don't understand—call me. Okay?"

"I will. Thank you. And thanks for taking care of this guy." He bent and put an arm around the big dog's neck and patted his back. "You be a good boy, like last time, okay?"

Dan licked his master's face.

"Don't worry about a thing here," Susan said. "I'll be thinking about you."

Josh pulled the door open. "This will be a special year for you, with Julia's first Christmas."

"It sure will."

"Your mom is so excited. You should see the number of Amazon boxes that arrived at her office with gifts for Julia."

Susan laughed. "That would be my mother!"

"She's been great to me. You all have." He stepped over the threshold toward his car. "Merry Christmas, Susan."

Chapter 21

"Something smells good!" Frank closed the back door behind him and followed the scent of baking into the kitchen.

Loretta was bending over the oven, removing a tray of cookies.

Marissa and Nicole were at the kitchen island. Five-year-old Nicole was carefully sprinkling red sugar onto iced cookies, while Marissa, the middle-schooler, struggled to pipe a decorative border with an icing bag. Sean, her oldest, was cracking eggs into a bowl at the sink.

Sally, Snowball, and Daisy kept watch at their feet, scooping up any dropped bits of food before they hit the floor. Sally reluctantly abandoned her post to halfheartedly greet her master, keeping one eye on the commotion in the kitchen.

"Good girl." Frank gave her ears a quick massage, noticing that her fur was matted with something sticky and blue. "What in the ... ?" He rubbed his fingers together. "This is icing."

Sally licked his fingers clean, then turned her attention to the other two dogs.

"Okay—you can go back."

Sally raised her eyes to his. "Go on," he said, "I know I'm not as interesting as food."

His border collie mix rejoined the other dogs in their search for crumbs.

"What've we got here?" Frank took off his coat and tossed it on a chair. He stood behind the island.

"Daddy!" Nicole said, reaching for him with red-sugar-stained hands.

She'd started calling him that over the summer and the name still brought tears that he blinked rapidly to control. He'd given up on being a father—until he'd married Loretta. Frank leaned in and accepted her hug. A year ago, he would have been more concerned about ruining his custom-made shirt. Now with the family he'd been aching for his whole life, he couldn't have cared less.

"What're you all doing in here?" He looked around the kitchen. Every surface was covered with Christmas cookies in various stages of completion. "You must have at least a hundred cookies." He reached across the island to pick up an angel that Marissa had just finished piping with white icing.

"A hundred and eighty," Loretta said, dropping the hot cookie sheet on a trivet and smiling at him. "You can have *one*"—she extended a stern index finger to him and her children—"but that's it."

"What're you going to do with all of these?"

"We're giving 'em to our friends and neighbors," Marissa said through a mouthful of cookie. She pointed up and down the counter. "We've made all of these this afternoon."

"Wow. You've been busy." Frank bit an iced wing off the angel. "This is delicious, too." He turned to Loretta. "Aren't we going to keep any for us?"

"That's what I asked," said Sean, grabbing a chocolate-sprinkled reindeer. "There's plenty here. We shouldn't give them all away."

Frank and Sean turned hopeful eyes to Loretta.

"We'll keep the ones that break," she said. "And don't you dare break any on purpose," she added, fixing Sean with her stare.

"This is awfully nice of you, honey," Frank said, pride evident in his voice.

"It's a Westbury Christmas Eve tradition," Loretta said. "You know that." She raised an eyebrow at him.

He had no idea, but then he'd never been part of the fabric of this warmhearted community until he'd met Loretta. He smiled at her and nodded to cover up his ignorance. "You two have made them look beautiful," he said to Nicole and Marissa. "Laura doesn't have better-looking cookies in her bakery."

Nicole wriggled with happiness and almost slipped off the chair she was standing on. Frank reached out to steady her.

Loretta stepped back to survey the cookies lined up on cooling racks. She brushed damp tendrils of hair from her temples and leaned against Frank. "I think we've got enough," she said.

"What about this batch?" Sean lifted the spoon from the bowl where he was mixing batter for more cookies.

Loretta sighed heavily. "I don't think I've got another batch in me. I need to get off my feet."

Frank helped her to a chair at the kitchen table.

"We can save that dough until tomorrow. We'll bake them in the morning."

Sean raised a worried eyebrow at his mother. "Okay…" he said as he put the dough into the refrigerator.

"Why don't you go lie down?" Frank asked. "I can help here."

Loretta looked up at Marissa. "Can you work with your brother and sister—and Frank—to finish up?"

Marissa nodded solemnly.

"We need a dozen plates with an assortment of cookies."

"I know, Mom." Marissa gestured to the decorative plates they'd found together at a Celebrations pre-Thanksgiving sale. "And I know how to put them in the cellophane bags."

"What about the ribbons and tags?" Loretta asked as she got wearily to her feet.

"I know how to do that, too."

Loretta edged toward the kitchen island. "I can help Sean and Nicole decorate." She teetered on her feet.

"You don't look so good, Mom," Sean said. "We can do this."

Frank put his arm around Loretta's waist. "Why don't you lie down for a bit?" He steered her out of the kitchen. "I'll make sure that everything's done and cleaned up. Take a nap and you can check on things when you wake up."

"I love you, Frank Haynes." Loretta placed her palm on the side of his face and leaned in to kiss him. "I don't know why I'm so tired lately."

"Maybe because you've taken on too much." Frank's lips set into a thin line. It was his stupid, selfish mistakes that had caused this. "I'm sorry that you're bearing the brunt of running Haynes Enterprises."

"That's just it," Loretta said, stepping into their bedroom. "I'm not doing anything more than I've done in the past. I don't know what's wrong with me." She kicked off her shoes and sank down on the bed.

Frank knelt and brushed the hair back from her forehead. "I didn't want the kids to hear me say this, but you're not yourself, Loretta. I'm—I'm concerned that something's wrong."

She shook her head. "I'm probably just coming down with something. I think the kids are all getting colds. I'm fine, Frank. Don't worry."

He wasn't convinced. "If you're still feeling this way after the holidays, will you go see the doctor?"

"If it'll make you feel better—"

"It will." He got up and tucked the covers around her.

"Then yes. But I'm sure I'll be fine by then." She turned to curl up on her side. "You'd better get back to the kids."

He planted a soft kiss on her temple and turned to go.

"And Frank," she called. "Don't you dare eat those cookies. They're for our friends."

Frank opened his mouth to reply but couldn't find words. Tears pricked the back of his eyes. He loved the idea of giving to their friends and neighbors. For the first time in his life, he felt like he belonged.

He cleared his throat. "Don't worry about a thing," he said. "I'll make sure you're proud of the Haynes family."

Frank motioned for David to follow him into the kitchen. "Thanks for stopping by so early," he said.

"No problem," David said. "I'm happy to help."

"Loretta and the kids worked on these cookie trays all day yesterday." He pointed to a dozen plates of cookies sheathed in cellophane and tied with red velvet ribbons.

"They look good," David said, leaning over to inspect the contents of one of the delicious-smelling packages.

"The tags tell you who they go to," Frank said. "You know all of these people, of course."

"You want me to deliver them?"

"Yes. Loretta said it's a Christmas Eve tradition in Westbury, and she wants to participate. She was going to drop them off today, but she's not feeling well. The kids are all coming down with colds, so I don't think they should be in and out of the car delivering cookies with me. And I don't want to leave them home alone with Loretta. She needs to get her rest without worrying about the kids."

"It'll be fun," David said.

"There's a plate for you and your mom, too," Frank said.

A smile spread across David's face.

Frank gestured to a paper lunch sack at the end of the counter. "And there's a few extra in there for the delivery boy."

David's smiled widened. "Thanks, Frank. Be sure to tell Loretta I really appreciate these." He held up the bag.

"I will. Now—let's get these out to your car."

David began placing the wrapped plates along his arm. Frank followed suit.

"How's Cooper doing?" Frank asked.

"He's great. You should see Dodger with him. They're the best of friends."

"Have you found out any more about becoming a service dog trainer?"

"There's a school in California I'm interested in. It's a three-year program. You start out working there first. Doing a lot of the same stuff I do now at Forever Friends."

"That sounds good."

"I'll be able to bring Dodger with me, so I like that. I wouldn't leave him for three years."

"No. I can see that."

"I don't think they'll take Cooper into the program," David said. "They have their own breeding program for animals that they'll later train."

"I wondered about that," Frank said. "Makes sense."

David opened the back door of his car and they began placing the cookie plates on the floor.

"What about Cooper? Will you take him with you, too?"

"I wanted to talk to you about him," David said, straightening to look Frank in the eye. "I have another plan for Cooper." David explained what he had in mind.

Frank clapped David on the back. "I think that's the best idea you've had yet."

"You don't mind?"

"Not in the least. When do you plan to do this?"

"I'm not sure."

"Can I make a suggestion?"

David nodded and leaned in, smiling as Frank laid out a terrific plan.

David stamped his feet against the cold while he waited for someone to answer the door. This was his second-to-last stop, with Cooper in tow, and he was anxious to complete his mission.

The overhead light on the porch came on and Sam Torres threw the door open.

"David!" the handyman exclaimed, reaching for the arm of the young man. He'd become very fond of the boy when David had worked as his assistant. "Come on in. Get out of the cold."

"I can't," David said. "My car's running. I just stopped by to deliver these." He thrust a plate of cookies into Sam's hands. "They're from Frank and Loretta and the kids."

"That's awfully nice of them," Sam said. "Joan dropped off cinnamon rolls to them this morning. I guess they're all sick."

David nodded. "Colds."

Sam peered into the driveway. "Is that Dodger you've got with you? Why don't you shut off your car and bring him in. I know Joan would love to see you. Are you hungry?"

David put an arm around the older man's shoulder in a half hug. After William Wheeler's suicide, Sam had stepped into David's life—another father figure that the boy had desperately needed back then. "It's not Dodger. He's a new dog—Cooper."

Sam raised an eyebrow. "Did you get a new dog? Is Dodger all right?" he asked with a note of alarm.

"Dodger's fine. I left him home with Mom tonight. I rescued Cooper from Forever Friends, but I'm not keeping him."

Sam looked at David. "You're taking him back to the shelter? On Christmas Eve? Doesn't he get along with Dodger?"

"It's not that. Cooper's a great dog." He turned to look at the animal sitting in the front seat, waiting patiently for his return. "Remarkable, actually. That's why I'm giving him away—to Susan and Aaron Scanlon. For Julia."

"Do they want a dog?"

"They do. And Cooper is perfect for them. It's a long story, but Cooper has the ability to calm Julia. I've got cookies to drop off at Susan's, so I'm going to give them Cooper, too. As a surprise."

"That's a nice surprise. I'll never forget the Christmas I got my first dog," Sam said. "I was ten."

"I think they'll be happy about it," David said.

"Your dad would be very proud of you. He was a kind man, and so are you."

David turned his face aside and swallowed hard. Cooper emitted a sharp bark.

"I'm going to their house as soon as I leave here."

"You know, Joan just came from Rosemont. She was delivering cinnamon rolls. I think she said that Susan and her family are at Maggie's for Christmas Eve." Sam rocked back on his heels. "Joan," he called. "Come say hello to David."

"I was wondering who was at the door." Joan's sweet voice preceded her to the entryway.

"David," she said, sweeping him into a hug. "I'm so glad to see you! How are you and your mother doing?"

"Fine, Mrs. Torres," David said.

"Good." Joan handed him an aluminum pan covered with foil. "These are for your breakfast in the morning. Pop them in the oven at three twenty-five for ten minutes and then drizzle this over them." She gestured to the Ziploc bag of thick white icing that rested on top of the foil. "You should have plenty."

David grinned. "Thank you. These smell wonderful."

"Just took them out of the oven half an hour ago," Joan said.

"David dropped these off," Sam lifted the plate of cookies he was holding. "He's making deliveries for Frank and Loretta."

"How nice," Joan said.

"He was on his way to Susan's. Didn't you say that her family is at Rosemont?"

"They are."

"That's great." David said. "I have cookies for Maggie and John, too. That'll be my last stop."

"You should see John. He's so excited to have Julia with them on Christmas Eve. That man is positively smitten with her," Joan said.

Sam and Joan put their arms around each other's waists and smiled at David.

"Merry Christmas, son," Sam said.

"I'd better be on my way," David said. "Merry Christmas."

"You've got a big job to do, boy." David put a hand under the golden retriever's muzzle and lifted it until their eyes met. "I love you. This isn't because I don't love you. It's because you've got a mission."

Cooper winked his left eye.

David raised his eyebrows. "You understand me, don't you, boy?"

Cooper swept his tail along the passenger seat.

David drew in a deep breath and held it. He knew he was doing the right thing, but that didn't make it any easier. He sighed heavily and forced himself into motion, grasping Cooper's leash and reaching into the backseat for the last two cookie plates before they got out of the car. They mounted the stone steps to Rosemont as the sun headed for the horizon.

David brought the iron lion's head doorknocker down onto its base, a resounding crack echoing through the still night. Cooper sat patiently at his side.

They waited as the sound of a crying baby on the other side of the door grew louder. John opened the door, bouncing an insoluble Julia in front of him.

"David," he said, raising his voice to be heard. "Nice to see you. Come in."

David stepped inside, tugging on Cooper's leash. The dog followed him.

Julia squirmed in John's arms and drew in a deep breath, preparing to unleash another wail. Her eyes fell on Cooper, and she closed her mouth. She sniffed loudly, then began to coo.

John looked between Julia and Cooper, then turned wide eyes on David. "I knew Dan had this effect on her but didn't know there was another dog that could calm her. We tried Roman and Eve, but they didn't help."

"There's something about Dan and Cooper, isn't there?"

"There certainly is. Does he belong to you?"

"Sort of," David said. "He's from Forever Friends."

John bent and stroked the dog. "Aaron just went home to pick up Dan. I offered to babysit while Maggie, Susan, and Aaron go to church after dinner. I thought I could get Julia to sleep, but I'm not sure I'll have any luck."

"Now you won't need Dan," David said.

"What do you mean?" John asked.

"I'm giving Cooper to Susan's family."

John turned to David and raised an eyebrow.

"They wanted to adopt Cooper," David said. "All three of them came to Forever Friends and were set to fill out the paperwork, but I'd already claimed him. I—I had an idea that he'd make a good service dog."

"He just might," John said, turning his attention back to Cooper.

"He had the same calming effect on Julia when they were at the shelter. So—I think that he's meant to stay with her."

"That's very generous of you, David." John looked David in the eye. "Very selfless."

David flushed.

"You're sure?"

David nodded.

"Maggie. Susan," John called. "There's someone here to see you. He's got quite a surprise."

"I've got my hands full in the kitchen," Maggie called back.

"You need to see this," John replied.

"Okay. Coming."

Susan preceded her mother out of the kitchen. Cooper let out a short bark when he saw her.

"What in the world?" Susan said, hurrying to the dog who was sitting quietly next to Julia. Susan glanced at David. "Are you his owner?" she asked, pointing to Cooper.

"I was, ma'am," he said. He took a deep breath and cleared his throat. "I'd like you to have him. I think you're his real family."

Susan looked at the tranquil scene in front of her and her eyes filled with tears. "You don't have to do that," she stammered.

"I want to do it," David repeated quietly.

Susan dropped to one knee and hugged Cooper. "We'll give you a good home. You'll be happy with us, won't you, boy?"

Cooper pressed his muzzle into her neck.

Susan looked up at David, blinking rapidly. "This is the nicest gift anyone's ever given us. We'll never forget this."

Maggie caught David's eye and mouthed the words "Thank you."

David looked from Maggie to Susan and swallowed hard. He reached toward Cooper and ruffled the fur between his ears. Cooper remained next to Julia and turned his nose into David's hand, giving it a slobbery kiss. "You're—the—best," David choked out.

He straightened and held out the cellophane-wrapped cookie plates to Maggie. "They're from Loretta," he said. "She wasn't feeling well, so Frank asked me to bring them by."

Maggie took the package. "Oh dear," she said. "It's no fun to be sick at Christmas."

"Loretta's just tired."

"It's easy to be tired, this time of year. Especially after a day of baking," Maggie said. "I've got something for you and your mom, David." She turned to the pile of wrapped loaves of bread on the entryway table. "Cranberry orange," Maggie said. "My mother's recipe. I hope you like it."

Susan stood and threw her arms around David. "I don't know what to say—thank you just isn't enough."

David stood stiffly in her arms. "I better get going." He took a step back and looked down at Cooper. "Bye, boy. Behave yourself." He turned and walked quickly to the door.

Susan hesitated, then went after him. He was almost to his car when she called to him. "You're a really good dog trainer, aren't you?"

"I think I am."

"Would you have time to train Cooper? Actually, work with me and Cooper? I have no idea how to train a dog."

"I'd be happy to," David said. Susan could see his shoulders relax.

"Perfect. We'll start next week. Let me know what you charge."

"You won't have to pay me."

"I insist. My mom has your phone number?"

David nodded. "I've done odd jobs for her."

"I'll call you." Susan paused, then raced down the steps into the cold night and flung her arms around David. "Thank you," she whispered into his ear. "Thank you for such a special Christmas."

Maggie, Susan, and Aaron came through the kitchen door of Rosemont after church on Christmas Eve.

"That was a beautiful service," Susan said. "I love when they dim the lights before the benediction, and everything is lit by the candles we're holding. It's so peaceful."

Maggie nodded in agreement.

"Speaking of peaceful," Aaron said, "I don't hear a sound from anyone here. Julia must be asleep."

The three of them walked quietly to the living room. The lights on the Christmas tree flickered in the empty space. A faint glow from the fireplace in the library beckoned them onward. They stepped into the room to find Roman and Eve curled up together on the dog bed by the fireplace.

Susan gestured to the sofa that sat in front of the fireplace. John was sitting upright, his legs stretched out on an ottoman. Julia was resting on his chest, her head tucked under his chin. Grandfather and granddaughter were both sound asleep, their deep breathing in rhythmic unison.

Cooper lay at their feet, his head on his paws. He raised his head when they entered the room and gave one wag of his tail. He didn't bark.

"Will you look at that?" Aaron said softly.

"I was feeling guilty that he didn't get to go to church with us," Susan said, "but it looks like he's had a wonderful evening."

"I think there's nothing he'd rather have been doing," Maggie agreed.

"I hate to disturb them, but we'd better head home," Aaron said.

Maggie tiptoed to the sofa and laid a hand on John's knee.

He cracked one eye open.

"Hey there, sleeping beauty," Maggie said.

John forced his other eye open.

Maggie reached for Julia. "Susan and Aaron are here to take Julia and Cooper home."

John stirred and held Julia out to Maggie.

The baby stretched and sighed but continued sleeping.

John and Cooper got to their feet and followed Julia and her parents to the garage.

Aaron buckled Julia into her car seat without waking her.

"Thank you, John," Susan said.

"I loved every minute of it," he replied.

Cooper swished his tail against John's leg.

John reached down to scratch between his ears. "This guy is a very special dog."

"I still can't believe that David gave him to us," Aaron said. He stepped to one side and Cooper jumped into the car and settled down next to Julia.

"This may be a quiet Christmas for us," Susan said, "but I think I'll remember it as one of the best."

Maggie kissed her daughter on the cheek. "I couldn't agree more. See you tomorrow. Come over whenever you like. We don't have to be at Alex and Marc's for dinner until four."

"I'll call you in the morning." Susan opened the passenger door. "I love you both. Merry Christmas."

Chapter 22

John shrugged into the jacket that hung by the back door and whistled for the dogs. Roman, Dan, and Cooper joined him. Eve, however, was nowhere to be seen. He had a good idea where he'd find her.

His footsteps crunched across the dead grass, dusted with a light coating of snow, as John made his way through the chilly air to the figure sitting on the low stone wall at the bottom of Rosemont's sloping lawn. Maggie was huddled in a down jacket, clutching a cup of coffee, the faithful Jack Russell terrier mix at her feet.

The dogs dashed ahead of him, bounding and circling in playful good spirits around her. Dan stuck his snout into Eve's face. She got to her feet and allowed him to sniff her, wagging her tail. When he was done, she turned to Maggie, gathered herself on her haunches, and sprang into her master's lap.

Maggie laughed, pulling her coffee cup to the side and sloshing the ground with the now-cold liquid. "It's okay, girl," she murmured, drawing her beloved companion to her chest.

"I wondered where you'd gone," John called as he crossed the last ten feet to join her.

"After Julia went down for her morning nap, I told Susan and Aaron that they should get some sleep, too. I decided I needed some air."

John joined her on the low wall. Roman rested his head on his master's knee, and John stroked the golden retriever's ears. "If I didn't know better, I'd say you're a bit—blue."

Maggie blew out a breath. "You know me so well, don't you? I guess I am."

"It's been a nice Christmas," John said. "Quiet and peaceful."

"That's just it," Maggie said, shoving her hair behind her ears. "I don't think I like quiet and peaceful."

"You thrive on a lot of commotion, don't you? Running around the kitchen at ninety-miles-an-hour, with every dish and glass dirty by the time the day's done."

"Exactly! I know I should be glad that I've got time to relax, but I miss having a houseful of people."

"Alex and Marc are so excited about hosting Christmas dinner."

"I know. They've been cooking for days," Maggie said. "It'll be wonderful, and I'll have a great time once we get there."

"But in the meantime, you're feeling at loose ends?"

"Yes." Maggie drew a deep breath. "I just need to embrace change. I've been down here, giving myself a pep talk."

Her jacket pocket vibrated. "This has been going off for the last twenty minutes," Maggie sighed, pulling out her cell phone. She punched at the screen and began scrolling through her texts.

"There's an electrical outage on the other side of town," Maggie murmured as she tapped through the messages. "Something about an accident taking out a transformer?" She tipped her face to John and her eyes shone. "Alex's electric oven doesn't work, and he wonders if they can use our kitchen and bring the dinner here."

Maggie set Eve on the lawn and hopped off her perch on the wall. "Of course!" she said aloud as she tapped on her phone.

The reply pinged back immediately. *On our way.*

Maggie scrolled through the other messages. "Sam and Joan don't have power either. She wants to know if she can come over to bake a ham in our oven."

"You bet," she typed back.

Maggie turned to John. "Your old house is near Sam and Joan's. I'll bet it doesn't have power, either. Why don't you call David and invite him and his mom for dinner?"

"Good idea. Frank will be affected by the outage, too," John said.

"You'd better invite them over," Maggie said, her growing excitement palpable. "You like this as much as I do, John Allen."

"Guilty as charged," he replied.

"We'd better get a move on," she said. "I've got tables to set and things to do. I wonder who else we should invite? I'll text Joan and ask her to spread the word. There's a Christmas potluck at Rosemont and everyone's welcome."

Judy Young was the first to arrive. "I've got a Crock-Pot full of my maca-roni and cheese," she said to John as he opened the front door. "It's absolutely decadent. Christmas is the only time of year that I indulge myself. I figure I deserve a treat after all the long holiday hours I work at Celebra-tions." She motioned for him to follow her to her car. "Would you mind carrying it in for me?"

John dutifully lifted the Crock-Pot out of her trunk.

"Let's set it up in the library. You'll need all the room you can get in your kitchen."

John raised an eyebrow at her.

"Set it on low, will you?" She turned back to the driveway as Joan and Sam Torres pulled up. "I'll see if they need a hand."

Joan got out of the car, and the two old friends embraced. She pointed to another car parked along the circled driveway. "Who's already here?"

"I'm pretty sure that's Alex's car," Judy said. "He and Marc were hosting Christmas dinner until their electricity went out. He called Maggie to see if they could move the meal to her house. You know Maggie—it all snow-balled from there."

"I'm so glad it did. This is going to be a lot of fun."

Sam opened their trunk and removed a large, foil-wrapped roasting pan.

"That's a ham I was going to bake," Joan said.

Judy clicked her tongue. "Perfect. I brought macaroni and cheese."

"The one you make in the Crock-Pot? With the beaten eggs that make it light and fluffy?"

"The very one."

"I love your mac and cheese!" Joan reached for a platter covered with cling wrap and handed it to Judy. "Snowball cookies," she said. She picked up a covered casserole dish. "This has my grandmother's ambrosia salad."

"I'm glad I'm taking a break from my diet," Judy said with a laugh. "Let's see what Maggie needs a hand with."

The piano in the conservatory came to life as they stepped into the en-tryway, and jazzy renditions of Christmas classics filled Rosemont.

"That's Marc, isn't it?" asked Sam.

"Nobody else can play like that," John replied. "Why don't you come back and meet me here when you've delivered that to the kitchen?" He motioned with the giant crock of mac and cheese toward the roasting pan Sam was carrying. "I'm keeping an eye on Julia," he said, gesturing toward the swing where the baby sat, wide-eyed and content. "And acting as doorman."

"I'll be right back," Sam said.

The kitchen was buzzing with activity. Susan was leaning over a large pot on the stove, a wooden spoon held aloft, enveloped by a cloud of fragrant steam. Alex was placing a tray of homemade rolls into the oven.

Maggie appeared out of nowhere, balancing a stack of dinner plates against her chest. She stopped abruptly, almost colliding with Sam. "Hey, everybody," Maggie said. "Merry Christmas."

The newcomers returned her greeting.

Sam carried the pan to the only open spot on the counter. "Do you need any help with those dishes, Maggie?"

"Nope. This should be the last of them. Why don't you go back to keep John company?"

Sam nodded, grateful to be able to step away from the frenzy in the kitchen.

"How many are we expecting?" Joan asked.

"I think we'll end up with eighteen of us," Maggie said. "Not counting Julia."

Judy stepped into the dining room, where a starched linen cloth draped the long table and silver, crystal, and china were set out for each guest. She looked over the top of her half-moon spectacles at Maggie. "You're amazing. Two hours ago, you thought you were going out for Christmas dinner, and now you've set a formal table for eighteen."

Maggie shrugged. "I've got all of this stuff. I may as well use it."

Judy chuckled and drew Maggie to her for a hug. They were stepping apart when Nicole, Sean, and Marissa Nash burst into the kitchen with John at their heels.

"I told them the dogs are in the back garden. I promised they could go outside to play with them until dinner," John said.

Maggie nodded at him. "Good idea. Let them burn off some energy."

John ushered them through the kitchen and into the yard.

Maggie glanced out the window to see the three children alternatively chasing—or being chased by—Roman, Cooper, and Dan. A slight movement below the windowsill caught her attention. Eve was slinking along the side of the house, making her way to the door.

Maggie threw the door open and called to her beloved terrier mix. "Is this too much commotion for you?"

Eve wagged her tail effusively.

"Would you like to go upstairs to take a nap in your basket?"

Eve emitted a short bark.

Maggie bent and scooped her up, receiving a shower of doggie kisses. "I'm going to carry you through the kitchen, so you don't get stepped on," she murmured into Eve's ear.

Maggie climbed the stairs and deposited Eve in her bedroom. The terrier made a beeline for her basket, circled three times, and settled in for her nap.

"I'll come get you when it's time for your dinner," Maggie said softly as she walked away. She was heading back to the first floor when Aaron emerged from the entrance to the attic. His hands were full, with an easel and a large pad of paper.

He grinned when he saw her. "Thank goodness that attic has everything. Well—almost everything. Where would I find markers?" he asked.

"There're several in the top right-hand drawer of my desk. In the library," Maggie replied. "Why? What have you got planned?"

"Christmas Pictionary," he replied. "After dinner. Is that all right? I figure everyone can play."

Maggie brought her hands together in a clap. "Brilliant idea!"

"Marc and I have written up all the answers," he said. "This is going to be fun."

"Frank and Loretta and the kids arrived a few minutes ago. We'll be ready to eat soon."

"I'll set this up in the conservatory."

Maggie and Aaron returned to the first floor to find Sam greeting Tim and Nancy Knudsen.

"Thank you for inviting us," Nancy said, holding out a salmon-colored poinsettia to Maggie. "I don't know what we would have done at home without electricity."

"I'm so happy you're here," Maggie said. "In fact, John and I are glad that the power outage gave us the excuse to get together. Christmas is about spending time with family and friends."

John stepped behind Maggie. "Alex sent me to announce that dinner is ready. The buffet is set up on the kitchen island. Let's eat!"

Everyone gathered in the kitchen. Judy was the first in line and was filling her plate when she stopped and shrieked. "My mac and cheese! It's in the library."

"I'll get it," David said from the back of the line. He handed his plate to Sean, who stood in front of him.

David returned with the Crock-Pot and placed it at the end of the array of dishes lined up on the island. He lifted the lid, and everyone groaned with pleasure at the aroma of cheesy goodness.

Judy resumed filling her plate.

Dinner proceeded in a leisurely fashion, with lively conversations and frequent trips back to the kitchen for seconds. When the final piece of pecan pie had been consumed and no one could find room for one more bite, Maggie nodded to John at the other end of the table. He rose from his seat, picked up his glass, and tapped it with his knife.

"Now that I have your attention," he said, "I want to thank you all for coming and bringing such excellent food. I don't think Rosemont has ever seen a better meal."

Sam Torres raised his glass in salute. Everyone clapped.

"Aaron has devised the evening's entertainment, which will be in the conservatory. Marc has issued us all a challenge," John continued. "He's going to play 'The Twelve Days of Christmas,' all verses, all the way through. If we can work together to clear the table, put away the leftovers, and load—"

"*And* start—" Marc interrupted.

"And start," John added, "the dishwasher before he's done playing, he'll draw a name out of a hat for a twenty-dollar bill."

Judy jumped out of her seat. "Come on, everybody. We can do this." She scooped up her silverware and plate and those of Jackie Wheeler, who was seated next to her.

Maggie caught Marc's eye and blew him a kiss.

He made his way to the conservatory and began playing the familiar melody at a slow tempo.

The group seated at the dining room table sprang into action. The table was cleared, and they were halfway through dealing with the leftovers, when Marc began the ninth verse. He picked up the tempo.

Susan shrieked and the group kicked themselves into high gear. Frank was taking the bagged trash to the garbage can and Maggie was pushing the button to start the dishwasher as Marc played the final chord with a flourish.

Marc joined them in the kitchen, bringing with him an old fedora that he had retrieved from the hall closet. He made a show of inspecting the counters and placed his ear against the dishwasher. He nodded and turned to the expectant crowd. "You did it. I never thought you could have cleaned up before I finished, or I would have played faster."

Alex whistled through his teeth and Sam and Tim cheered.

Marc held the hat high over his head and motioned to Joan to step forward. "Will you do the honors?"

Joan smiled and reached into the hat, churning the slips of paper inside it until she drew one out and handed it to Marc.

He reached into his wallet and removed a twenty-dollar bill. He unfolded the paper and looked at the faces trained on him. "David," he said. "The winner is David Wheeler."

The group clapped as David stepped forward to claim his prize. "I never win anything," he mumbled. "I can't believe this."

"Maybe it's karma," Marc said to him quietly as he handed David the twenty. "I heard what you did for Susan, Aaron, and Julia."

A line of red crept up David's neck and he shrugged.

Marc shook his hand. "Thank you for giving up Cooper. And congratulations. You deserve good things to happen to you."

"The Nightmare Before Christmas!" Aaron shouted.

"Yes!" Alex dropped the marker he was holding onto the tray of the flip chart. David hooted and Aaron gave Alex a high five as he rejoined his team.

"We're breaking up the Scanlon brothers the next time we play Christmas Pictionary," Susan said. "No more being on the same team. You can read each other's thoughts."

Aaron arched a brow at his wife. "Sounds like sour grapes to me."

"Whatever." Susan rolled her eyes at her husband and rose from the arm of the sofa where she had perched. She picked a slip of paper out of the bowl and approached the flip chart. "Okay, team, we need to get back in the game."

Julia, asleep in her swing in a corner of the room, startled and began to cry.

Maggie jumped to her feet. "I'll take her," she said. "I'm hopeless at this game, anyway." She picked up her granddaughter.

Cooper and Dan, stretched out in front of the fire, began to rise.

Maggie motioned for them to stay. "I've got this," she said.

The dogs watched her walk to the door and then laid their heads back on the hearth rug.

Maggie tucked Julia's face against her neck and felt the tension ease out of Julia's tiny body. By the time they had crossed through the living room, Julia was once again asleep.

Maggie headed for the library and the overstuffed chair by the French doors overlooking the garden. The room was dimly lit by moonlight streaming through the French doors—just like her first night, so many years ago, at Rosemont.

Maggie sank slowly into the chair and allowed her eyes to adjust to the low light. She rocked Julia gently, rubbing her back. The rhythmic sound of Julia's breathing was interrupted by a low, buzzing snore emanating from a furry white lump in a basket next to the chair.

Maggie smiled and peered over the side of the chair. Eve had taken herself away from the noise and commotion of the after-dinner games and conversations and was sound asleep in her basket.

"Good idea, girl," Maggie said softly. "I'm about ready for bed, too."

She stretched her hand toward her beloved pet and gently scratched her ears.

"This is the exact spot where we met, do you remember? Except you were outside of these doors, in a blizzard. I still don't know how you survived all night, out in the cold." Her voice caught. "But you saved me, girl. You led me to John, and you helped me build a happy life."

She blinked hard and didn't notice the figure in the entryway.

"Maggie," David's mother, Jackie Wheeler, said.

Maggie looked up sharply.

"I don't mean to interrupt," Jackie said. "I—I wanted to have a word with you before I left. In private."

"Of course," Maggie started to rise.

"Don't get up," Jackie said. "You and Julia look comfortable." She cleared her throat. "I want to apologize—for the way I've treated you—in the past."

"Nonsense," Maggie said. "You've got nothing—"

"I do and we both know it," Jackie said. "I was horribly rude to you after William died and our house was foreclosed. I blamed you for our troubles and you had nothing to do with them."

"It was a very difficult time for you," Maggie said. "I understood that."

"I used you as a scapegoat and you repaid my pettiness with kindness. You and John. You've been caring and helpful to David, and now you've invited us to Rosemont for Christmas."

"I know what it's like to have the rug pulled out from under you—to have everything you thought you knew about someone turn out to be a lie."

Jackie nodded. "That pretty much sums it up."

"How are you doing now?" Maggie asked.

"Things are getting better," she said. "I love my new job and I've been promoted twice. In fact,"—she took a deep breath—"I was going to ask if John would like to sell his house to us. We love it there, and, unless he wants to keep it as a rental, we'd like to work something out to buy it."

"That's wonderful." Maggie's voice rose, and Julia stirred. "I'm sure he will. I'll mention it to him," she whispered. "Give him a call."

Jackie turned at the sound of approaching footsteps.

Sam and Joan Torres came into view, followed closely by Judy Young.

"We wondered where you'd gone," Judy said.

"Us old folks are ready to head home to bed. It's been a wonderful day, Maggie," Joan said. "Thanks for coming to our rescue by letting us use your oven."

"And the rest of the house," Sam said.

"Thank you for including David and me, Maggie," Jackie said. "We've had a terrific time. I have to work tomorrow, so I'd better corral David and be on my way."

"He's having the time of his life in there," Sam said. "Why don't we give you a ride home so he can stay awhile longer? The young folks seem like they're going strong."

Jackie paused. "He's been down in the dumps since he and Grace broke up. I haven't seen him this happy in quite a while."

"Yes—let him stay," Joan said. "That first heartbreak is a doozy. It'll do him a world of good."

"I don't want to take you out of your way," Jackie said.

"We're dropping Judy off and I think you're close to her? It'll be no trouble."

"Well—then—yes. I'd appreciate that."

Maggie rose slowly and walked her friends to the door.

"It was so nice to all be together," Joan said. "Even Frank and Loretta and the kids. After the last few years, we've become a big extended family."

"She didn't look too good by the time they left," Judy said. "I hope she's all right."

"Frank said she's been really tired," Joan said. "She's going to see her doctor after the New Year for her annual checkup."

"Having three kids in school and running Haynes Enterprises would wear anyone out," Maggie said. "Thank you for coming. Rosemont and I weren't liking the new quiet Christmas."

Sam laughed. "You still think Rosemont has feelings, don't you?"

"What a thing to ask, Sam Torres," Judy said as she leaned in to kiss Maggie's cheek. "We all know that it does."

"We should be thanking you, Maggie," Jackie said. "They didn't restore power until an hour ago. We would have had cold cereal for Christmas dinner."

"It was absolutely no trouble for me," Maggie said. "All of you brought the food. In fact, I think we should do this every year."

"Christmas potluck at Rosemont?" Judy and Joan said in unison.

"What do you think?" Maggie asked.

"I think we've got ourselves another Rosemont tradition," Sam said. "Now, let's hit the road. I've got a full schedule of handyman work tomorrow." He ushered the three women to the door.

"Take that baby back into the library," Joan said. "We don't want her near the door when we open it. Too cold."

"Would you tell David that I've gone home, and he can stay as long as he likes?"

"I will," Maggie said, retreating to the library. "Merry Christmas. I love you all."

Chapter 23

Maggie got out of her car and tucked the ends of her scarf into the neck of her coat. The breeze was brisk on this morning after Christmas, with heavy snow in the forecast by late afternoon. She made her way to the sidewalk that flanked the library and headed toward the administration building. The walk to her office would only take ten minutes. Even so, she regretted giving the go-ahead to close the admin parking lot during winter break so the maintenance crew could repair sewer lines.

She came around the side of the library and passed the wide concrete steps leading to the bank of doors sheltered by an elaborate carved stone cornice. She paused in the cold, rubbing gloved hands over her arms as she admired the handsome building.

A young woman stepped around her and began her ascent to the doors. She glanced over her shoulder at Maggie, stopped abruptly, retraced her steps, and extended her hand.

"President Martin," the woman said. "Sunday Sloan. I'm one of the librarians here."

Maggie took her hand. "Of course. And, please—it's Maggie. We talked earlier this fall. When you were in London?"

Sunday swallowed hard. She'd hoped that Maggie had forgotten their conversation. "Yes—that was me."

"I've been meaning to come over to meet you and take a tour of the rare book room," Maggie said. "My schedule has been packed since I started here."

"No worries," Sunday said. "I'd be happy to show it to you whenever you have time."

Maggie pulled the cuff of her coat away from her wrist and checked her watch. "I don't have any meetings. I'm planning to spend my day in my office, catching up."

Sunday smiled and nodded. She was planning to do the same thing.

"Would you have time to show me around the library, now?"

"Of course," Sunday said. "This'll be the perfect time. You and I may be the only two people on campus today."

Maggie laughed. "I'm hoping you're right. I'll really be able to get a lot done."

The two women proceeded up the steps and Sunday unlocked the door, holding it open for Maggie.

"Did you have a nice holiday?" Maggie asked.

"I did. Best in years," Sunday said. "I spent it with one of the other librarians. How about you?"

Sunday led them across the main reading room to a corridor that ran toward the back of the building.

"My daughter and her husband just had a baby and they were with us. My son and his wife and their twin daughters were with Amy's family this year. We started out as a small group, but it morphed into something bigger." She shifted her purse to the other shoulder. "Do you have any family here?"

"No. Just me." She pushed keys around her keyring until she came to the one she was seeking. Sunday inserted the key into the lock of a door with the words "The Hazel Harrington Rare Book Room" etched into the glass. They stepped inside.

Maggie stood in the middle of the space and looked at the mahogany bookshelves lined with volumes. Four glass cases stood in two rows running down the center of the space. One of the cases held a copy of *Gone with the Wind* with placards and illustrations describing the history of the groundbreaking bestseller and pedigree of the rare first edition displayed in the case.

"*Gone with the Wind* is one of my favorite books," Maggie said breathlessly, leaning over the case. "This is fascinating." She swiveled her head to Sunday. "Did you make this display?"

Sunday nodded, holding her chin high. "I'm going to fill the other cases with similar displays. Rare books don't have to be dusty volumes written in old English. We've got some very interesting books in our collection."

Sunday stepped to the case and searched for another key. "Would you like to see it up close?"

"I'd love to!"

Sunday inserted the key and removed the volume. She turned to the copyright page. "If you look at the date," she began, and stopped, mid-sentence.

"What's wrong?"

"This isn't our first edition," Sunday said. "This is a Book of the Month Club copy." She turned to Maggie, her eyes wide.

"How can you tell?"

Sunday pointed to the dates on the page. "The first edition is dated May 1936."

"This one is June." Maggie peered at the page that Sunday held out to her.

"The covers look the same. The only way to tell the difference is by the date."

"Did we have both editions in our collection?"

Sunday shook her head no. "Someone must have obtained this one," she held up the volume in her hand, "to cover up the theft of our valuable first edition."

"You're sure that the original was in the display?"

"Yes. I placed it here myself and double-checked the date. When I locked this case, the first edition was in there."

"When was that?"

"Last March."

"Have you opened the display to show our copy to anyone else?"

"No."

"Who else has access to the key to this display?"

"The other librarians," Sunday said. "I know I locked this case." She lifted her eyes to Maggie again. "I'm positive."

Sunday took a deep breath and straightened her shoulders. "You probably think I'm a kook after my call about the Tennyson volume," Sunday began, "but something's going on with our rare book collection. I believe books have been stolen in the past. Our collection is worth millions of dollars. We left it out in the open for years. Anyone smart enough to know its value had easy access. Based upon this"—she gestured to the case—"I'm concerned that the thief is still active."

Maggie and Sunday stood quietly, looking at each other.

"I don't think you're a kook, Sunday," Maggie said. "I learned long ago that we should trust our intuition. We can get a sense of something long before we can prove it."

Maggie took off her coat and folded it over her arm. "Would you mind showing me the Tennyson that you thought you'd seen in the London bookshop?"

"Sure." Sunday motioned for Maggie to follow her into the maze of bookshelves. She stopped and pulled out an ornately tooled leather-bound volume and handed it to Maggie.

Maggie began carefully turning pages. "It's beautiful, isn't it?" Maggie said. "The cover, the paper, and the typeface. It's lovely."

"Some of these old volumes are little works of art."

"Wasn't there a distinctive mark on our copy that you also found on the one in the bookshop? That's why you thought our volume was in London?"

"Yes. May I?"

Maggie handed the book to Sunday who turned it to page [ix]-8 and gave it back to Maggie.

"This tear?" The pitch of Maggie's voice rose slightly.

Sunday nodded.

Maggie drew a deep breath. "This can't be," she said. "Surely there can't be two books with this exact same tear." She looked into Sunday's eyes. "You're sure it's the same."

"I am. I've tried to talk myself out of thinking that, but I'm sure. I just can't see how the book went from the bookshop to our library between the time of my visit and when I returned home."

"Things get shipped around the globe overnight all the time," Maggie said.

"But the proprietor must have known to be suspicious of me," Sunday said.

"Did he know where you work?"

Sunday was silent, tapping her index finger on the shelf where the Tennyson volume had been housed. "I don't exactly remember, now," she said. "I could have mentioned it."

"There you go," Maggie said.

"How are we going to prove it?"

"We may not be able to," Maggie said. "We need to gather some information first."

"What do you mean?"

Maggie felt her pulse quicken. "First, I want you to tell me everything you've found. Don't leave anything out."

"I can do that," Sunday said, pointing to a table in the corner.

"Not here," Maggie said.

"We can go to my office," Sunday said. "Or yours. That would be more convenient for you."

Maggie shook her head. "Not at the university. If something's going on, we need to discuss this out of the public eye." She looked at Sunday. "Let's stick with our original plan. Can you come to my home tonight?"

"Sure."

"Do you know where it is?"

"Rosemont? Yes. I know where Rosemont is."

"Right after work? Say six o'clock? I've got a refrigerator full of holiday leftovers, so if you don't mind something warmed up, I'll feed you dinner."

"That's not necessary, but I'd like that."

The two women looked at each other and smiled.

Maggie turned and shrugged into her coat as she headed for the entrance. "One more thing," she said. "Do you have any trustworthy contacts in London?"

Sunday began to shake her head no but stopped. She'd been emailing almost daily with the Cambridge librarian she'd befriended at the conference.

"Well, yes, actually. He's a fellow rare book librarian."

Maggie's eyes gleamed as she turned back to Sunday. "Perfect. Exactly what we need. I'll see you tonight at Rosemont. You can bring me up to speed, and we'll come up with a plan."

Sunday watched as Maggie walked down the steps into the blustery morning, then turned and hurried to her office. She needed to finish her comparison to Hector Martin's inventory by the time she left for Rosemont.

Chapter 24

The cab inched through snarled London traffic, and he resisted the urge to direct the driver to pull to the curb to let him out. He still had at least another two miles to go before he arrived at his destination, and the late December weather was too inclement for him to walk the rest of the way.

He reached for the leather satchel at his feet and felt the outline of the volume that he knew was nestled safely inside. Satisfied that he had the package he wanted to deliver with him, he sagged against the ripped leather of the seat. How in the hell had he, a respected professional, gotten himself mixed up in all of this?

His addiction had crept up on him slowly. He'd enjoyed penny ante poker with his buddies for years and hadn't gotten into trouble. It was only when he'd made that first trip to Las Vegas that he'd glimpsed the compulsion that would soon lead him to empty his bank accounts and retirement fund. When the house had gone into foreclosure and his wife had threatened to leave him, he'd dug himself out of the hole he was in by stealing and selling rare books from the Highpointe collection.

He'd only meant to take a few books from those dusty old boxes in the basement of the Highpointe College Library. Hadn't they been talking about disposing of the mountain of books that Hector Martin had given to the college? For years, they'd wanted nothing more than to clean out that basement. The only thing that had prevented it from happening was inertia. The elevator didn't service the basement, and no one wanted to carry all of those boxes up the steep stone steps.

The cab pulled to the curb lane and picked up speed, only to stop suddenly, throwing him forward. His foot knocked his satchel over. He bent and set it upright, making sure its precious contents remained in place.

"Sorry, mate," the cabbie said. "Traffic's a right bugger today."

He didn't respond. He peered out the window at a street sign. Another mile to go.

He'd done them a favor, really. Relieved them of the need to dispose of what they had been so anxious to get rid of. No harm, no foul was how he looked at it. At least until Hazel Harrington had stuck her nose into it.

The old librarian had insisted that she go through each box before they got rid of any volumes. She'd wanted to make sure that they weren't disposing of anything valuable. The books sat in their boxes in the basement another seven years while she worked her way through them.

He'd held his breath that first year, waiting for her to discover that some of the boxes weren't as full as they should be. When she'd never raised the issue, he'd resumed his pilfering. They'd made it so easy for him. His compulsion had expanded to the local racetrack and, later, to online gambling. He'd had a ready market for the stolen items in the London bookshop that he was now en route to. And he'd never worried about getting caught—until recently.

Nigel had seemed to be a mild-mannered accomplice in the early years. As time wore on and the thefts had climbed into the hundreds of thousands of dollars, however, he had revealed himself to be a demanding and ruthless co-conspirator. Still, it had been a bloodless, victimless crime—until Hazel died.

He shivered in the damp chill of the cab. Hazel had been found unresponsive at her desk in the library early one Tuesday. She was typically the first person to arrive in the morning, usually at her desk by six-thirty. When the front desk clerk clocked in at seven that fateful day, Hazel was slumped over her desk. She'd been pronounced dead on the scene.

Nigel had been in Westbury that Monday. Their meeting at a deserted freeway rest stop was seared into his brain.

"Here's what I promised," he had said, handing Nigel two volumes of Thomas Jefferson's personal copy of *The Laws of the United States*. Bearing Jefferson's annotations, they were extremely rare and comprised the single most valuable items he had ever stolen. With these Jefferson volumes, the thefts from the library would exceed one million dollars.

Nigel calmly opened the package and slowly inspected its contents. "Very nice, indeed," he said, carefully replacing the volumes in their padded packaging.

"These'll be the last items you'll get from me." He'd become increasingly uneasy that his luck would run out and his thefts would be discovered. The money from this sale would allow him to replenish the funds his wife believed were in their children's college accounts. He'd get counseling—join a twelve-step program—whatever it took to control his compulsion. He needed to quit.

Nigel caught his elbow in a vise-like grip. "That's not a plan that works for me," he hissed. "Thanks to everything I've received from you over the years, I've got a clientele with a voracious appetite for items from Hector's collection. I depend on your supply."

"The librarian's getting suspicious."

"Why do you think that?"

"She's made a list of missing items and posted notices about them. She's reminding people that they need to check things out when they take them from the library and that they need to return them on time."

Nigel snorted in response. "Is that all?"

"She's very protective of this collection. That list of missing volumes contains everything I've taken … and nothing more." He swallowed hard. "These Jefferson volumes will resolve any doubts she may have that somebody's been stealing. It's one last big haul. We're both going to have to be satisfied with that."

Nigel leaned into him, bringing their faces within inches of each other. His voice, when he spoke, was a low hiss. "Librarians can be eliminated."

The very next day, the formerly hale and hardy Hazel dropped dead at her desk.

The paramedics attributed it to a heart attack.

Nigel claimed he was more than three hundred miles away from the rest stop by Tuesday morning.

The man hadn't been convinced.

The cab pulled to the curb, jarring him out of his reverie. He paid the driver, grasped his satchel, and stepped onto the pavement. He caught his reflection in the shop window as he hurried to the door. His usually precise hair was unkempt. The pallor of his complexion was mirrored by the gray skies reflected there. The chill that ran down his spine had nothing to do with the icy breeze.

He paused on the pavement, his hand on the door to Blythe Rare Books, and took several deep breaths. This would be the last of it; he'd stand his ground this time. He was done with all of it.

He pushed the door open and the bell tinkled. There were no customers in view, and Nigel didn't appear.

He waited, shifting his satchel from one hand to the other. The only sound was the muffled traffic noise from the street outside.

He stepped around the display case in the front of the shop and pulled aside the curtain that obscured the tiny office behind the case. The space was empty. He'd told Nigel that he'd come by the shop today. Where could he be? He leaned toward the desk, littered with papers, straining to read the day's entry on the calendar propped against the wall.

"What the hell do you think you're doing?" came the familiar British voice from behind him.

He jumped back and spun to face Nigel. "I didn't hear you," he said, clutching the front of his coat with one hand.

Nigel took his elbow and pulled him into the office, shutting the curtain behind them. He gestured to the satchel with a jerk of his head. "Got something for me?"

"A first edition *Gone with the Wind.*"

Nigel rubbed his hands together. "Not many of those around. They're highly sought after—even over here."

"You'll be able to sell it quickly."

"If it's really a first edition." He removed the volume and turned it over in his hands. "Excellent condition."

"Martin only acquired the very best."

"This better not be a book club edition or a second printing," Nigel said.

"It's not," the man said, a hard edge to his voice. "I know the difference."

The proprietor looked at him over the top of his glasses. "Since when are you an expert?"

"I had to take this from a display case and replace it with something so the theft wouldn't be discovered. I picked up a book club copy that looks identical to this first edition. Unless someone opens the case to inspect the copy on display, no one will know it's been switched out."

The proprietor's head snapped up. "You took a display copy? What kind of an idiot are you?"

"Relax." The man's jaw set in a firm line. "It'll be fine. No one will look at it since it's in a locked case. They're still assessing condition and establishing value on the remainder of the collection. They put this one," he pointed to the book in the proprietor's hands, "in the case when they were done cataloging it. I figured it was the safest volume in the collection to take without it being noticed. And it has the value you need."

The proprietor stared at him, then moved his eyes slowly to the copyright page. He ran his fingers down the spine, then gently flipped through the pages.

"It's a first edition." The proprietor placed it carefully on his desk.

"We're done. The account's been settled."

The proprietor stared at him.

"I'm not doing any more."

The proprietor opened the curtain and motioned for the man to precede him to the door of the shop.

"I understand that we're done—for now."

"For good." The man wheeled on him. "I'm not doing this again. They're suspicious—I can feel it."

"Maybe," the proprietor said. "Time will tell. I've been through these things before. We'll let the dust settle for a while."

"I'm not—"

The proprietor stepped close. "You're sitting on a gold mine in that collection. I made more on the sale from those two Jefferson volumes than I have from the rest of this shop in the last two years. We'll be patient and let things settle down, but we're not going to give up."

"You've met our new librarian. She's very savvy. You think so, too— that's why you returned the Tennyson. She's taken inventory and made sure that the collection's secure. She'll notice if anything goes missing."

The proprietor leaned in, stale coffee and bourbon on his breath. "Librarians have a funny way of dying at their desks."

A river of fear coursed over the man, and he wrenched his elbow free.

"Go home and get me a copy of that inventory."

"I can't do that. I don't have access to it."

"You got access to the rare book room to replace the Tennyson volume without being found out," Nigel said. "And to get the book you just brought me. You'll find a way." Nigel opened the door, and the man stepped over the threshold.

"Just do it and sit tight. I'll tell you what to steal and when to steal it. You'll be hearing from me." The door to the shop slammed shut.

Chapter 25

"Sit. Stay." Maggie commanded the two dogs barking at the front door. Eve and Roman obediently took their customary spots in the entryway as Maggie opened Rosemont's massive mahogany door. Sunday stood on the other side, clutching her laptop and a file bulging with papers.

"I'm sorry I'm late," Sunday said, stepping inside. "I wanted to finish my analysis, and I lost track of time."

"I just got home a little while ago," Maggie said. "It's wonderful how productive you can be when everyone else is out of the office." She turned toward the kitchen. "I was just pulling leftovers out of the fridge. Are you hungry?"

"Starving, actually," Sunday said.

"Work through lunch?"

Sunday smiled at Maggie and nodded.

"Me, too," Maggie said. "There's ham and turkey and a killer lasagna. Plus salads and sides. Anything out here"—she swept her arm toward the counter—"is fair game." She handed Sunday a plate. "Help yourself. The microwave is over there."

"Wow. You must have had a large gathering," Sunday said.

"It turned out that way." As they filled their plates, Maggie recounted the circumstances that led to the Rosemont Christmas potluck. "It was a lot of fun. What would you like to drink? I've got sodas and iced tea, or water."

"Water, please," Sunday said.

Maggie filled a pitcher and took it to the kitchen table. "It'll be just the two of us. My husband had to go back to the animal hospital for an emergency. Would you like to get started while we eat?"

"If you don't mind, yes." Sunday set her plate on the table and opened her laptop.

"I don't know much about the history of the rare book collection at Highpointe. Can you give me an overview?"

"We acquired all of our rare books from your late husband's great uncle, Hector Martin. He was an avid collector of both Americana from the Revolutionary War era and nineteenth- and early-twentieth-century British and American literature."

Maggie reached for the pepper shaker. "I'm guessing he would have had some very valuable items. I know he was extremely wealthy."

"He was also a savvy collector. I haven't had time to make a comprehensive assessment of the collection, but what I've seen has been very impressive." She paused and looked at Maggie. "I think we may have one of the most valuable rare book collections of any college or university in the United States."

Maggie rested her fork on her plate, suddenly uninterested in her dinner. "That's saying something. I Googled the subject today. Yale and the University of Virginia have significant holdings. Did he leave his collection to us in his will? Wouldn't his estate have established a value on it then?"

Sunday shook her head. "He gave it to us piecemeal, over time. The first gift—that I've found a record of—was in 1979. Most of the books were contributed to us in the 1980s, with the last record of a gift in 1992."

"That's all fairly recent," Maggie said.

"It is. Unfortunately, no one knew—or inquired into—the value of what we received from him. I understand that whenever he donated boxes of books, they were carted down to the basement and left unopened."

"Good grief," Maggie said.

"Thankfully, the basement is cool and dry. The collection is in excellent condition. It was forgotten until someone wanted to clean out the basement. They were planning to throw them away."

"That would have been tragic."

"One of our former librarians—the one the book room is named after—prevented it. She went through the boxes and had the books shelved in a corner of the library."

"Did she know that they were valuable?"

"I don't think she did at first. She was interested in them, however, and kept researching what we had."

"I take it she isn't here any longer? Can you contact her?"

"That's one of the odd things." Sunday paused and looked into Maggie's eyes. "Hazel Harrington died at her desk. In the library."

Maggie leaned back in her chair. "What happened?"

"They say she had a heart attack. She was usually the first person in. A coworker found her in the library one morning."

"Did she have heart problems? Was she in poor health?"

"No. Not that anyone knew of. She was in her early sixties, so no one was suspicious of a sudden heart attack."

"You're not so sure, are you?"

Sunday dropped her eyes to the table. "I hate to sound like a conspiracy theorist, but I'm starting to have my doubts. There's too much that doesn't make sense."

"Tell me the rest of it."

"By all accounts, Hazel was a very sharp woman. Those who knew her said that she'd become obsessed with those old books of Hector's. If that's the case, why haven't I found any of her notes? What librarian wouldn't have kept precise written records of something they're interested in? If there's one thing we're good at, it's keeping records."

"Good point."

"The library's accounting manager had Hector's handwritten inventory of the books he donated. It contains detailed notes on the volumes—where he acquired them and how much he paid for them."

"That must be incredibly useful," Maggie said.

"It is. Hazel had a copy, but it wasn't anywhere to be found in her papers. I only found out about it recently. Lyla Kershaw, the library's accounting manager, asked me why I wasn't using Hector's list to help me research the value of our collection. When I told her I had no idea what she was talking about, she made a copy for me. She's the one who told me that Hazel had a copy, and that she kept the original in the accounting files."

"And you never found Hazel's copy?"

"No. And I'm sure Hazel was very careful with it."

"That is odd." Maggie agreed.

"Once I got my hands on a copy of the list, I started comparing Hector's inventory with the one I prepared when we moved the books into the rare book room." Sunday slid a document out of the folder and handed it to Maggie. "This is Hector's list. I've highlighted in yellow all of the books that are no longer in our collection. They're not—and never have been—in our rare book room."

Maggie turned the pages slowly, examining all of the highlighted entries. She looked up at Sunday. "There are a lot of missing volumes," she said. "And they're among the most valuable in the collection, based on what Hector paid for them."

"Exactly."

"Any idea when they went missing?"

"None. That's the frustrating part. These thefts—if that's what they were—could have been done while the books were in the basement or on open shelves in the back of the library. We had no control over them until they were moved into the secure room. For most of these books, that's almost forty years when anyone could have taken them." Sunday rested her head in her hands. "I don't know how we'll ever unravel this."

"We may never figure out what happened to these"—she tapped the list—"if they were stolen so long ago. But you think books are still disappearing?"

"I do. That Tennyson volume had me wondering, but with our first edition *Gone with the Wind* missing—I'm convinced they were stolen. Recently."

"Rare books are an obscure subject," Maggie said. "Someone would have to have specialized knowledge to know what they were looking for. My guess is that we're looking for one person. Whoever took these recent volumes probably took the others."

"That's what I think," Sunday said. "Our thief has had access to the books for a very long time. It could be anybody who used the Highpointe Library. I don't know where to begin."

"Countless used bookstores came up when I did my Google search this afternoon, and most have a small selection of rare books. If we were only missing one or two books, I'd imagine they could be in just about any one of them. If the theft is as widespread and systematic as you suspect, our thief probably knows how to get top dollar. They wouldn't have sold to just any used bookstore."

"That makes sense."

"There's a tight network of stores that specialize in rare books. I'm guessing our thief only sold to a couple of them. And you," Maggie's eyes gleamed, "may have stumbled into one in London."

Sunday sucked in her breath. "That would be an incredible coincidence."

"What's that saying? There are no coincidences?"

The two women looked at each other.

"Tell me about that person you know in London."

"Robert Harris? He's not in London, but he's close by. He's the rare book librarian at Cambridge. We met at the conference, and we've been in touch since I came home. He recommended the shop to me while I was there."

"So he's probably been in the shop before?"

"Yes. He said it was his favorite. If I only visited one shop while I was in London, Blythe Rare Books was the one to go to."

"Excellent. Can you ask him to do you a favor? Do you know him that well?"

"I—I think so."

"Is he trustworthy? Can he keep a secret?"

Sunday pursed her lips and paused. "I've only known Robert for a short time, but I believe so."

"We're going to have to trust someone. He sounds like a good candidate." Maggie took a deep breath. "Let's find out if the Tennyson volume you saw is still in that bookstore."

"I've been wondering about that," Sunday said. "If there really are two copies with an identical tear on that page, then we don't have a theft."

"I'm with you on that," Maggie said. "Can you ask him to make a trip to Blythe Rare Books? Ask him to look for the Tennyson volume. While he's there, have him look for a first edition *Gone with the Wind* and some of these other volumes that we believe Hector donated but aren't currently in our collection."

"I'll have to fill him in on why we're asking him to do this," Sunday said.

"I agree. He'll have to be discreet. If the proprietor is buying stolen books, we don't want him to know that we're onto him. If Robert marches in with a list of stolen books, the proprietor is sure to get suspicious."

"The proprietor might not know that he bought stolen books," Sunday said.

"That's possible," Maggie agreed. "Our thief might have concocted a believable story about how he or she came into possession of the books."

"Or the proprietor might not be as up-and-up as everyone thinks."

"We need to find out," Maggie said. "Can you contact Robert?"

"Yes. I'll call him. It'll be easier to explain over the phone."

"That's wise."

"I'll send him the list of our missing items. If he goes into the shop often enough for the proprietor to know him, I'll bet that he'll be able to browse to his heart's content." Sunday sat up straighter. "I'm so glad that we have a plan."

"Who else knows of your suspicions?"

"No one. Lyla Kershaw—the accounting manager—is aware that I've been working on an inventory, but not that I suspect these thefts."

"Good. Let's keep it that way. The fewer people who know about this, the better. The thief is likely to be someone close to the library. We can't rule out the possibility that they're a Highpointe employee."

"I hate to think that, but it's true."

"Will you tell me when you've spoken to Robert?"

"Of course."

"For now, why don't you call me on my cell phone in the evenings to update me? If you've got something urgent during the day, text me and I'll get back to you."

Sunday nodded her agreement. "You believe me, don't you?"

"I do. I hope you're wrong and everything's in order, but I don't think so. We'll find out soon."

Chapter 26

Low clouds hugged the horizon, bringing an early dusk on the last day of the year. Maggie pulled into the garage at Rosemont in the late afternoon and was relieved to see that John was already home. She hated the thought of either of them being out on the roads after dark and was glad that they'd decided to ring in the New Year at home.

Maggie received a hero's welcome from Eve and Roman when she stepped inside. She accepted their effusive greeting and hung her coat on its hook by the door.

She could hear John mumbling to himself in the kitchen and found him standing at the island, unpacking containers from a large cardboard box. "What in the world?" she asked as she inspected the label on the box.

"I told you I'd be supplying dinner tonight," John replied.

"I figured it'd be a pizza from Tomascino's or takeout from Pete's." Maggie leaned in to kiss him. "Either of which would be fine," Maggie added-ed.

"It's New Year's Eve and I wanted to make it special for you. After all—I proposed to you on New Year's Eve. I've got a lot to live up to."

"You don't have to do anything to convince me that I'm the luckiest gal alive. And don't even try to top an evening where a girl gets a marriage proposal."

John pulled a brown paper bag out of the box. "Even so, I decided I'd surprise you with a fancy home-cooked meal."

Maggie raised her eyebrows. "That's what all of this stuff is?" She gestured to the countertop.

"Yes. It's one of those meal kits that you order online. Everything's measured out and they give you a detailed recipe to follow." He held up a letter-sized brochure, printed in full color. "Two of the techs at the clinic recommended this. They claim they're delicious—and really easy."

Maggie took the brochure and scanned the contents. She raised her eyes to his.

"Do your techs know that you don't—well—you don't know how to cook?"

John shrugged. "How hard can it be? All I have to do is follow directions. And I've watched you in the kitchen plenty of times."

Maggie placed the brochure on the counter and reached for her apron. "Why don't I give you a hand?"

John snatched the apron out of her reach. "Not a chance. I've got this covered. Go soak in the tub. You love to do that." He pointed to the brochure. "This says that dinner can be ready in forty-five minutes. I've already lit the fire and set the table in the library. Report back here in your pajamas." He consulted the clock on the wall. "At six fifteen."

Maggie hesitated, eyeing the mountain of containers, bags, and boxes on the counter.

"Go on. This'll be a piece of cake."

Maggie toweled off and put on her best silk pajamas. John had been right—it had been heaven to relax in the tub. She still had another fifteen minutes before she was supposed to appear for dinner, but her curiosity was getting the better of her. Susan used an online meal service and spoke highly of it but conceded that some of the meal kits required a lot of work.

She was halfway across the living room when she heard the unmistakable sound of breaking glass. She hurried to the kitchen and found John sweeping shards into the dustpan. A pot of what looked like pasta was on the verge of boiling over on the stove. The counters were littered with cutting boards, knives, and vegetable scraps. John's shirt and the brochure with the recipes were both stained with tomato sauce.

He looked up when she entered the kitchen. "What the hell is braising?" he asked. "I was just about to Google it."

"Can I please help you?" Maggie asked.

"I'm afraid you'll have to—if we're ever going to eat. This," he stabbed a finger at the large cardboard box at the end of the counter, "is way harder than I thought."

"No worries," Maggie said. "I'll bet you're almost done and I'm sure it will be delicious." She stepped to the stove, turned down the flame under the pasta, and began to stir the sauce.

"I'm sorry, honey," he said. "I didn't want you to have to lift a finger."

"I love to cook, you know that. And being in here, with you, is fun." She consulted the recipe, found a small labeled package of spices, and added them to the sauce. "Maybe we should try another of these kits when we can work on it together."

"I'm certainly not going to do one on my own again."

"I love you for trying." Maggie tasted the sauce and nodded approvingly. "This is good." She put down the spoon and smiled at him. "We've had a wonderful year."

"Hard to believe that you started the year as mayor of Westbury and ended it as president of Highpointe."

"And you got to hold your baby granddaughter."

John nodded. "I can't deny it—she's got me wrapped around her little finger."

Maggie laughed. "You think?" She consulted the recipe one last time. "This is done. I predict it'll be fabulous. Well done, Dr. Allen."

"Thanks to you, coming to the rescue," John said. "Let's take our plates into the library and talk about all the things we have to look forward to next year."

Chapter 27

Susan sorted through the tall stack of mail on her desk, tossing direct mail solicitations in the trash and setting bills in a pile. She separated out two envelopes bearing return addresses of reunion registries—the final two that she was waiting to hear from.

She paused and tapped the letters against her desktop. If neither of these registries had any information about Josh's birth mother, she'd widen her search into DNA matching services. She hoped—for Josh's sake—that the answer they sought was in one of these envelopes.

She slit them open. The first letter contained the familiar rejection language and was placed in the "NO" folder. She was leaning toward the folder, the second letter in her hand, when she suddenly froze. She blinked and read the opening of the letter again.

We are delighted to inform you that the birth mother you are seeking is registered with us and has authorized the release of her information, set forth on the attached document.

Susan's hand shook as she pulled the document from behind the letter.

There, on the enclosed paper, was the name of Josh's birth mother as it appeared on the original birth certificate. The form had been updated only five days prior to the date of the letter. The birth mother was right here—in Westbury.

Susan drew in a sharp breath as the woman wearing a herringbone coat stepped into the coffee shop and stood, searching for someone in the crowded interior. Susan raised her hand over her head and waved, catching the woman's attention.

The trim woman looked to be in her early fifties and nothing like Josh, but there was something about the way she carried herself and the set of her chin that reminded Susan of him.

The woman smiled at Susan and made her way across the room. She reached for the back of the chair opposite Susan. As she pulled, the chair caught on something sticky, escaped her grasp, and tumbled toward the floor.

Both women lunged for the chair and set it upright.

"Sorry 'bout that," the woman said. "I'm nervous."

"I imagine you are. To tell you the truth, I'm nervous, too." She gestured to the counter where baristas were scurrying to and fro, producing complicated coffee drinks with precision. "Would you like to order something?"

"No. I'm jittery enough as it is, without caffeine." The woman cleared her throat and leaned toward Susan. "You say you represent my son?"

Susan smiled into the woman's eyes. "I do."

"How is he?" Her voice cracked. She swallowed hard and continued. "Is he well? Is he happy?"

"He's very well. He's an extremely nice, successful graduate student. He's had a good upbringing and a happy childhood."

The woman released the breath she'd been holding, and tears spilled down her cheeks. She opened her mouth to speak but couldn't form the words she wanted to say.

Susan paused, allowing the woman to compose herself. Now that she, herself, was a mother, she could imagine what the woman was feeling. "His adoptive parents told him that his birth parents had both been killed in an auto accident. That's why he had been put up for adoption."

"I see," the woman replied softly.

"He never looked for his birth parents when he became an adult. He wasn't interested in genealogical information. His father made a deathbed confession—that you were alive when he was adopted."

The woman furrowed her brow. "That must have been a shock."

"It was. When your son learned that you had been alive—might still be alive—he decided to try to find you."

The woman nodded. "And he hired you?"

"I'm a friend and offered to help. I've been searching all over social media and contacting reunion registries. I came up empty-handed until last week."

The woman turned tear-filled eyes to Susan. "I recently updated my contact information with the registry in the state where he was born. Was that what did it?"

Susan smiled broadly. "Yes, it was."

"Thank God," the woman said in a tremulous voice.

"What prompted you to update it after all of these years?"

The woman turned her palms up. "I was talking to someone, and it reminded me to do it."

"Sounds like divine intervention to me," Susan said.

"What does my son think of all this? Does he want to meet?"

"I haven't told him yet. I wanted to find out what you'd be willing to do. I didn't want to get his hopes up if things wouldn't—work out—with you."

"I understand that," the woman said, nodding her head vigorously. "I'm glad you're putting his interests first." She leaned over and took Susan's hands in hers. "I want to meet my son," she said. "I've dreamed of this moment every day since I gave him up. I need to meet my son."

Josh sent the tennis ball sailing high into the air. Dan crouched, then pushed off, eyes locked on the ball as he raced across the dead grass to catch it on the first bounce. Josh clapped his hands and his dog bounded back to him.

"Last one," Josh said before he threw the ball again. "I've got to get ready to meet a woman at a coffee shop."

Dan was loping back to his master when Josh's cell phone rang. Josh's father had always called him at about this time. Now that his father was gone, his phone never rang on Sunday afternoons.

He dug the phone out of his pocket and the caller ID showed that Susan Scanlon was on the line. He swiped the screen and answered the call.

"I hope I'm not disturbing you," Susan said.

"I'm at the park with Dan," he replied. "This is a perfect time."

"Good," Susan said. "How was your holiday?"

"Very productive," Josh said. "I got my parents' house all cleaned out. It's being painted inside and out next week."

"I know this isn't my business, but are you sure you want to sell it?"

"I'll never move back to Atlanta," Josh said.

"So long as you're sure," Susan said. "You've had a lot of changes in your life. I know that we barely know each other, but I feel very 'sisterly' about you. Don't make any rash decisions."

"Thanks, 'sis.' Don't worry about me." He cleared his throat. "Do you have news?"

"I do. That's the reason I called. I found your birth mother."

Josh froze as Dan dropped the ball at his feet and looked at him, expectantly.

"Are you there?"

"Yes—I'm here." Josh cleared his throat. "Is she still alive?"

"She most certainly is. I've met her, in fact."

Josh reached down and picked up the ball and threw it for Dan. "Where? When?"

"This morning. Right here in Westbury."

"She lives here?"

"Yes."

His voice quavered when he asked his next question. "Does she want to meet me?"

"She does. She said that she's thought about you every day since she gave you up."

"Did she say why she—why she gave me up?"

"We talked about all of that, but she would like to tell you herself. Is that all right with you?"

The line grew quiet.

"I'm trying to respect her wishes, Josh, as well as yours. I hope you understand that," Susan said softly.

"I guess I do."

"Would you still like to meet her?"

"Yes—of course I would. Did you tell her about me?"

"Only that you are a graduate student and she'd be very proud of you."

"But not my name or how to contact me?"

"No. You asked me not to. She wanted to know about you, and I told her that you'd had a good upbringing and a happy childhood."

Dan returned to his master, set the ball on the ground, and sat quietly at his feet.

"Do you want me to tell you her name and give you her information?"

Josh bent and absently ruffled the fur on top of Dan's head. "I—I don't think so. I read on one of those reunion websites that it's sometimes best to meet for the first time without a lot of information about your birth relative. That way you don't go into it with a bunch of preconceived notions about the other person." He sighed heavily. "You won't be so disappointed that way—if things don't go as you've imagined."

Susan wanted to tell Josh that she didn't think he'd be disappointed, but she bit her tongue. "Would you like me to set up a meeting? She said she'd be available anytime or anywhere you choose."

"Would you mind being there, too?" Josh asked. "To break the ice?"

"I'd be happy to," Susan said. "When would you like to do this?"

"Any evening this week."

"I'll contact her right away. Why don't we meet in one of the conference rooms at Scanlon and Associates? It'll be neutral ground and you'll have as much time and privacy as you need."

"That'll be fine."

"I'll text you the address when I confirm a date with her."

"Okay," Josh said. "And thank you."

Susan smiled. She had a gut instinct that this meeting would be the start of something wonderful for both mother and son.

Chapter 28

Josh kept his eyes trained on the door as he drummed his fingers on the table. Now that he was here, he regretted agreeing to meet Lyla's coworker. He was perfectly happy being single and had enough going on in his life with his graduate studies and the upcoming meeting with his birth mother. He didn't have time for a blind date.

He'd adopted his father's practice of always being early. She still had another fifteen minutes until the time they'd agreed to meet.

He watched an attractive woman stride past the plate-glass window to the door, her long blond hair cascading over her shoulders. There was a confidence in her purposeful step that he found compelling.

She stepped into the coffee shop and searched the room with eyes that looked almost purple. They found him and paused. She lifted her brows and a smile played at her lips.

Josh's heart leapt to his throat. Could this be the woman Lyla had set him up with? He rose from his chair and raised his hand in greeting.

She made her way to his table. "You must be Josh," she said as she squeezed through the small opening between tables in the cramped cafe.

He held out a chair for her.

"I'm Sunday Sloan." She extended her hand and he took it in his, hating when he had to release it.

"Nice to meet you," he said. "What would you like?" He gestured to the chalkboard on the wall above the barista station.

"I'm fine, actually," Sunday said. "I just came from work and I've been drinking coffee all day. By all means, get yourself something. I'll hold the table."

Josh shook his head. He wasn't going to step away from her.

"Maybe after the line dies down." He shifted his chair to face her directly. "Lyla tells me you're a librarian at Highpointe."

"I am," Sunday said. "I've been a lifelong bookworm, and now I get paid for it."

"Doing what you're passionate about. That's the ideal."

"I'm very lucky," Sunday said. "I even get to be in charge of our rare book collection, which is a particular interest of mine. Not many colleges have such collections, so finding this position was a dream come true."

"Highpointe has a lot to offer. I'm getting my master's in educational administration."

"Lyla told me that you work part-time for President Martin."

Josh nodded. "That job is one of the best things about being there. I know she's new to her role, but she's a terrific leader. I can study college administration in the classroom, but nothing beats learning from someone who's doing the job well."

"I agree with you on both scores," Sunday said. "Maggie is one-of-a-kind."

"Have you worked with her?"

Sunday hesitated. Maggie had been very clear about keeping their involvement quiet. "I've admired what she's done for the college in her short time here." She unzipped her jacket and Josh helped her drape it across the back of her chair.

"Lyla tells me you're a very talented painter."

Josh shrugged. "I don't know about that, but I enjoy it."

"Were you one of those kids who was always good in art class?"

He smiled. "I guess I was."

"I envy you. I can't even draw a stick figure. What mediums do you like working in?"

"Acrylics, mostly. Some pen and ink, too."

"Do you have any pictures of your work on your phone?"

Josh punched at the screen and scrolled until he found what he was looking for. He slid his chair next to hers, and she put her hand over his, tilting the phone, so she could view the images.

"These are fabulous," Sunday said, leaning back in her chair to face him. "The colors are vibrant. Cheerful. Your use of light makes them seem to—glow."

Josh shrugged his shoulders, but Sunday could tell that he was pleased by her reaction.

"This is only the second class I've taken," he said. "Most of my work is unschooled. I love being outside and painting in the morning light."

Sunday tapped the screen of his phone. "Who's this dark-haired beauty in so many of your pictures?"

"That's Dan: the best black Lab on the planet."

"He's beautiful," Sunday said. "And it looks like he's really big."

"One hundred eight pounds," Josh said.

"Wow. That's a lot of dog!" She scrolled through the pictures again. "Were these all painted around here?"

They huddled together, going through each picture, as Josh explained each one.

"Lyla says the canvas you're working on in class is exceptional. Very emotional."

"She's sweet to say so." He pursed his lips and looked aside. "I lost both of my parents this past year, so painting has been a great release for me."

"She told me." Sunday set his phone on the table. "And that you just got back from Atlanta—closing up your parents' home and putting it on the market. I'm sure that was hard."

"It had to be done."

"I'm so very sorry. I know what it's like to lose your parents."

Josh raised his eyebrows.

"Both of mine were killed in a car accident on Christmas Eve," she said quietly.

"That's horrible. How long ago was that?"

"Seven years. I was in college at the time."

"I'm sorry."

"When you say it—you know, seven years—it sounds like such a long time ago, but sometimes it hurts like it happened yesterday."

Josh nodded.

"For the most part, it gets better," Sunday said. "Those sad feelings don't derail me like they used to."

"How did you deal with your grief?"

"I threw myself into my studies," Sunday said. "That's when my interest in rare books took off. I got a scholarship to the Rare Book School at the University of Virginia and the rest, as they say, is history."

"I know very little about rare books and even less about Highpointe's collection. Tell me about it."

Sunday cocked her head to one side and smiled. "Are you really interested or are you just being polite?"

"I'm interested."

"Okay," Sunday said. "I tend to get lost when I start talking. Don't say I didn't warn you. If you feel like you're about to lose consciousness from boredom, just raise your hand."

Josh laughed. "I'm certain that won't happen. I'd like to hear about it."

Sunday took a deep breath and the color rose in her cheeks as she launched into the topic.

Josh listened attentively, interrupting occasionally with questions. "Fascinating!" he exclaimed when she'd finished. "I can't believe I didn't know any of this."

"Really?" Sunday asked. "You're not just saying that?"

"Absolutely. I'm intrigued."

"Why don't you come by the library, and I'll give you a tour of the collection? If you'd like to see it."

"I'd love to."

"I'm there Monday through Friday. Maybe you'd like to stop by one afternoon."

"I'm done at four on Tuesday. Will that work for you?"

"Sure."

"Would you like to grab dinner afterward?"

"I'd love to."

"What do you like to eat?"

Sunday looked at him and he felt like he could get lost in the depth of her eyes. "Surprise me. I'm not picky. And it doesn't have to be fancy. I love little hole-in-the-wall places."

"Excellent," he said. He'd be sure to ask Maggie for suggestions. He wanted to impress Sunday Sloan.

The overhead lights flickered, and they looked at the clock above the door.

"It's seven o'clock," Sunday said. "We've been here more than three hours."

"I had no idea it was getting so late." He rose from his chair. "And we never ordered a thing."

"I can't believe it. I talked your ear off," Sunday said.

Josh pulled out his wallet and put a ten-dollar bill on the table.

"That's kind of you," Sunday said.

"I've been a barista before—in my undergraduate days."

Sunday smiled at him. "I'll look forward to hearing more of the Josh Newlon story. Come prepared to talk about yourself."

They moved onto the pavement and faced each other. Josh took her elbow and leaned toward her.

She tilted her face to his.

A teenager on a skateboard barreled toward them, swerving at the last moment and clipping Sunday's purse. The contents spilled on the sidewalk.

"Hey!" Josh protested but the teen kept going.

Josh and Sunday knelt to pick up the items strewn at their feet. Her cell phone began ringing and Josh picked it up, handing it to her.

"It's a number in the UK," he said.

Sunday frowned as she looked at the screen. "I'd better get this," she said, stepping back.

"See you Tuesday," Josh said.

Sunday nodded as she answered the call and turned to walk away.

Josh watched until she rounded the corner and was lost from view.

"Sunday Sloan," she said into her phone.

"It's Robert Harris," came the voice at the other end of the line.

"Good heavens, Robert," Sunday said. "It's the middle of the night there."

"I was planning to call you in the morning, but I couldn't sleep," he said.

"You've found something?"

"I have."

"Tell me everything."

"I was in London this weekend, as I told you. I'd planned to go to Blythe Rare Books this afternoon because he'd found a volume I've been anxious to acquire for my personal collection."

She heard his deep intake of breath. "Nigel was expecting me, so it was perfect. He showed me what he'd obtained for me, and we agreed on a price. I then said I had some time to kill before my train and did he mind if I browsed." Robert chuckled. "Of course, he said yes. He was busy and said he'd be in his office if I needed anything."

"Perfect," Sunday said, willing him to get to the point.

"I was the only customer the whole time I was there." He paused, choosing his words. "I went through the entire list," he said. "Nigel had six of the volumes on the spreadsheet you sent me."

"That's a coincidence, but doesn't necessarily prove that they were from Highpointe," Sunday said.

"He also had a first edition of *Gone with the Wind*."

Sunday's heart thudded in her chest. "Did he have other copies of it? Maybe not as valuable, but other editions?"

"Nope. It was on display near the register and I chatted him up about it."

"What did he say?"

"That it was a very unusual item for him to carry. Said it might be the only first edition in the entire UK."

"And the Tennyson volume—with the tear on page [ix]-8? Did you find that?" She held her breath.

"It wasn't there."

Sunday felt her pulse quicken.

"There's more," Robert said. "When I collected my parcel on my way out, Nigel asked if there were any other volumes I was searching for. I told him that I have a particular interest in Tennyson and that I was looking for a copy of *The Princess*. He said that he'd never seen that particular work for sale."

Sunday came to a halt on the sidewalk as she approached her car. "You've got to be kidding. He had *The Princess* in his shop—I held it in my hand."

"I know."

"So, he was lying."

"Appears so."

"What was his demeanor when you asked him about *The Princess*?"

"It's hard to say." Robert paused. "He's not the friendliest person on a good day. It might be my imagination, but I felt like he was suddenly anxious to get rid of me. Thanked me for coming in and said he wouldn't want to keep me. He started to walk me to the door."

"Hmmm—"

"I asked him if he could try to acquire a copy of *The Princess* for me—like he'd found the book that I'd just picked up."

"And?"

"He said he'd try but that he didn't expect he'd be successful."

"Do you think he knows that someone's onto him?"

"Maybe. I'm not sure. I could be reading things into his reaction. *The Princess* might be that hard to find."

"Did you ever suspect this guy of selling stolen goods?"

"That's the funny part. He had a partner until three or four years ago. I always dealt with his partner."

"What happened to him?"

"Died of a sudden heart attack."

Sunday was silent.

"Sunday? Are you there?"

She forced herself to breathe. "I am. There are just too many coincidences."

"What do you mean?"

"We had a librarian here—the one I replaced—who died of a sudden heart attack."

"That's—unbelievable," he said.

"Don't go back in there," she said.

"I don't believe I will," Robert said. "What do you plan to do now?"

"I'm not sure," Sunday said. "I need to talk to President Martin. She'll know how to proceed."

"Keep me posted. This is the most interesting thing to happen in my world for a long time."

"I will. And thank you so much for your help. I don't know what we would have done without you."

"Of course. And you can count on me in the future, too. Who knows where this will lead?"

"I can't imagine. I hope you can get some sleep now. It's almost time for you to get up and go to work."

"Don't worry about me. Just take care of yourself."

Chapter 29

"We have a problem," came the English patrician accent on the other end of the line.

Anthony stepped out of the kitchen where his wife was busy packing her lunch, the local morning news show blaring from the television in the corner. "What're you talking about? What's happened?"

"One of my regular customers came in to pick up a book I'd procured for him."

"So?"

"So, he saw the copy of *Gone with the Wind* on display and asked about it. I know what he's interested in, and it'd never be *Gone with the Wind*."

"You're being paranoid."

"That's not all. He asked if I had a copy of *The Princess*." Nigel paused to let his words sink in.

"Maybe it's a coincidence."

"I'm not a believer in coincidences."

"What did you tell him?" Anthony held his breath.

"That I'd never seen a copy of *The Princess* for sale. He asked me if I could procure one for him. I told him I would try, but that I didn't think I'd be successful."

"That's smart." Anthony relaxed. He was glad Nigel hadn't assured the customer that he'd find the book, thinking Anthony could remove the copy he'd recently restored to Highpointe's collection.

"We've got a problem," Nigel repeated. "One that needs to be solved. Now."

A trickle of sweat ran along the back of Anthony's neck. "What d'you mean?"

"That new librarian who came into my shop. What's her name?"

"Sunday Sloan."

"That's the one. I think she's onto us."

"I thought you just said that the person who came in asking questions was a customer of yours. What does that have to do with Sunday?"

"This customer is a rare book librarian at Cambridge."

The line crackled with static while both parties remained silent.

"See what I mean about coincidences? That woman came into my shop while she was at a librarian's conference. I'll bet she met my customer there."

"And sent him in to check on whether you've got any of the volumes that are missing from Highpointe."

"Exactly."

"How would she know what's missing? Except for *Gone with the Wind*, everything was removed before the secure room was completed."

"I don't know how she knows, but she knows."

Anthony cleared his throat. "This proves it. We need to be done with each other. I can't feed you any additional volumes from Highpointe's collection. It's too risky."

Nigel emitted a dry, raspy laugh devoid of mirth. "I've got a better idea." He lowered his voice. "We can eliminate the risk."

"What do you mean?" The vein at Anthony's temple pulsed.

"It's time to take out Sunday Sloan. Librarians at Highpointe have an unfortunate habit of dying. Maybe she has a heart attack at her desk like her predecessor?" he said. "I don't care how you do it, but get rid of her."

Anthony spun around when his wife stepped out of the kitchen, her purse over her shoulder and lunch sack in her hand. She smiled and waved at him as she crossed to the garage door and left the house.

Anthony's knees buckled, and he slumped against the wall. "You crazy bastard," he said, gulping air. "I'm not going to kill Sunday."

"One of us has to. Either you do it or I do and you're an accessory to murder. Does it really make much of a difference? Either way, you're still part of it."

"NO! No way," he cried. "I'm not a killer. I can't do this."

"I'm not asking. Either take care of her or—"

"Or what?"

"I'll be in Chicago for the annual rare book show. Not that far from Westbury. I can make arrangements while I'm there, or I can nip down and do the deed myself."

Anthony heard him draw in a deep breath.

"It'll be inconvenient for me and you don't want to inconvenience me, Anthony. It makes me very angry. You won't like it if I'm angry at you." He released the breath. "Think carefully, Anthony. If one of us gets nailed for the thefts, we'll both go down for them. My country will extradite me. Given the amounts, we'll both be looking at long jail sentences. I'm too old to spend my remaining days in custody. Get rid of her." Nigel disconnected the line.

Anthony lowered his head to his hands. How in the hell had he gotten himself into these dire straits? He didn't want to go to jail, but he wasn't a murderer. He wasn't going to kill Sunday and he couldn't let anyone else kill her, either.

Chapter 30

Loretta held Julia against her shoulder as she swayed from side to side.

"What's taking them so long?" Frank asked. "I thought we were just dropping Marissa off. This is supposed to be our night off—without any kids at home."

"It's Susan's first time to leave her baby with a teenaged babysitter," Loretta said. "She wants to make sure that Marissa's all set to take care of Julia."

"I guess I don't know much about those types of things," Frank said.

"They've been at it quite a while," Loretta said. "I think I'd better get in there to see how things are going. Here." She held Julia out to Frank.

He took a step back. "What'm I supposed to do with her?"

Loretta rolled her eyes. "Honestly, Frank. Just hold her."

"But I don't know how."

"You've never held a baby before?"

"No."

Loretta's tone softened. "There's nothing to it. She's old enough to support her own head. Just take her here—under the arms—and move her up and down and talk to her."

Frank grasped Julia gingerly.

Julia began to coo.

He moved her slowly up and down. "What's up, doc?" Frank said in his best Donald Duck imitation.

Julia's eyes crinkled and she emitted a throaty baby chuckle.

Frank flushed and cut his eyes to Loretta.

She gave him a thumbs-up.

"I'll be doggone," came the Donald Duck voice again, followed by peals of laughter from Julia.

Loretta leaned in and kissed Frank on the cheek before she left the room in search of her oldest daughter and Julia's parents.

"You're sure everything's clear?" Susan pointed to the list she'd handed Marissa.

Loretta stepped behind her daughter. She leaned over Marissa's shoulder to read the list of instructions.

"Marissa's a seasoned babysitter, honey. I'm sure she'll be fine," Aaron said.

Susan turned her head swiftly to face her husband. "I'm just making sure," she said in a frosty tone.

Loretta caught Aaron's eye and they exchanged a knowing glance. "It's very scary to leave your child with a babysitter for the first time," Loretta said.

"She's had babysitters before," Aaron said.

"Grandparents don't count," Loretta said. "This is the first time with a teenager. Marissa is very responsible—Julia's in good hands."

Susan looked at Marissa and smiled. "I guess I'm just being silly."

"You're being a new mother," Loretta said. "Nothing silly about that."

"I know how responsible you are, sweetie," Susan said, giving Marissa's shoulder a squeeze. "That's why we picked you." She looked to Aaron. "Why don't we go to dinner and check in before the movie?" Turning back to Marissa, she added, "We can come home if you need us to—"

"I think we'll be fine," Marissa said. "Dinner and a movie aren't that long."

"Why don't Frank and I stay here—with Marissa?" Loretta said. "Would that make you feel better?"

Susan's countenance lightened. "Don't you have to get home to Sean and Nicole?"

"They're both spending the night with friends," Loretta said.

"Don't the two of you have plans?" Aaron asked.

"To tell you the truth, we were going to order takeout and stay in to watch a movie. I've been so tired lately that I'm beat by the end of the day."

"You could watch a movie here," Susan suggested.

"That's what I was thinking," Loretta said. "I'll let Marissa take care of Julia. We'll be here if she needs us. Otherwise, we can do the same thing here that we'd be doing at home."

"That would be—" Susan glanced at Aaron, "so very nice of you. This first time is harder than I thought it would be."

"Then it's settled," Loretta said.

"I left money on the kitchen counter for Marissa to order dinner," Aaron said. "There should be enough for all of you."

"And there's a television in both the living room and the family room, so Marissa doesn't have to watch the same movie that you and Frank watch."

"Perfect," Loretta said, sweeping her hand to the door. "Off you go. Enjoy yourselves and don't worry about a thing."

"I'll just go say goodbye to her." Susan started toward the family room where Frank was entertaining Julia.

Aaron caught his wife around the waist. "You can hear that she's having the time of her life with Frank," he said. "If you go in there, you might upset her. You don't want to do that. We're already running late."

Susan stopped and looked at her husband. "You think she's fine?"

"I know she is." He ushered her toward the door.

Susan stepped across the threshold and Aaron turned back to Loretta. He mouthed "thank you" and the new parents were out the door.

"Boy," Marissa said. "I hope I'm not that nervous when I have a baby."

"You will be, honey. It's part of it."

"Is that the way you felt with us?"

Loretta nodded.

Marissa looked at her list. "I need to feed Julia her dinner. I want to make sure I do everything exactly how Susan wants."

"That's very responsible of you," Loretta said. "Let's see if we can pry her out of Frank's arms."

Marissa and Loretta stepped into the family room.

Frank was lying on his back on the floor, tossing a delighted Julia up in the air a few inches and catching her.

"Do you mind if I take her?" Marissa asked.

Frank drew Julia to his chest and sat up. "My arms are getting tired. I'm glad you came in."

Marissa took Julia and headed toward the kitchen.

"If she gets fussy," Frank called after them, "I'd be happy to take her again."

Loretta reached a hand out to Frank and pulled him to his feet. "You're completely smitten with her, aren't you?"

"I have to admit that was more fun than I would have imagined." He tucked in his shirt and ran his hands over his hair.

"I'm sorry we won't have children of our own, Frank."

"There's nothing to be sorry about, Loretta. I never expected we'd have a baby."

She placed her hands on the sides of his face and turned it to hers. "You are the dearest man on the planet. I'm grateful that you feel that way."

"Marissa, Sean, and Nicole are enough for me."

"I've been hoping that I'd get pregnant, but after I developed endometriosis, the doctors told me that it's almost impossible."

"We discussed this before we got married. Don't worry about it." He took her in his arms and drew her to him.

"The way I've been feeling lately—I think I need to see the doctor."

"Good," he murmured against the top of her head. "I've been wanting you to go for weeks."

"I'm just afraid that they'll tell me I need a hysterectomy," she said with a small sob.

He held her away from him and looked into her eyes. "If that will make you feel better, then that's what we need to do."

She nodded silently.

"The only thing I care about is what's best for you. I've got everything in life that I've ever wanted with you and the kids."

He enfolded her in his embrace, and they stood, arms entwined, drawing strength from each other to face whatever lay ahead.

Chapter 31

"Two, please," Josh said. "I made reservations under Newlon."

Pete placed a checkmark next to the name on a list at the hostess stand. "Right this way." Pete said, leading them through the dining room. "You work for Maggie Martin, don't you?"

"I do."

"She mentioned you when she and John were in on Saturday night. Said to give you her favorite table."

Sunday cut her eyes to Josh.

He smiled.

Pete led them through an arched opening at the back of the dining room into an alcove fitted with a pair of circular tables surrounded by half-moon upholstered booths. "We normally reserve these for overflow on the weekends when the dining room is full, but we always sat Maggie and John back here while she was mayor. If she sat in the main dining room, constituents were constantly interrupting her."

"Very cozy," Sunday said as she slid along the bench. Josh sat next to her.

Pete handed them menus. "Your server will be right over to tell you about the daily specials. If there's something you're hungry for that's not on the menu, let your server know. We're not busy tonight and our chef loves to accommodate special orders if he can."

Pete stepped away as Sunday and Josh opened their menus.

Sunday studied the dinner selections, then closed the menu and placed it on the table. She leaned toward Josh. "I've only been to Pete's for lunch, and I've never been in this section. This is so nice." She turned her head to survey the alcove. "Beyond charming. What a wonderful choice of restaurant."

Josh felt his cheeks grow warm. "I've never been here before," he said. "Too busy studying and working, I guess."

"That can happen."

They smiled into each other's eyes as their waiter approached. He gave a detailed recitation of the evening's specials, highlighting the inclusion of local ingredients and explaining methods of preparation.

They kept their eyes on each other. Neither of them focused on what the waiter was saying. When he was done, they had no questions on the menu. They each ordered the special entree.

Sunday put her hand to her forehead and grinned. "I have no idea what I just ordered. I was paying absolutely no attention."

"That makes two of us," Josh said. "I guess we're in for a surprise."

"For two such highly educated people, that was pretty dumb," she said.

"I don't know about that. We just had our minds on other things. I'm still thinking about everything you showed me in the rare book room."

"Seriously?"

"Yes. It was part literature and part history lesson, with a generous sprinkling of art thrown in. Some of those old leather-bound volumes were breathtaking. Like the Tennyson you showed me. The craftsmanship in the tooling of that leather is a lost art."

Sunday turned her head to one side. "I'm glad you understand. I've spent my life being the odd bookworm girl. When I was in college, most boys found me dull and way too serious."

"Then they were idiots," Josh said. "I find you fascinating, funny, and brilliant." He placed his hand over hers. "And beautiful."

Sunday felt her cheeks grow warm. "What do you plan to do when you graduate?" She held her breath, waiting for his answer.

"I'm staying here in Westbury," Josh said.

Sunday exhaled.

"I'll have a master's in educational administration. There are a number of private liberal arts colleges in this area. I won't be able to work at that level until I have some experience, but there are plenty of high schools here as well. I'm starting to line up interviews for the spring."

"Did you ever want to go back home when you graduated?"

"To Atlanta?" He shook his head no. "I never saw myself there—even when my parents were alive. And now ..." he hesitated. "I don't plan to ever go back."

"I see." Sunday picked up her fork as the waiter set cups of a spicy roasted red pepper soup in front of them. "How *are* you doing with the loss of your parents?"

He brought his spoon to his lips and blew on the steaming liquid. He took a sip and then put the spoon on the saucer under the bowl. "Their deaths have led to some unexpected discoveries."

She raised her eyebrows.

"I was adopted. I think I told you that?"

Sunday nodded.

"My adopted parents told me that my birth parents were killed in a car accident."

"I'm so sorry," Sunday murmured.

"Turns out, that wasn't completely true," Josh said. He launched into the tale of his father's deathbed confession and his subsequent efforts to find his mother in Westbury.

Sunday listened with rapt attention. "That's incredible, Josh. What a brave thing your father did, telling you at the end like that."

"You think so? I was mad at him at first for hiding it to begin with."

Sunday put her hand on his arm. "Your adoptive parents sound like wonderful people. You've told me enough about your childhood for me to realize that it was very happy."

"It was."

"Then don't condemn them for decisions that they surely would have made out of love for you. Your adoptive parents are both gone now, so you'll never know why they did it. Don't invent a hurtful narrative to explain their actions."

The waiter approached their table. "Was the soup not to your liking?" He looked at Josh's still full cup.

"No. It's fine," Josh said, pushing it away from him. "I got caught up talking. You can take it."

The waiter cleared their dishes. "Your entrees will be right out."

Josh took both of Sunday's hands in his. "You think I should stop trying to figure out why my adoptive parents didn't tell me the truth?"

"I really do." She squeezed his hands. "You said that your birth mother lives in Westbury? What an extraordinary coincidence."

"That's what I thought. It's like it's meant to be."

"Will you meet her?"

"As a matter of fact, yes. This Friday afternoon."

The waiter entered the alcove with their entrees and they reluctantly dropped hands.

"I told you about the attorney who helped find her? It's Maggie's daughter, Susan, actually. She's going to let us use the conference room at her law firm. She'll be there to make the introduction."

"That's exciting. I'll be around this weekend. If you want to talk after you meet her, just give me a call."

"I was thinking about that," Josh said. "Do you have plans Saturday?"

"I don't," Sunday said.

"Can we start with breakfast and spend the day?"

"Sure." She looked at him and raised one eyebrow. "What do you have in mind?"

Josh grinned. "There's something I've wanted to do since I read about it online over a year ago. It's kind of intellectual and nerdy," he said. "I figured I'd have to do it by myself, but after this afternoon, I think you'd really like it."

"You are a man of mystery, Josh Newlon."

"Do you want me to tell you what it is?"

She shook her head. "Nope. Nerdy and intellectual suits me to a T. Just tell me what to wear."

"Warm and casual. We'll be outside a fair amount and doing a lot of walking."

"Hiking? In the woods?"

"Not that rustic." He caught her eye and smiled. "That's the only clue I'm going to give."

"I can't wait. And if you want to talk on Friday after you meet your mom, my phone will be on. You can always call me."

Chapter 32

"I'm going to walk Sally and Daisy," Sean said, pushing his chair back from the kitchen table. "I don't have much homework."

"Wait," Frank said, holding up his hand.

"It's not my night to do the dishes," Sean began to protest. "It's Marissa's."

"It's not that," Frank said. "Your mom has something she wants to tell you."

The three children seated at the dinner table turned their eyes to their mother.

Loretta drew a deep breath, then stood quickly. "It's okay. We'll do it later."

"What, Mom?" Marissa narrowed her eyes as she searched her mother's face.

"Nothing. We can talk when Sean gets back." She nodded to him. "Go on. And Nicole—go put your toys away. Marissa, get your homework done."

Marissa got up from the table and began gathering plates and silverware.

"You can leave that. Frank and I'll take care of the kitchen tonight." Loretta took the plates from Marissa. "We'll talk at bedtime."

Marissa and Sean exchanged worried glances.

Loretta flicked her hand to motion them out of the kitchen. She walked to the sink and began loading the dishwasher.

Frank came up behind her and drew her against him, resting his chin on the top of her head. "What's all this, sweetheart?"

Loretta leaned back into him and sighed heavily. "I don't know what came over me." She turned in his arms to face him. "I thought it would take weeks to schedule my hysterectomy. I thought I'd have more time to get used to the idea."

"We told the doctor that you'd be happy to move the surgery up if he had a cancelation. When his office called this afternoon, you said you were relieved that you wouldn't have to wait."

"I know. And I was all set to tell the kids about the surgery. That it's a routine procedure and I'll be fine. But the minute I knew I had to say the words," a sob escaped her lips, "I couldn't do it."

"If you're not ready to have the surgery, we can wait. I just hate to see you so worn out all the time."

"It's not only fatigue," Loretta said. "I've had a lot of abdominal pain, too."

"What? Sweetheart—you should have told me. That's all the more reason to go forward. The doctor told us your symptoms will go away once you've had the surgery."

"I'm ready to get it over with," Loretta said. "But I feel selfish. If I have this surgery, there's no chance that I'll ever be able to give you a child, Frank." She tilted her face to his and tears welled over her bottom lids. "I've seen how you are with my kids, Frank. And how dear you were with Julia. You're a terrific father. You deserve to have a child of your own. I—want—to give you a child of your own," she said, choking on the words.

He drew her to his chest and held her, swaying gently. "I've got the family I always dreamed of with you and the kids. I don't think of them as *your* kids—they're *our* kids. Please don't put yourself through any more pain because you're trying to give me something I don't need."

"Maybe if we waited awhile longer? Another six months?"

"And watch you suffer? No way." He dropped his voice to a whisper. "The doctor told us that he doesn't believe you can conceive anymore. You'd be putting yourself through a miserable six months for nothing. Don't wait on my account. I want you to feel better."

She leaned back and took his face in her hands. "Are you absolutely sure?"

"I'm positive," Frank said. "We should go forward as planned. The surgery is scheduled for day after tomorrow. You'll be in the hospital two or three nights, and you'll recuperate at home for four to six weeks."

"I'm sure I'll be able to go back to work in three—"

Frank cut her off. "Absolutely not. You'll not darken the door of Haynes Enterprises until I have a 'release to work' note from your doctor."

"Aren't we the stickler?" Her eyes sparkled.

"The woman who's been running the place lately has gotten us on the straight and narrow. We're up to snuff on our HR compliance."

"Good for her. Sounds like my kind of gal."

"You should see how sexy she is." Frank nuzzled her neck. "Positively drives me wild."

Loretta stepped out of his embrace. "All right, Mr. Haynes," she said. "Enough of that. Sean will be back with the dogs any minute."

Frank snatched the dishtowel from its hook. "Then it's set? We go forward as planned?"

Loretta turned on the hot water and began to wash a frying pan that was too big for the dishwasher. "Yes. I'm miserable as I am. I want to get this over with and start feeling good again." She handed Frank the clean pan.

He swiped at the pan with the cloth and hung it, still dripping, on the pot rack over the stove. "And you'll tell the kids tonight?"

She rested her hands on the edge of the sink and sighed heavily.

"Would you like me to tell them?"

She shook her head. "No. It should be me. I don't know why I'm making such a big deal of this."

"You're worried that they'll be afraid?"

Loretta nodded.

"They're tougher than you think. Look at all they went through when Nicole received the kidney from Susan."

"That's true."

"Don't underestimate the kids, Loretta. Our kids. They're strong and resilient, like their mama."

They finished cleaning the kitchen and gathered the three children together at bedtime. They explained the procedure and Loretta's expected recovery time. Sean, Marissa, and Nicole were strong and resilient, as Frank predicted.

"You'll feel better, Mommy?" Nicole asked.

"Yes, I will."

"Like when I got Susan's kidney?"

"I won't be getting a new organ, but yes. The surgery will make me feel better."

"I want my mommy to feel good," Nicole stated firmly.

"I'm supposed to babysit for Julia the night before the surgery," Marissa said. "I'll call and cancel."

"You don't need to do that. This is very routine."

"I understand, Mom. The mother of a girl in my math class had a hysterectomy and she was okay. I'll still want to be with you."

"Daddy might get scared." Nicole swung her big eyes to Frank. "We should all be here with him."

Frank swallowed the lump in his throat. "That's very thoughtful of you," he said. "I'm not worried. Your mother will be fine."

"It's all set, then. I know you'll be the best kids ever for Frank. And I'll be home before you know it."

Chapter 33

Susan leaned into the booth to hug her mother before taking a seat on the bench opposite Maggie.

"This is a nice surprise," Maggie said. "I can't remember the last time we had lunch together, just the two of us."

"It was before Julia was born. That little lady has changed everything."

"She's worth it," they said in unison.

"I thought that your babysitter couldn't come until later," Maggie said.

"Grace Acosta doesn't have classes on Friday afternoon and offered to babysit as soon as she got done at school. I almost told her not to come, but then I decided to see if you could get away for lunch."

"I'm glad you did." Maggie smiled at her daughter. "And I'm proud of you for leaving Julia with a babysitter for the entire afternoon."

"I know I've been crazy and overprotective of her."

"You're a new mom—you're entitled to be crazy and overprotective." Maggie glanced around the restaurant in search of their waiter. "How much time do you have? Should we order?"

"I don't have to be at my office until three. We can relax. Unless you need to get back to the college."

"My calendar is clear. This is the first personal lunch I've taken since I started as president. I'm going to enjoy this." She patted Susan's hand. "What made you feel so comfortable with Grace?"

"I guess the fact that she's a senior in high school and an honor student. She's got tons of five-star reviews on the babysitting service's website. We talked on the phone for at least forty-five minutes."

Maggie cocked one eyebrow at her daughter.

Susan laughed. "You don't have to say it—I know that was a bit much. Anyway, she was very professional and reassuring."

"And reminded you of yourself at that age?"

"Exactly. How did you know?"

"I've met her before and that's exactly how she struck me."

Susan grinned. "Great minds think alike."

The waiter was making his way across the dining room to them when Pete intercepted him. The waiter turned toward the kitchen and Pete came to their table, a slip of paper in his hand.

"This is a sight for sore eyes," he said as both women rose to hug him. "We used to see Maggie all the time when she was in charge of Town Hall, but we thought she forgot about us now that she's president of Highpointe."

"I can't get over here at lunch anymore, but you see John and me at least one night a week."

"True," Pete said, "but we still miss you at lunch. The kitchen crew is different at lunch than at dinner. At any rate, I'm here to take your orders." He recited the daily lunch specials. "I see that you haven't opened your menus," he said. "Do you need a minute?"

Both women shook their heads no.

"I thought so," Pete said, unfolding the paper in his hand. He raised his brows and looked expectantly at Maggie.

She placed her order for a Cobb salad, dressing on the side, hold the bacon, with extra avocado.

Pete looked at the paper and checked off each item as she spoke. He turned to Susan.

"I'll have the same," she said.

He made a show of crumpling the paper into a ball and tossing it through the kitchen window. Someone in the kitchen cheered.

"What in the world is all that about?" Maggie asked.

Pete laughed. "When you walked in today, the kitchen staff got a betting pool going on whether you'd still order what they came to refer to—when you were at Town Hall—as the 'Mayor's Special.'"

Maggie flushed. "Was I that predictable?"

"No 'was' about it, Maggie. You ordered it exactly as they remembered it."

"Well—I'm dependable, that's for sure." She smiled up at Pete. "Which way did you vote?"

"Let's just say that I lost ten bucks."

"I'll be sure to leave you an extra big tip."

"You'll do no such thing," he said. "In fact, lunch is on the house. We're all so happy to have you back with us. I'll go put your order in." He turned without waiting for them to protest.

"That's awfully nice of him," Susan said. She turned her head to one side. "I still can't get over how good the people are in this town. Like Judy and Joan helping with Julia when she had colic, and David giving us Cooper."

"It's remarkable, isn't it?" Maggie agreed. "I don't think I'll ever forget David giving you that dog on Christmas Eve. He's been through so much tragedy, his father's suicide, he and his mother losing their home, but he's never lost his kind heart."

"David's coming over later this afternoon to start training Cooper."

"Does he know you won't be home? That Grace will be there?"

"He's only going to be working with Cooper. He said that he'll train with both of us after a couple more lessons." Susan brought her eyebrows together. "He knows that a babysitter will be there. He's going to knock, and the babysitter will let Cooper out into the backyard."

"But does he know the babysitter is Grace?"

"I—I don't think so. When we set this up, the babysitter was going to be Marissa Nash."

"What happened to Marissa?"

"She had to cancel. Loretta is having a hysterectomy tomorrow and Marissa wants to be home tonight."

"I hadn't heard that. I hope everything's all right?"

"I should have told you. Marissa said it's all routine. Her mother has endometriosis."

"That would explain Loretta's recent fatigue. No cancer?"

"I didn't ask, but I don't think so. Marissa wants to be with her mother. If you were having surgery, routine or not, I'd be at your side."

"So you had to scramble to get a replacement babysitter?"

"Yep. I can't reschedule the appointment at the firm this afternoon."

"Hmmm—" Maggie pursed her lips.

"What does that mean?"

"Just that David and Grace were going steady until right before Christmas. They broke up, and I understand he's been pining for her ever since."

Susan rested her elbows on the table and cradled her head in her hands. "Good grief. This could be really awkward for them. Do you think I should call him and cancel dog training for today?"

Maggie put her index finger on her lips and thought. "Grace's father is a professor at Highpointe," she said. "I remember talking to him at the holiday staff breakfast, and he said Grace was nursing a broken heart. Maybe this is fate trying to bring them back together."

"Are you saying I should leave things alone? Let the chips fall where they may?"

Maggie nodded slowly. "That's exactly what I'm saying. Let nature take its course."

Pete arrived and placed their salads in front of them. Mother and daughter exchanged a conspiratorial glance.

"What are you two up to?" Pete asked.

Maggie shrugged and Susan picked up her fork.

David rounded the corner to Susan's street and squinted at the car parked in the driveway. It was a very popular SUV. He passed that make, model, and color on the street every day.

As he came to a stop behind it, he knew it wasn't just anyone's vehicle. He recognized the fuzzy pom-poms hanging from the rearview and the slight crease in the bumper from the post in the high school parking lot. There could be no mistake: Grace Acosta was at the Scanlon's. She must be the babysitter Susan was talking about.

He turned off his engine and sat in his car. Should he text Susan that something had come up and he couldn't make it? That he'd reschedule for next week? He looked at the house, solid and impassive in front of him.

He hadn't seen Grace for weeks. They no longer had any classes together, and they were both going to great pains to avoid each other. She would be inside, taking care of Julia. He probably wouldn't see her.

A loud "woof" from the gate to the backyard got his attention. Cooper was already outside, waiting for him. He swung his car door open and got out. He was not going to renege on his promise to Susan.

David strode toward the gate. Cooper spun in a circle and wagged his tail, ecstatic to see David.

David's pulse quickened. He was glad to see Cooper, but he couldn't deny it, he wanted to see Grace.

He opened the gate and Cooper leapt up, resting his paws on David's shoulders and covering his face with sloppy kisses, his tail beating the air.

"Okay, boy," David said, running his hands roughly over Cooper's back and rubbing his ears. "This is not a polite way to greet me. You can't jump on people. You'll knock them over if you do."

Cooper sat at David's feet and stared up at him, swishing his tail back and forth.

David slipped a training leash over Cooper's head and grabbed a handful of small treats from the ziplock bag in his backpack. "You're a smart boy. You're going to learn really fast."

He led Cooper into the backyard. "We're going to start with 'come.'"

David kept his eye on the house as he worked with Cooper for the next hour. The back door remained closed, and Grace didn't appear at any window. He continued to train the dog until the light began to fade and Cooper's patience had worn thin.

David stood, giving Cooper a thorough rub down, as he surveyed the back of the house. If Grace were inside, she had no intention of letting him see her.

He squatted next to the dog and rubbed Cooper's belly. He had to accept it—he and Grace were done.

He sighed heavily as he stood and stuck his hands in the back pockets of his jeans.

Cooper got up and shook himself.

"Go on back inside," David said. He gestured to the doggy door with one hand.

Cooper looked where he was pointing, then back at David.

"Go on, boy."

Cooper bounded inside.

David swept his gaze over the back of the house one last time, then turned and headed around the side of the house to his car. He was pulling the driver's side door shut when the front door opened.

Grace stood in the open doorway; her face shrouded in shadow.

He got out of the car and walked to her.

Grace moved toward him, one arm outstretched, as he climbed the steps to the front porch.

"David," she said, and her voice cracked.

He took her hand in his.

"I—I miss you," she said.

He brought her hand to his chest.

"I'm so sorry. I had our futures all mapped out together. My way—we were living my dream."

"I should have told you how I was feeling."

"I think you tried to, but I wouldn't listen. I get so bossy sometimes."

"You're just definite," David said. "You know what you want. That's not being bossy."

"I thought we had agreed to go to Highpointe together."

"I'd like to—eventually. But I want to check out some other things, first."

"Service dog training?"

"Yes."

"So you don't want to be a vet anymore?"

"I'd like to be a vet. Maybe I'll specialize in service dogs."

"You're remarkable with animals and people," Grace said. "I saw how you and Dodger helped my brother Tommy in the hospital. You've got a gift."

"I feel like Dodger saved me, after my dad died," David said. "I know animals help people in all sorts of ways. I want my life's work to revolve around that."

Grace squeezed his hand. "Then that's what you should do, even if that means that you need to go away to school."

"Thank you. Neither of us knows what the future holds, Grace. But right here, right now—I miss you. Can we go back to seeing each other?"

Grace swiped at a tear. "I'd like that. I promise I won't hold you back. I want you to do what'll make you happy. Even if that means we'll be apart."

They both took a step toward each other.

David put his finger under her chin, lifted her face gently, and kissed her.

Chapter 34

"We're ready to take you back, Mrs. Haynes," the nurse said. She pulled open the curtain that surrounded the hospital bed and stepped on a lever to release the brake on the hospital bed wheels.

Frank clutched Loretta's hand in both of his and leaned over to kiss her. "I'll be right there—in the waiting room—the whole time."

"I'm going to be fine, Frank. Why don't you head to the cafeteria and get some breakfast?"

"I'm not going anywhere."

The bed began to move. "The doctor will talk to you when she's done," the nurse said.

"I love you," he said, squeezing Loretta's hand before the nurse eased her down the hallway. Frank watched until a set of automatic doors closed behind them.

He sighed heavily and turned to his right, searching for the waiting room. A sign mounted on the wall pointed him in the right direction.

Frank paused at the waiting room door, fighting a rising sense of panic. He knew he was being ridiculous. Everything was going to be all right. It was just that he had finally found the love he'd always dreamed of; he couldn't bear the thought of losing Loretta.

He drew a deep breath. All he had to do was get through the next few hours of waiting. He could do that.

Frank pushed the door open and found a vacant chair off to one side, far from the other families waiting for news of their loved ones, and settled himself into the seat.

He didn't see the man on the other side of the room motioning to him. Frank picked up a day-old newspaper from the end table next to him and tried to get interested in it.

The man crossed the room and said, "I thought you might need some company, Frank. Time in a hospital waiting room crawls by. It's like spending eight hours on the rock pile."

Frank looked up quickly. "Tim! What are you doing here?" He began to get to his feet, but Tim motioned for him to remain seated.

"I didn't want you to be alone," Tim said, sinking into the chair next to Frank.

"How did you know I'd be here? How did you hear about Loretta's surgery?"

"Nancy told me," Tim said. "She heard it from Joan who talked to Susan. Or Maggie. I'm not too sure. You know how things are around here—there's no such thing as a secret in Westbury."

Frank laughed. "I guess not."

"Do you mind if I sit with you?"

"I'd be grateful, actually. I know that this is a common surgery, but I'm really nervous. I can't shake the feeling that something isn't right."

"It's natural to be nervous," Tim said. "She's in great hands here. She'll be home in no time."

"You think so?"

"I do. If I were you, I'd decide on a nice getaway—just the two of you—when she's recovered. You deserve it."

"I can't leave town," Frank said. "I still need to work with you on the sale of those condos."

"We're almost done—thanks to you and your hard work. You've more than fulfilled your court-ordered community service." He looked Frank squarely in the eyes. "You've made good on it, Frank. Everyone knows it."

Frank dropped his gaze to his lap. "I never should have allowed the fraud and embezzlement to happen, Tim. I'll never forgive myself."

"Everyone else has, Frank. It's time you did, too. You owe it to yourself—and Loretta and the kids. It's time for a fresh start."

A nurse appeared at the door to the waiting room, propping it open with her hip as she consulted a clipboard. "Frank Haynes," she called.

Frank's brows furrowed. It was far too early for Loretta to be out of surgery. He raised his hand over his head.

The nurse acknowledged his hand with a jerk of her head. "Come with me, please."

Frank stood quickly and turned worried eyes to Tim.

"I'm sure it's just—paperwork," Tim said.

Frank sensed that Tim was concerned, too.

"I'll be right here," Tim said.

Frank nodded and hurried to join the nurse.

"The doctor would like to talk to you," she said.

"Did something go wrong? Is Loretta in surgery?"

"Your wife is over here." The nurse led him to a curtained enclosure.

Loretta was sitting up in her hospital bed. The IV bag that had been in place when she'd been wheeled into surgery had been removed.

Frank crossed to her side and took her hand in both of his. "What is it?"

"I have no idea," Loretta said. "They never even started the anesthesia. It seemed like I was waiting in the operating room forever and then they rolled me back here."

"What did they tell you?"

"Just that they were going to bring you back and the doctor would talk to both of us." She turned frightened eyes to his. "They took some blood this morning. Maybe they've found something—"

Frank and Loretta turned as the curtain opened and her doctor, dressed in surgical garb, stepped into the enclosure. Her mask hung around her neck.

"I've only had this happen one other time in my thirty-eight years of being a gynecologist," the woman said.

Loretta gripped Frank's hand.

"We're unable to do a hysterectomy on you today." The doctor's face broke into a huge grin. "Because you're pregnant!"

Frank and Loretta both leaned forward, eyes wide. Neither of them spoke.

"You're four weeks along," the doctor said. "All of your signs are normal. You'll need to be seen by an obstetrician as soon as possible, but everything looks good."

"How?" Loretta began to cry.

"I think you know the answer to that." The doctor's eyes twinkled.

"I didn't think I could get pregnant," Loretta choked on the words.

"It's very unusual for someone with your condition," the doctor said, "but not impossible. Obviously."

Frank leaned over the bed and took Loretta into his arms.

"I'll leave the two of you alone," the doctor said. "Call my office if you need a referral to an obstetrician." She backed out and closed the curtain behind her.

"Oh, Frank," Loretta whispered in his ear. "Are you happy about this?"

Frank leaned back and smoothed the hair out of her face. He took a deep breath and tried to speak. Tears streamed down his face. He leaned his forehead against hers. "I'm happier than I've ever imagined I would be. I— I feel blessed beyond measure."

They clung to each other.

"I'll never let you down, Loretta. I'm going to be the father our baby deserves."

Chapter 35

Susan pushed through the door of Scanlon and Associates at two forty.

The receptionist waved Susan over to her desk. "May I place you on a brief hold?" she said into the mouthpiece as she tapped on her keyboard. She looked up at Susan. "Your three fifteen is in the conference room." The woman narrowed her eyes. "I told her that she's more than thirty minutes early. She insisted that she couldn't stay out here in the waiting room—that you told her she should go straight to the conference room."

"I did." She nodded at the receptionist. "You did the right thing. Did you ask if she wants coffee?"

"She said no. I put a pitcher of ice water and cups in there for you."

"You are so efficient. Thank you." Susan headed toward her office. "A young man should arrive at three fifteen. Let me know when he gets here."

"Of course."

"He'll be meeting with the woman in the conference room, but I want to be the one who takes him in there."

"I'll let you know the minute he arrives."

Susan stepped into her office and put her satchel, heavy with papers, on the desk. She sat and carefully reviewed her notes detailing the information she would provide at their introduction. She'd decided to keep her initial remarks brief, allowing mother and son to proceed at their own pace.

Susan had unearthed a lot of information about them but didn't know if they'd want to learn all of it now—or ever, for that matter. She wasn't there to give them a report; she was facilitating a reunion.

The outcome wasn't up to her, but every fiber of her being wanted this to be a joyous reunion. This was the most emotionally charged matter she'd ever handled. She folded her hands in her lap and lowered her head, sending up a prayer for divine guidance.

The buzzer on her phone sounded. Susan pushed the button to connect with the receptionist.

"He's here," the woman said.

Susan noted the time—three-fifteen on the dot. She'd told him not to be early—she didn't want this reunion to take place in the waiting room. He'd heeded her advice.

She carefully picked up her papers and made her way to the lobby.

Josh stood with his back to her, looking out the window to the street.

"Right on time," Susan said.

Josh turned to her. "I did exactly what you told me to." He gave a nervous cough. "Is she—is my mother—here?"

"She is. As a matter of fact, she got here almost half an hour early. She's in the conference room." Susan extended her arm in the direction of the room. "Shall we?"

Josh sucked in a deep breath and didn't move.

"Are you ready to do this?"

He tapped the side of his head with his index finger. "I'm ready, here," he said. He pointed to his stomach. "I'm not sure about here."

Susan put her hand on his elbow. "It's natural to be anxious. I'm sure your mother is feeling the same way."

Josh swallowed hard.

"You don't have to do this," Susan said. "I can go in there and tell her you've changed your mind."

He stared at her.

"I don't think you should do that. I know I shouldn't make predictions, but I think this will turn out to be one of the happiest days of your life. Both of your lives."

He took a step forward.

Susan led him down a corridor to the conference room. She knocked softly on the door, then pushed it open. She entered the room, then moved aside, leaving Josh framed in the doorway.

The woman at the table rose slowly to her feet, fumbling to push her chair out of the way.

Josh was across the room and at her side in an instant.

"Lyla!" Josh exclaimed.

"Josh!" cried his mother.

They stood, holding each other at arm's length, staring.

"The two of you know each other?" Susan asked.

Lyla took an instinctive step forward and Josh swept her into a hug. They swayed together and soon began to laugh.

Susan set her papers on the table and watched the scene unfolding in front of her.

"I can't believe I didn't know it was you," Lyla said, her voice thick with tears. "You don't look like your father, but your mannerisms are all his."

"You didn't suspect when I told you I'd been adopted and was searching for my birth mother?"

"There've been other times—over the years—when I've encountered a man your age looking for his birth mother. I've always wished that it would turn out to be me. But it never did—until now." She lowered her head and sobbed.

Susan found a box of tissues on a credenza and slid it across the table to where Lyla and Josh stood.

"That's why I signed up with the reunion registry. If you ever wanted to find me, I wanted you to."

Josh handed her a tissue and took one to dab at his eyes. "Remember what you said to me that morning when we were both painting the tree? About my mother?"

"I do. I kept wishing that my son was out there somewhere, asking someone the same questions you were asking me. I was hoping that they would answer them the way I answered you."

"You convinced me to go forward."

She tilted her head to look at him. "Your father would have been so proud of you."

He pulled out her chair and she sat.

Susan hung back on the other side of the room.

"So he died in the accident. And you were injured?"

"There was never an accident. Your dad and I were in graduate school together. We were very much in love and planned to get married." She turned her head aside. "He was from England and was over here, getting his master's in library science. He got very sick at the end of our last semester. Cancer. It wasn't supposed to be that bad. He was young—he was supposed to survive."

Lyla turned to Josh with eyes filled with pain. "We didn't have health insurance, so he went home after graduation to live with his parents while he got treatment. He was getting better, then things took a turn for the worse. I found out I was pregnant and wanted to tell him—in person. I thought it would give him"—her voice broke—"something to live for."

"I sold my car to raise money for the trip and flew to England. When I got to his house, his parents told me that he'd died the week before. They hadn't had any way of contacting me."

"Did they know you were pregnant with—me? Their grandson?"

"I told them."

"What did they say?"

Lyla struggled to compose herself. "They didn't believe their son was the father. They said he'd never mentioned me."

"That's outrageous."

"They didn't even invite me into their home. I heard all of this, standing on their doorstep, in the rain."

Josh leaned over and put his arm across her shoulders. "I'm so sorry."

"I was stunned and heartbroken," Lyla said. "I'd lost the man I loved."

"Did you ever try to prove paternity?"

"I didn't know how to go about all that in a foreign country. I only had enough money to get back to the U.S., so I came home. I looked for jobs but, being pregnant and soon to be a single mother, I didn't find any. I had no car, no money, and no job. I was renting a room in a seedy part of town. It wasn't what I wanted for you and I couldn't see a way to change my circumstances."

Lyla leaned toward him and took his face in her hands. "So I gave you up for adoption. And I've regretted that every moment of every day since I signed those papers."

Josh nodded slowly. "I can understand why you did what you did."

"It was never because I didn't love you," Lyla said. "Giving you up was the biggest mistake of my life."

"Did you ever get married? Do you have other kids?"

"I never met another man who I loved like I loved your father. It wouldn't have been fair to marry a man who would always be second-best in my eyes. And I punished myself for giving you up for years." Her voice was barely audible. "I didn't feel I deserved children."

Susan, who had remained motionless on the other side of the room, now reached for a tissue.

"I think you've been way too harsh on yourself," Josh said. "I'm so sorry that you've denied yourself so much happiness."

"It was my choice," Lyla said. "I understand—from Susan—that you've had a good life. I already know that you're a talented artist and you're in graduate school here at Highpointe, so you're smart."

"Sounds like I've got you and my dad to thank for my brains," Josh said.

"Your dad was one of the smartest people I've ever met," Lyla said. "I'd love to hear all about you, all the details. Your hopes, your dreams." She glanced at him and quickly lowered her head. "That is, if you'd like to go forward—have some sort of a relationship. I know that your adoptive mother raised you. I'm not trying to replace her."

Josh remained silent.

"Maybe all you wanted to do was meet me. Nothing more." Her voice quavered. "If that's it, I understand. I agreed to that before we met."

"You don't have to decide right now," Susan said. "This has been a very emotional afternoon. You both might need time to process everything."

Josh held up his hand to stop them. "I already liked you from painting class," he said. "I'm thrilled that you turned out to be my mother. I was just thinking," he said, a grin spreading across his face.

Lyla's shoulders straightened.

"You introduced Sunday and me," he continued.

"Yes. She likes you—says you have a lot in common and she could talk to you for hours." Lyla cocked her head to one side. "What does she have to do with—us?"

"Sunday and I are spending all day together tomorrow, ending up with dinner at The Mill."

"That's great," Lyla said.

"Sunday knows I'm meeting my mother right now. She'll be expecting me to tell her all about you tomorrow."

"I'm sure she will."

"Why don't I keep your name a secret? You can join us for lunch at Pete's."

Lyla laughed. "That will certainly be a big surprise."

"I think she'll love it. What do you think?"

Lyla took a deep breath and smiled into his eyes. "On one condition. You let your mother pick up the tab."

"That's not why I'm inviting you," he protested.

"I know, but it would give me joy. I've been waiting to do something for you your entire life. This will be a tiny start."

Chapter 36

Sunday stepped onto her front porch. "Good morning. You're right on time." She pulled her door shut behind her and checked to make sure it was locked.

"I'm punctual to a fault," Josh said. "Ready to go?"

She smiled and the chilly morning felt warmer to him.

"I've been ready for more than an hour. I've been thinking of you non-stop since yesterday afternoon." She slipped her gloved hand into the crook of his arm and looked into his eyes. "How did your meeting go yesterday? With your mother?"

"It was—" he paused, searching for the right word. "Perfect."

Sunday released the breath she had been holding. "I'm so glad. Do you want to tell me about it?"

"In time," he said. "I'm still processing it all."

"But you liked her?"

"Very much. I felt like I knew her." He began to lead the way to his car.

"Did you get some of your questions answered?"

He opened the passenger door and she got in.

"She explained what happened to my father and why she put me up for adoption." He shut her door, came around the front of the car, and got into the driver's seat. He reached for the ignition but stopped and leaned back into his seat.

He recounted Lyla's story.

Sunday reached across the console and put her hand on his arm.

"She said she's regretted giving me up every day of her life since I was adopted."

"That's so tragic." Sunday swallowed hard.

Josh blinked rapidly and started the ignition.

"Thank you for telling me," Sunday said.

"There's more to the story. I'll fill you in later." He pulled away from the curb. "We'd better get going. We've got a full day ahead of us."

"Do tell." Sunday took a pair of sunglasses from her purse and put them on. "I still don't know what you've got planned. I'm wearing my walking shoes." She pointed to her flat-soled boots. "And I'm dying to know."

Josh reached into the backseat to retrieve a large paper, rolled into a cylinder and secured with a rubber band. He handed it to Sunday.

"I got this from the Chamber of Commerce."

"It's a map," Sunday said, unrolling it and turning it around until north was facing up. She peered at the title at the top of the document. "Historic Westbury."

Josh nodded.

Sunday held the map in a ray of sunshine streaming through the windshield and studied the document. She placed her finger on the numbered items on the map and traced her way to the key in the corner.

"Oh, my gosh! These are all historic sites of Westbury. I had no idea this was available. No one's ever mentioned it."

He grinned. "So you think this is interesting?"

"Are you kidding me? This is the kind of thing that makes my pulse race."

"Mine too," Josh said. "Now that I've decided to stay in Westbury—especially now that I've got family here," his voice cracked, "I want to learn everything I can about this place."

Sunday swiveled her head to look at him.

"That's what we're going to do today. We're going to follow the map and visit all of these places." He cut his eyes from the road to glance at her.

Sunday squealed. "I've never been on a more interesting—or original—date. This is fantastic."

"I thought it would be right up your alley. To tell you the truth, I don't know of another girl who would enjoy this." Josh pulled into a turn lane. "First stop is Rosemont," he said. "There's information on the back of the map about each stop."

Sunday opened her mouth to tell Josh that she'd been inside Rosemont when she'd met with Maggie but stopped herself. "I can't wait to see it. Do you think Maggie minds people driving up to gawk at her house?"

"I saw her at work yesterday morning. I told her about the map and that I'd planned to do the tour today—with my date."

"What did she say?"

Josh chuckled. "She thought it was a neat idea for a date, too. She hadn't heard of the map, either," Josh said. "Said it explains why they sometimes find people in their driveway, looking up at Rosemont." He completed his turn onto the long, winding driveway that would take them to Rosemont. "She said that she wished they would be home to show us the inside, but John's at the animal hospital and she's at her daughter's. She told me to be sure to walk around the grounds."

"That was nice of her."

He pulled to a stop on the circular drive, and they got out of the car. "Some of the oldest oaks and maples in the state are right here, on Rosemont's back lawn."

Sunday tilted her head to examine the roofline. She counted the chimneys with her finger. "Six. Can you imagine having six fireplaces? It's lovely, isn't it? There's such a sense of permanence and calm about the place."

Josh nodded.

"Let's find those trees," Sunday said, heading around the side of the house. "As I remember, you love to paint landscapes."

"I'm drawn to nature," he replied, looking at his watch. "We can spend twenty minutes here. I'd like to make two more stops before we get to Town Square later this morning. We can visit Town Hall and the points of interest along the Square before we have lunch at Pete's."

"That sounds nice."

"After lunch, we'll head into the countryside. There are four more stops before we come to the end of the tour."

Sunday nodded.

"It ends at The Mill," Josh said. "We've got reservations there at six thirty—if you aren't tired of me by then."

Sunday grabbed his arm and hugged it to her. "There's no way I'll be tired of you," she assured him. "I can't wait to tell Lyla about this," Sunday gushed. "She'll think this is so cool."

Josh held the door as Sunday stepped into Pete's Bistro.

"I didn't know Westbury was such a bustling metropolis at the turn of the twentieth century," Sunday said. "It's fun to get a glimpse of what life was like then."

Sunday looked over her shoulder at Josh, who stood in the open doorway, scanning the room. He raised his hand in greeting to someone seated by the window.

She turned and saw Lyla waving back.

"I've got someone I want you to meet," he said, grabbing her hand and pulling her with him.

"Lyla?" Sunday stammered. "I've already met Lyla. We work together. You know that. She's the one who set us up."

Josh stopped at the table as Lyla got to her feet. He turned to Sunday. "I'd like you to meet Lyla—my biological mother."

Sunday took a step back and swiveled her head from mother to son and back again. "Your—your mother?"

Josh's smile lit the room.

Sunday leaned into Lyla and they hugged each other hard.

Lyla was the first to step back. "Can you believe it?"

"I'm—I'm so happy for you. For you both." Sunday's eyes welled with tears. "I had no idea."

"I never talked about it. To anyone," Lyla said. "I was too filled with regret and heartache. I've been grieving this my whole adult life."

"That's all over now," Josh said, pulling out a chair for Sunday.

Sunday plopped into her seat. She leaned over the table to take Lyla's hands. "I don't have words for how happy I am for both of you."

"I've been praying about this every day, and my prayers have been answered." Lyla said.

Sunday turned to Josh. "How on earth did you keep this to yourself all morning?"

"It was hard not to blurt it out," he admitted, "but I wanted to surprise you. I knew you'd be happy for both of us."

"That's the understatement of the century," Sunday said, rummaging in her purse for a tissue. "I may sit here and cry all through lunch."

Lyla patted her hand. "Don't do that. I want to hear all about your morning. Josh explained his plan for your day, and I told him it was a genius idea."

"It most certainly was." Sunday bathed Josh in her smile. "It's been riveting, and we're only halfway through the map."

They placed their orders and discussed the town with great animation as they ate.

"We're lucky to live in such a peaceful place," Lyla said. "After Maggie and Alex cleaned up the corruption at Town Hall, we're back to our safe little town."

Sunday bit her lip. She wasn't so sure that Lyla was right—someone in their safe little town had been stealing a fortune in rare books from the Highpointe Library, and maybe offing librarians.

"Are you all right, Sunday?" Lyla asked.

"Yes. Fine. I was just thinking about the upcoming stops on our Historic Westbury tour this afternoon."

"You'd better be on your way," Lyla said, "if you want to finish before dinner. The Mill is fabulous—you won't want to miss that."

Josh reached for the check, but Lyla was too quick for him.

"You two get out of here. This is on me." She looked between the two of them. "I've never been happier in my life."

Sunday leaned across the table and kissed Lyla on the cheek. "Thank you," she whispered in Lyla's ear. "For everything."

"I'll call you tomorrow," Josh said. "If that's okay?"

Lyla beamed. "Of course it is. Now," she pointed to the door, "be gone with you."

Josh and Sunday spent the rest of the afternoon winding their way along country roads. The afternoon was sunny and calm, with a hint of spring in the air.

The map was mostly accurate and when it wasn't, they worked together to find their destination. They visited an abandoned church and a forgotten mercantile center.

The sun was dropping low in the sky when they approached an overrun homestead. Their elongated shadows transformed them into giants striding across the barren field. They hiked through stiff grass until they came to the crumbling foundation of a farmhouse.

Sunday consulted the description on the back of the map. "It says here that the family farmed the largest plot in the state in the eighteen nineties. They attributed their success to the fourteen sons who worked the farm." Her head snapped up. "Good heavens. Fourteen children—all boys. I can't imagine."

Josh pointed to the foundation. "This would have been a large house for that period of time," he said. "By today's standards, it would be cramped for a family of four."

"They were tough back then," she said.

Josh shielded his eyes with his hand and turned slowly in a circle, surveying the spot. The house sat at the top of a gentle rise. A stand of trees stood to one side, with empty fields stretching in every direction. "Beautiful land."

"It sure is."

He spun to her. "Wait right here," he said and took off at a run for the tree line two hundred yards away. When he reached his destination, he bent and pulled something out of the ground, tucking it into his jacket.

She watched as he jogged back to her and held his treasure out to her.

"Crocus!" she cried, taking the white, yellow, and purple flowers from him. "The first flowers of spring. They're beautiful."

"They must have been blooming there for decades," he said. "According to this," he pointed to the map, "the land hasn't been farmed since the nineteen fifties."

"It's sweet to think that these people had spring flowers to look forward to every year," Sunday said. "It must have been very lonely out here all winter long. It's so easy to feel sorry for our forebearers—to imagine that their lives were hard and joyless. I like knowing that they had the optimism to plant these."

Josh drew her into his arms. "You have a poetic soul, you know that? Kind and insightful."

She turned her face to his. "And you're a romantic." she said, holding the flowers up for him to smell.

Josh moved her hand gently aside and kissed her deeply.

They stood, wrapped in each other's arms, as the sun dipped below the horizon.

"We've got one more stop," he said. "The Mill. Are you hungry?"

"You bet," she said. All she wanted was to be with him.

Chapter 37

"You've disappointed me."

Anthony shook with an involuntary shiver. His phone showed a number from a Chicago area code. Nigel was there. "What do you mean?"

"Ms. Sloan is still with us," the Englishman hissed. "I just called the library and was told she's in a meeting. Would I like to leave a message?" He snorted. "No, I would not. What I really want is for her to be six feet under."

"You're crazy. You think they'll believe another librarian had a fatal heart attack at her desk? Especially one as young as Sloan?"

"You don't have to poison her. I agree that would be suspicious. There are other ways to take care of business. We've already been through this, Anthony. She's got to go."

"I told you—NO!"

"You're sure about that? Knowing how mad that will make me?"

"I'm sure."

"Didn't you once tell me that you were almost beaten to death over a gambling debt? Weren't you hospitalized for weeks? Would you like to go through that again?"

Anthony was silent.

"I can make that happen if you don't do as I've requested."

"Roughing me up won't change my mind."

"It'll be more than roughing *you* up. I think it's time I met your wife and kids, don't you?" He paused. "I'll give you another twenty-four hours to think about it. If the switchboard operator at the library confirms that she's there tomorrow, I'll be forced to take action. Against her—and you."

Anthony pulled his phone away from his ear and stared at the screen. He knew what he had to do.

Chapter 38

"I'm going to work in the library today," Anthony said as he walked up to Fanny Hodson. The administrative assistant that kept everyone and everything in the English Department running smoothly looked up from her desk and smiled.

"Thank you for letting me know," Fanny said, making a note on a paper calendar on the corner of her desk. "You'll be there all day?"

"Yes. I've got an article to write, and I plan to hide in an out-of-the-way cubicle."

"Good plan. Nobody will disturb you there."

He leaned over her desk and whispered conspiratorially. "You'll keep my secret?"

"You bet."

"I'm also going to see if I can get a tour of the rare book room. Now that I'm part of the Friends of the Library, I'd like to know more about it."

"I heard you'd joined that group." She pushed her readers onto the top of her head. "I'm so glad that you're going to help them. Hazel would have been very proud of what that new librarian and the Friends of the Library have accomplished."

He rested his fingertips on the edge of her desk. "Did you know Hazel?"

"Oh my, yes. We were best friends—ever since grade school."

"Horrible that she died so suddenly."

"Yes. It was quite a shock. I'm still not over it." Her voice caught. "Still—she didn't suffer, and she died in the place that she loved best."

"There's comfort in that." He watched her carefully. "They said that she'd never had any health issues. Was that true?"

"I wasn't aware of any. But she never went to the doctor, even when she was sick. She had a horrible cough the winter before she died, and I told her over and over that she needed antibiotics, but she wouldn't see anyone." Fanny shook her head slowly. "I should have dragged her out of that library and forced her to go in. Maybe they would have found her heart problem then. Every women's magazine you pick up has an article about how heart disease is the silent killer of women—that it's treatable but you have to pay attention to the symptoms."

"Don't blame yourself," Anthony said. "You can't force someone to do what they don't want to."

"I've been telling myself that every day since she died," Fanny said. "She had a massive heart attack. They did a thorough investigation at the time, and her daughter told me that she wouldn't have survived even if they'd gotten her to the hospital. I have to accept that."

Anthony took a step back. "I'm sorry to drudge all of this up again."

Fanny swiped her hand across her eyes. "You'd better get going before one of the other professors comes looking for you."

He got into his car and set out for the library. If Nigel was going to harm Sunday, shouldn't he go to the police now? How could he protect her by hanging around the library? He couldn't tail her twenty-four hours a day. And what about his own family?

He pulled into the library parking lot. If he went to the police, what would he say? He'd have to come clean on everything he'd done. He'd lose his job and probably go to jail. His wife and kids would be humiliated. They'd lose their house. Was it fair to his family to set all of this in motion if Nigel wasn't serious?

He brought his head to his hands, replaying the conversation with Fanny in his mind. The medical examiner's investigation had found that Hazel had died of a heart attack. Death by natural causes. He remembered all of the ruckus about it at the time.

Nigel was blowing smoke—trying to scare him. Nigel wanted their arrangement to continue. Anthony did not. Desperation had pushed him into this dirty business, but that was no longer a problem. He had worked hard in his twelve-step program and he was not about to relapse. It was time to end his participation in these thefts, and make sure that nothing worse ensued.

Anthony opened his door. He'd continue with his plan to watch Sunday. If anything, or anybody looked out of place, he'd go to the police.

A cold rain had begun to fall. The roads would soon be icy. He made his way carefully to the entrance. He'd spend the entire day at the library and, if everything seemed normal, he'd stop worrying.

⁂

Anthony walked down the long hallway toward Sunday's office. Her door was open, and she was hunched over her desk. Her left hand held the front cover of a book open while she made notes on a spreadsheet. Stacks of books stood on either side of her desk.

He stepped into the doorframe.

She didn't look up but continued in her work.

He cleared his throat. "Sorry to disturb you," he said. "Looks like you're in the middle of something."

Sunday's head jerked up. She smiled when she saw him. "Come in. Nice to see you," she said, starting to rise.

He motioned for her to remain seated. "Don't get up. I'm working in the library today and wanted to say hello."

She lowered herself back into her chair. "I'm glad that you did. The library is a good place to hide if you don't want to be interrupted."

"Exactly."

"You'd be surprised the number of professors that do that."

"Glad I'm not the only one. I'll get out of your hair and let you return to your—" he gestured to her desk.

"This is the inventory of our rare book collection," she said. "If you need anything while you're here, just let me know. I'm going to run some errands on my lunch hour but other than that, I'll be in the building all day. I'm almost done with this," she said, resting her hand on the spreadsheet, "so I'm going to stay after hours. If you'd like to work late, let me know and I'll sign you in. You can be here until I leave."

"That's very nice of you." He took a deep breath while he considered this. "I'll take you up on that."

"Good," she said. "Let me know where you'll be working after hours so I can come get you when I leave."

"Will do," he said. He'd let his wife know that he wouldn't be home for dinner. With any luck, it would be a quiet day and he'd lay to rest any fear of Nigel harming Sunday.

Sunday returned to her spreadsheet as Anthony stepped away. She was performing an internet search on one of the Revolutionary War items when her phone chimed, alerting her to a text. She leaned back in her chair and brushed her hand across her eyes. She reached for her phone and her pulse quickened when she saw the text from Josh:

Clear skies predicted tonight. I'm stargazing. Perfect spot along the highway by abandoned farm we visited. Join me?

Sunday tapped in her response: *Sure. I'm at library until closing. I can leave by 9:30.*

Josh: *I'll pick you up in back of library then.*

Sunday felt herself flush. She should have told him that she was too busy—she needed to finish the inventory—but she couldn't turn him down.

Sunday: *Great!!! See you soon!*

Anthony set his satchel in a cubicle that afforded him an unobstructed view of the entrance. He pulled out his laptop and opened the commentary he was writing. With any luck, the day would unfold uneventfully and he'd make significant progress on the article so that he could submit it by the spring publication deadline.

The doors opened and a group of students entered the library. A blast of cold air drifted to him, and he pulled his jacket from the back of his chair. He'd like to move to a cubicle where he wouldn't be subjected to drafts from the entrance. Anthony shrugged into his jacket. He'd chosen this cubicle for its vantage point—none of the others fit the bill. He needed to see every person entering the library. He'd have to cope with being cold.

He turned to his article but found that all the frequent interruptions made it impossible to concentrate on his writing. The library was a busy place, and he couldn't work for more than a few minutes at a time before the doors opened and someone came through them. He finally closed the document. He'd pick up the day's *New York Times* and *Wall Street Journal* from the rack on the far wall and spend the day reading newspapers.

He was crossing the reading room, newspapers in hand, when the doors opened, and a stocky man slipped into the library.

Anthony froze. It had been almost ten years since he'd seen the man. It had only been once, but he'd never forgotten him. The balding man with a scar along his jawline had beaten Anthony to within an inch of his life. Whether he'd intended to put Anthony in the hospital for weeks or not, the man had attacked him with an unleashed psychopathic fury that caused Anthony's blood to run cold even now.

Anthony lowered himself into the nearest chair and opened a newspaper to hide the lower part of his face. He kept his eyes on the thug who had been hired to punish him for his unpaid gambling debts—the beating that had been the impetus for his thefts from the library.

Anthony's breath came in short bursts. Could the man be looking for him? Had Nigel sent him?

The man slunk around the edge of the room, picked a tall book off a shelf without glancing at the title, and settled into a chair fifteen feet in front of the spot where Anthony sat. The thug opened the book and kept his face pointed at the door.

Anthony considered crossing behind the man to resume his seat at his cubicle, then abandoned the idea. He didn't want to risk catching the brute's attention. He'd stay where he was.

The clock over the entrance chimed twelve and the library was busy with people coming and going on their lunch hour. At one fifteen, the thug sat forward in his chair and set the book he'd been holding on the floor.

Anthony spotted her as the thug began to rise out of his seat. Sunday tied the sash of her coat, wound her scarf around her neck, and stepped out of the library.

The thug hurried after her, lunging at the door she'd just gone through.

Anthony tasted bile in the back of his throat. The thug was after Sunday! Nigel had meant what he'd said: He'd sent the thug to kill her.

Anthony leapt to his feet. His cell phone and laptop were in the cubicle, but he had no time to retrieve either of them. He ran to catch up to Sunday and the man he was certain would be following her.

Anthony took the steps two at a time, slipping on a patch of ice on the bottom step. He fought to regain his balance and rounded the corner to the parking lot as Sunday pulled her car out of her spot. A large black SUV started its engine. The thug was at the wheel. He slipped into the lane behind Sunday.

Anthony reached his car and threw himself behind the wheel. There were now two other cars between him and the black SUV. He pulled in line behind them.

Sunday led the way on the icy roads to the big-box pet store in a strip center three miles from campus. The black SUV stayed with her.

Anthony pulled into a parking spot one lane over from the SUV. He didn't think the man had spotted him. Despite the cold day, Anthony's collar was wet with perspiration. He was in over his head and he knew it. If he'd had his phone with him, he would have called the police. He should have done it earlier. Sunday was in danger. He couldn't let anything happen to her. He'd have to figure out how to protect her.

The thug remained in his car, the motor idling. The automatic doors to the pet store opened, and Sunday emerged pushing a shopping cart laden with a large box of cat litter and a bag of cat food. She proceeded slowly to her car, struggling to maneuver the cart across the rutted, snow-packed parking lot.

The SUV suddenly pulled out of its parking spot and barreled toward her, picking up speed.

The scene in front of Anthony appeared to play out in slow motion. He knew what the thug was going to do. He was going to run her down with his car. The icy asphalt was the only excuse he'd need to claim he lost control of his vehicle.

Anthony put his foot on the gas and headed down the lane of parked cars. Back-up lights came on to his right and he leaned on the horn. He couldn't stop to let someone pull out.

The SUV was in the lane to his left, slightly ahead of him. Anthony was gaining on it. Sunday was parked in the lane to his right, oblivious to the devastation about to befall her.

Anthony pressed the gas pedal to the floor. His car lurched forward and into the lane that ran directly in front of the pet store.

He heard the sickening crash and felt himself being thrown forward before being pushed back and to the right as his air bags deployed. The SUV hit him squarely on the rear passenger door.

Anthony sat as his car rocked back and forth, then came to a stop. He coughed on the residue of powder unleashed by the air bags, took a deep breath, and turned to look over his left shoulder.

The front driver's side of the SUV was crumpled, and the thug was hunched over the steering wheel, motionless. Blood was splattered across the windshield.

Anthony's ears rang. A face appeared in his driver's side window. The man's mouth was moving as he peered in at Anthony, but Anthony couldn't make out what the man was saying.

The face belonged to a powerfully built young man who grasped the handle of Anthony's driver's side door. He pulled once, and then again. The door opened and cold air rushed in, chasing away the mental fog that had engulfed Anthony.

"We called 9-1-1," the young man said. "Help's on the way."

Anthony fumbled with his seat belt, finally finding the button to release it. He shifted his body and put one foot out of the car.

"Why don't you stay put?" the young man said. "You've been in a terrible accident. You may be hurt."

"I'm okay," Anthony mumbled.

"Let's have the paramedics check you out."

Anthony ignored him. He grasped the doorframe and hauled himself to his feet. He swayed and leaned against the door for support. He glanced toward the store and saw Sunday standing by the entrance, cell phone to her ear.

The unmistakable sounds of sirens could be heard in the distance, getting louder as they approached the scene.

"How's—?" Anthony gestured toward the SUV with one finger.

The young man shook his head. "We don't know. It doesn't look good."

Anthony nodded. "I lost control on the ice."

"Don't try to talk. The police will be here any minute to take your statement."

Anthony nodded.

"I saw him hit you," the young man said. "He was going way too fast. That's what I'll tell them."

Anthony stepped away from the car and glanced in the direction of the sirens. He was about to turn back to the SUV when he spotted a man in the next aisle standing in front of a gray sedan. Their eyes met and locked. The man put two fingers to his brow and saluted Anthony.

Anthony's chest seized with fear and he struggled to take a breath. The man was Nigel. He hadn't just sent the thug; he'd come to make sure Sunday was eliminated. He swayed and the young man reached out to steady him.

An ambulance arrived and two paramedics leapt out. A second ambulance pulled in behind the first.

A paramedic approached Anthony and the young man. "Are you able to walk?"

Anthony nodded.

"We'll need you to step away so we can assist the other driver," the paramedic said. "Wait over there." He pointed to the sidewalk. "Someone will be with you shortly."

"I'm fine," Anthony said. "I don't need medical attention." He and the young man moved to the sidewalk.

"You should go to the hospital and get checked out," the young man said. "It was quite an impact. You don't look fine to me."

Anthony turned away from him. What he needed to do was to keep Sunday in his sights. He couldn't let Nigel get to her.

The police arrived on the scene as the paramedics removed the thug from the SUV and placed him on a gurney. They quickly transferred him to the ambulance, and it sped away.

The police took Anthony's statement. He kept an eye on Sunday as another officer interviewed her. They finished with her before Anthony was done. He saw her load her purchases into her car and leave the lot. His heart hammered in his chest as he watched Nigel pull out after her.

"Sir?" the officer said.

Anthony swallowed his rising panic and turned back to the officer.

"Is that all?"

"Yes. It happened so fast," he said, which was true. "I lost control on the ice and the next thing I knew, that SUV had T-boned me."

"All right," the officer said.

Anthony brought his fingertips to his temples. Should he tell the officer about the stolen books and how the man in the SUV had been trying to kill Sunday? That another man was following her to do the same? Even to his own ears, the story sounded like the ravings of a lunatic. They'd never take him seriously and, even if they did, it would take too long. Sunday might already be dead by the time the police launched into action.

The officer pointed behind Anthony to a paramedic. "They're ready for you."

"I'm fine," Anthony said, gathering all of his strength to impress on them that he didn't need medical attention.

"I'd at least like to take your vitals," the paramedic began, reaching for Anthony's arm.

Anthony took a step back. "Not necessary." He spun on the officer. "Am I free to go?"

The officer nodded in the affirmative.

"I need to get back to Highpointe. I'm a professor, and I have a lecture to give this afternoon."

The young man who had come to Anthony's aid had finished giving his statement and stood behind them.

"You're really not going to the hospital?"

"No, I'm not." Anthony used all of his restraint to keep the irritation out of his voice.

"I'm a student at Highpointe, so if you want a ride," he gestured to Anthony's inoperable car, "I can give you a lift."

Anthony forced a smile and nodded.

"Go ahead," the officer said. "I've got your information and we've called in a tow. It'll be a while before it gets here. They've been busy today with these icy roads. You don't need to wait."

"Thank you," Anthony said. He turned to the young man. "I'd be very grateful. I'd like to get back as soon as possible."

The young man pointed to a pickup truck at the end of the lane in front of them. "Let's go. I've got a class in twenty minutes."

Anthony set off at a fast pace, ignoring the stiffness that was beginning to set into his back. He had no time to lose. He had to reach the library before Nigel got to Sunday.

Chapter 39

The young man unlocked his truck and hoisted himself into the driver's seat.

Anthony grasped the handle of the passenger door and lurched forward, sliding to his knees.

The man got out of the truck and came to Anthony's side. "I think we should go to the ER," he said.

"Nonsense," Anthony said, pulling himself to his feet. "I just lost my footing on the ice."

The man stood, silently appraising Anthony.

"Really. I'm fine. And you've got to get to class."

The man opened the passenger door and put his hand on Anthony's arm as Anthony maneuvered himself into the seat. The man sprinted around the front of the truck to reclaim his seat and started the engine. A hard rock station blared from the radio, the pounding bass reverberating inside the truck's cab.

Anthony brought his hands to his temples and began to massage them as they pulled onto the road that would take them back to Highpointe. "Could you turn that down?"

The man punched the button to turn the radio off. "Headache?"

"Yes."

"That's a sign of a concussion. I played football in high school—I know what that's like."

"I had a headache earlier today," Anthony lied.

The man glanced at Anthony, then turned his attention back to the road. "There's an unopened water bottle in the pocket of your door. Maybe that'll help."

"Thanks," Anthony mumbled. He found the bottle and fumbled with the cap.

"Here," the man said, reaching over and taking the bottle with his right hand. He quickly removed his left from the steering wheel, twisted the cap, and handed the bottle back to Anthony.

Anthony brought the bottle to his lips with a shaking hand and took a sip of water. He swallowed and brought the bottle to his lap, then leaned forward and vomited on the floor at his feet.

"That's it," the man said, checking his mirrors and swinging the truck in a U-turn. "We're going to the hospital. You're not okay, and I'm not going to let something happen to you on my watch."

Anthony remained hunched over, his head in his hands. He didn't protest as they headed away from Sunday and Nigel, and the danger she must certainly be in.

———

Anthony pressed his hands to his temples and concentrated on not throwing up again as they made the short drive to Mercy Hospital.

The young man drove to the emergency room entrance and left the engine running while he raced inside to get help.

Anthony sat still, trying to stop the pounding in his head. The passenger door opened, and a pair of nurses assisted him out of the truck and into a wheelchair. Anthony lifted his head and saw the young man who had been so concerned about him in the corner of his vision.

"They'll take good care of you, okay?" the young man said. "I'm sorry— I know you didn't want to come here, but I had to."

Anthony attempted a smile and raised a finger in acknowledgement as one of the nurses pushed him through a set of automatic doors. He was whisked past the crowded waiting room and through another set of automatic doors.

"Possible concussion from that fatality at the shopping mall," he heard the nurse call to someone sitting behind a desk to his right. "This guy's the other driver."

"Take him to trauma eleven," the person behind the desk said. "It's just opened up."

Anthony was wheeled into a small area cordoned off by curtains.

"Let's get you into bed and see what's going on with you," the nurse said.

Another person joined the nurse and, together, they helped him out of the wheelchair and onto a bed. The other person began asking him his name and insurance details.

Anthony managed to remove his wallet from his pants pocket and found his driver's license and proof-of-insurance card. He handed them to the person and the questioning stopped. He closed his eyes as the nurse poked his arm and started an IV.

"Stay with me, sir," the nurse said.

Anthony concentrated on remaining alert. He had to get out of there to save Sunday.

A doctor introduced himself, shined a light into Anthony's eyes, and ordered an MRI. "I understand that you were the driver of a car that was T-boned earlier today?"

Anthony focused on the doctor. "Yes. I walked away. I'm fine."

"You may not have broken any bones but that doesn't mean that you didn't suffer a concussion. Symptoms may not present themselves for several hours after an injury occurs. Can you tell me what happened?"

Anthony accurately recounted the details of the accident.

"Your memory is fine," the doctor said. He looked at the chart hanging off the end of Anthony's bed. "Your blood pressure is elevated. I understand you have a headache and are nauseated."

"My head still hurts but I don't feel like throwing up anymore. Can you give me something for the pain?"

"It's already being administered in your drip." The doctor pointed to the IV.

"I need to get out of here." Anthony propped himself up on one elbow. He was starting to feel better.

"I'm not ready to release you. Let's wait to see what shows up on the MRI. We may want to keep you overnight for observation."

Anthony sank back onto his pillow.

"I'll be back once we've seen the MRI." The doctor pulled the curtain aside and stepped away, leaving Anthony with a nurse hooking him up to a monitor.

"How long before I get my MRI?"

"We're busy tonight. Yours wasn't the only car accident today. It may be a while."

"What time is it?"

"Six o'clock," the nurse said. "Anything you need before I go?"

"Can I make a call?"

"I can arrange that. Give me a minute." She wrote on his chart and disappeared through an opening in the curtain.

Anthony pushed the button to raise the head of his bed. He was formulating a plan. He'd call the library and ask for Sunday. If the operator told him that she was there, he'd hang up before they could transfer his call. The library didn't close until nine, and she'd already told him that she'd planned to stay after hours. The library was always busiest in the evenings. If she was there, she'd be safe until the library closed. He'd need to leave the hospital in time to be at the library by nine. If she wasn't at the library when he called, he didn't know what he'd do. He'd have to figure out something.

The nurse came in. "I've got a phone for you. Here you go," she said, handing it to him. "Would you like me to dial the number for you?"

He shook his head no. "I've got it. Thank you." He looked at her, his hand hovered over the keypad.

"I'll let you make your call in private," she said. "Just hit the buzzer for me when you're done."

He began punching in the number as she departed. He held his breath as the operator answered his call and he asked for Sunday.

"She's on a call," the woman informed him. "I'll put you through to her voicemail."

He heard clicking on the line and quickly hung up. If they came for him in the next thirty minutes, he'd have the MRI that the doctor had ordered. If not, he'd slip out of the hospital by eight at the latest so that he could be at the library by nine.

The orderly assisted Anthony off the MRI table and onto his emergency room bed. Anthony sank back against the pillow. "Are you doing all right? All that banging inside the MRI machine can cause excruciating pain."

"I'm fine," Anthony lied. The test had been torture.

"Be sure to ask for something if you need it when you get back upstairs," he said. "I've got to bring someone down from the ICU and then I'll take you up. It'll only be a few minutes."

"What time is it?" Anthony asked.

The orderly checked his watch. "Eight twenty." The orderly patted Anthony's shoulder. "I'll leave you here in this alcove where no one will bother you. Why don't you close your eyes and relax? I'll be back as quick as I can."

Anthony watched the orderly walk away. He hoisted himself up on one elbow and swung his legs over the side of the bed. He didn't have time to waste in the hospital. He had to get to the library.

He stood and grabbed the bed rail to steady himself. He could do this.

Anthony squatted and found a plastic bag filled with his clothes, watch, and wallet on the shelf below the hospital mattress. He poked his head out of the alcove and looked right, then left. No one was in sight.

He tore open the bag, threw on his clothes, and was climbing back onto the bed to put on his shoes when he heard a noise at the end of the hall. Anthony grabbed the shoes and his wallet and headed through a door marked Exit to his left.

He found himself in a long, deserted hallway with numerous doorways and signs that identified different divisions of the radiology department. He leaned against the wall, shoved his feet into his shoes, and headed toward a large set of double doors. He needed to get to the hospital entrance.

Anthony hurried down the hallway, breaking into a run. Whether he was feeling better or adrenaline was pumping through his veins, he couldn't say. All he knew was that he was feeling stronger. And that he had to get there in time.

He burst through the double doors and found himself in front of a bank of elevators. A placard on the wall told him he was in Basement 1. He pushed the elevator button and paced until the car arrived. He jabbed the button labeled 1/Lobby. He'd be out of here soon.

The doors closed and the elevator whirred into motion. He jerked his head up. His cell phone was in the reading room of the library. He couldn't call an Uber. He'd have to find a pay phone to call his wife. He would explain that he needed to pick up his phone and laptop. Anthony checked his watch. The library closed in fifteen minutes. She'd tell him that he could get them in the morning. It wouldn't work.

His head began to throb. He exited the elevator and joined the crowd of people leaving the hospital at the end of visiting hours.

He emerged from the automatic doors and took a step back as a blast of biting air hit him. He looked around. A taxi idled at the end of the circular drive in front of the entrance. He cut in front of an elderly man moving slowly with the assistance of a walker and ignored the startled cry of the man's wife. He had to get that taxi.

He raced down the sidewalk and flung the door open. "Highpointe Library!" he shouted.

The driver looked in his rearview mirror. "Good evening, sir. I know Highpointe, but I'm not sure about the library. I'll look it up on my GPS."

"Start driving," Anthony said. "I'm in a hurry to get there before it closes."

"If it closes at nine, we're not going to make it," the driver said. The taxi didn't move.

"Just get going," Anthony snapped. "I'll give you directions when we get to campus."

The driver put the taxi in gear and pulled away from the curb. "Suit yourself," he said, "but I'm not guaranteeing that we'll make it."

Anthony sat back. He needed to think. What would he do if the library were closed?

Chapter 40

Sunday heard the chime on the overheard public address system, followed by the familiar announcement that the library would be closing in ten minutes. She leaned back, lifted her arms over her head, and intertwined her fingers, stretching to the ceiling.

She glanced at the papers strewn across her desk. She'd made good progress. If she stayed late, like she'd planned, she might actually finish. She gathered her papers into a stack as she thought about the evening ahead with Josh. An unaccustomed warmth radiated from her toes to the top of her head. When was the last time she'd been so excited to spend time with a——? She paused, searching for the right word. Was he her boyfriend? Yes. She decided he definitely was her boyfriend.

She picked up her half-full coffee cup and headed to the break room to dump the cold liquid down the drain. On the way back to her office, she stepped to the railing of the massive marble staircase that ran between the first and second floors. It rose twenty feet above the vaulted main reading room before splitting into two branches that continued another ten feet to the second floor. The commotion from the main reading room at the bottom of the staircase told her that the library had been busy that evening.

She wondered if Anthony was still at work. She'd looked for him when she'd returned from her errands, delayed by that hideous accident. She stayed on the scene long enough to make a statement. Not that she'd seen much—she was wrangling a shopping cart across the snow-packed parking lot when it happened. The police told her that one of the cars was going so fast it would have hit her if not for the other car.

She skirted the reception desk, and an involuntary shiver ran up her spine when she remembered the terrible crunch of metal and the concussive blast that followed.

There was no sign of Anthony, she'd searched both floors. He must have changed his mind about remaining after the library closed. She was relieved she didn't have to tell him she'd changed her plans and was leaving on time.

Sunday returned to her desk. She wanted to comb her hair and touch up her makeup. She'd be leaving soon to go stargazing with Josh.

Nigel heard the chime and the announcement in the stall of the men's room in a far corner of the library. After Anthony had taken out his hitman in that unfortunate accident, Nigel knew he'd have to take matters into his own hands.

The Hazel Harrington Rare Book Room was adjacent to the men's room. He'd been sorely tempted to seek admission to review the collection on his own but had restrained himself. He'd have to show identification and interface with a human being in order to gain access to the room. Even though he was carrying several fake IDs, he couldn't risk someone being able to identify him and place him at the library on the same day that Highpointe's young librarian met her demise.

A deep chuckle escaped his throat while he waited in the dank, dreary stall. When he had entered the library, he overheard Sunday tell the receptionist that she would close up and set the alarm for the night. He checked his watch. It was time.

Quietly he eased several paper towels out of the dispenser and ran them under the tap. He shoved the soggy mass under the soap dispenser and slathered it with gooey pink soap.

He flipped off the bathroom switch, plunging himself into darkness, and cracked open the door. The library was dimly lit and silent—assuring him that he and that nosy parker of a librarian were the only two left in the building.

Clutching the soap-laden wad in one hand, Nigel slowly opened the door with the other and stepped into the shadows.

He made his way noiselessly across the reading room to the staircase that led to the staff offices. He rubbed his free hand across his mouth to stifle another chuckle. Really—could this be any easier for him?

On the first landing, he peered over the railing to the cold marble floor below. This would do it. No one could survive a fall from this height.

He knelt in the middle of the space and surveyed the scene on either side of him. His plan would work. He smiled as the slimy towels eased across the marble landing under his fingertips, leaving a thick slippery paste in their wake.

When he was done, he rocked back on his heels and nodded in satisfaction at his handiwork. It was invisible in the low light. Careful to avoid the soap, he walked on his knees to the railing, where he pulled himself to a standing position.

When Sunday Sloan crossed the landing, she was sure to slip. And if she didn't fall over the edge on her own, one firm push from him would be all it would take.

He clutched the railing as he made his way up the remaining steps. A sign at the top of the stairs pointed to the staff offices. He set off to find his victim.

The taxi dropped Anthony at the library at nine thirteen. He peeled off three twenties for the thirty-dollar fare and leapt out of the taxi.

"Do you want me to wait?" the driver asked.

"No." Anthony slammed the door and hurried through the snow and up the steps to the entrance. The building was locked.

Anthony looked up at the library's impressive edifice. Only dim interior lights could be seen from the front window. Sunday's office was at the back of the building.

He raced down the steps, catching his foot and stumbling on the last one. He managed to regain his footing on the icy path and rushed to the back of the library.

What he saw made his blood run cold.

A single light from Sunday's second-story office window pierced the inky darkness of the back lot—where two cars sat. One of them was Sunday's. The other, a looming gray sedan, was Nigel's.

The stairs to the back door looked treacherous, but he climbed them, and pulled at the back door. No luck. He moved to one of the ground-level basement windows, looking for a latch or a crack in the glass. He had to get into the library.

His eyes scanned the parking lot and caught the glint of a large rock in one of the landscape planters. He wrestled out of his jacket, then dashed to the planter and back to the window. With the jacket tightly wrapped around his fist, he heaved the heavy stone against the pane. Glass shattered into the basement, but no alarm sounded. He prayed that window sensors and a silent alarm were summoning police, but he couldn't afford to wait. Anthony bashed at the window again, using the rock to break enough glass to allow him to squeeze through.

As he eased his bruised body through the small opening to the basement floor, a shard of glass caught at his left cheek, scraping a clean and nasty gash from his jaw to his temple. He ignored the injury and blinked, letting his eyes adjust to the dark room.

Through the broken window, the streetlamp cast an eerie glow on what looked to be a storage room filled with musty-smelling tables and old wooden chairs. There was a door no more than five feet away. He pushed his way through the furniture, sending a stack of chairs crashing to the floor as he opened the door to total darkness.

He reached out, feeling his way along a wall, shuffling his feet forward. His head was throbbing. The blood from his newest wound trickled into his mouth, and the warm metallic taste made him gag.

Suddenly the wall turned a corner and he jammed his toe on something. He leaned forward and felt the outline of a stair. Above he could see a shaft of light coming from what looked to be a door. If he were lucky, these stairs would lead him to the first-floor reception desk. Clinging to the railing, he took the first step slowly, careful not to bang another toe. As the second step creaked beneath him, a blood-curdling scream came from above.

Chapter 41

"We're close to Rosemont, aren't we?" Sean leaned forward in the backseat.

"It's about a mile ahead, on the right," Frank said.

"I love that we drive by it on our way home." Marissa said. "I always look for the lights through the trees."

"We should stop," Sean said. "We need to tell them."

"That's a great idea!" Marissa cried.

"We can't barge in on them," Frank said. "Not at this time of night. It's after nine."

"Pleeeeze," came the chorus of the three children in the backseat.

"We were married there," Loretta said softly. "They've been more like family to us than anyone else."

Frank cut his eyes to hers. "You want to stop?"

"I'd like them to hear it from us," Loretta said. "Not from the grapevine."

"Since we just celebrated our news by having dinner at Pete's, I'd say the grapevine may already be buzzing."

"All the more reason to do it now," Loretta said. "Why don't you turn in and go up the driveway? If their lights are on, we can call to see if they're still up."

Frank turned onto the driveway that wound its way up the hill to Rosemont. They cleared the last stand of trees and pulled in front of the house. Two oblongs of light spilled onto the lawn.

"They're up," Loretta said. "That light is coming from the library."

Marissa pointed out the window to a light farther back, along the front of the house. "I think that's the kitchen."

Frank put the car in park and reached for his cell phone. He turned in his seat. "You're sure you want to do this?"

"Yes," came four excited replies.

Frank scrolled through his contacts, found Maggie's number, and placed the call.

"Frank." Maggie answered on the first ring. "Is everything all right?

"Yes, thank you."

"You scared me, calling so late."

"I didn't mean to alarm you. Have you—have you and John gone to bed already?"

"No. We're still up. Why?"

"Can we drop in? Just for a minute."

He heard her draw a deep breath.

"Of course, you can. When?"

"We're right out front. We're in your driveway."

"Who's 'we'?"

"Loretta and the kids. And me."

Maggie paused. "Be right there."

The massive mahogany front door of Rosemont swung open and light from the entryway chandelier tumbled down the stone steps and onto the driveway.

Maggie and John stood in the open doorway, silhouetted by the light from inside the house.

"Okay everybody," Loretta said. "We can all go in, but you need to let Frank do the talking." She smiled at her husband as she unbuckled her seat belt. "I think he deserves to be the one to deliver our happy news."

They piled out of the car.

"I expect you to be on your best behavior. We're only going to stay a few minutes. Tomorrow is a school day, and you've been out too late as it is."

They all marched up the stone steps.

"Come in," Maggie said, motioning them inside. "How are you feeling?" She asked Loretta. "I heard that your surgery got canceled—that you no longer needed the procedure."

"I'm wonderful, actually," Loretta said.

"That's why we're here," Frank said. Sean, Marissa, and Nicole lined up behind Frank and Loretta.

Maggie looked at Frank. The happiness pouring off him was palpable. He bore no resemblance to the bitter, conniving man she'd met when she'd moved into Rosemont all those years ago.

She looked from Frank to the children behind him. They were straining to keep a secret; she was sure of it.

"We have news." Frank took Loretta's hand in his. "Since Loretta and I began our married life here, we wanted you to be the first to know."

Maggie's eyes began to water. She glanced at John out of the corner of her eye and saw that he was blinking rapidly.

"Loretta and I are going to have a baby. Turns out her recent fatigue and queasiness was for a happy reason."

Maggie clapped her hands together and had to restrain herself from jumping up and down. "Oh Frank—Loretta—I'm thrilled for you." She stepped forward and stretched her arms wide to draw them both into a hug. "This is fabulous news."

Maggie stepped back and looked at the three children, obediently quiet behind Frank and Loretta.

"And you three will be the best big brother and sisters, ever," she said.

John extended his hand and clasped Frank's. "Congratulations, man," he said, pumping Frank's hand.

"Thank you." Frank shook his head slowly. "I still can't believe it."

"When are you due?" Maggie asked.

"I saw an obstetrician for the first time today," Loretta said. "I'm only four weeks along."

"How are you feeling?"

"About the same. Tired and nauseated. Sort of like I did with endometriosis, but now that I know the reason, I don't mind."

"Are you trying to keep this a secret?" Maggie asked.

"In this town?" Loretta asked. "I know better than that. We just had dinner at Pete's to celebrate, so I suspect half the population knows by now. We wanted you to hear it from us." Loretta slipped her hand through Frank's arm.

"I'm so glad you came over," Maggie said. "We're thrilled for you. Do you mind if I call Susan to share your news? Or do you want to tell her?"

"That's fine," Loretta said with a yawn. "We need to get going. These guys have school tomorrow, and I'm bushed."

Maggie put her arm across Loretta's shoulders as they turned toward the door. "I'll throw a baby shower for you. At Rosemont."

"Don't you think I'm a little old for a baby shower? I already have three children."

"Nonsense," Maggie said. "That was a while ago. Do you still have any of the stuff you'll need?"

Loretta shook her head. "I donated it all years ago."

"There you go," Maggie said. "It's settled."

Loretta laughed and looked at Maggie. "Whoever would have thought that we'd become friends? You've been so kind to me, Maggie. More than I ever deserved."

Maggie flushed and patted her shoulder. She addressed the children. "Would you like to help with the shower?"

Marissa and Nicole nodded enthusiastically.

"You and Frank and I will find something fun to do that day," John said to Sean.

Sean gave him a thumbs-up.

Loretta and the children started down the steps to the car.

Frank hung back.

He and Maggie faced each other, then hugged. "I couldn't be more delighted for you, Frank. You deserve this."

Frank swallowed hard. "I'm not sure I agree with that, but I'm going to make sure I'm worthy of it." He followed his family to the car.

Maggie and John stood in the doorway, arm in arm, until Frank's taillights rounded a bend and were lost from view.

"How about that?" John asked.

"I can't wait to tell Susan," Maggie said. "I don't care what time it is; I'm going to call her. She'll be so excited to hear this."

Chapter 42

Nigel crept down the hallway to the square of light outside the open door of Sunday's office. This was going to be so easy. He had to restrain himself from cackling.

He peered into the open door. His target was bent over the desk, her back to him. She was a tall woman, thin and in shape. Still, his plan was foolproof.

He knocked softly on the doorframe.

Sunday uttered a small yelp and turned to the door.

"I'm sorry to startle you," he said.

Sunday gulped for air and studied him. The man looked familiar. "What are you doing here? The library is closed."

"That's my problem," he said. "I was so absorbed in my work that I didn't realize it was closing. And now I don't know how to get out."

"You didn't hear the chime and the announcement?"

"Alas"—he pointed to his ears—"my hearing's not very good anymore. I really should get hearing aids."

She stared at him. *How did she know him?*

He cleared his throat. "You're obviously working late. You must have a key. Can you let me out?"

A chill ran down Sunday's spine. The sooner she got rid of him, the better. "Certainly." She retrieved her keys from her purse. "Follow me."

"Thank you."

As they exited her office, he stopped short. "Where are you going? Isn't the front that way?" he asked, pointing in the opposite direction.

"I thought we'd take the elevator," she said.

"Oh—no need of that on my account," he said. "I'm fine with taking the stairs."

Sunday paused to look at him.

"The white stone is beautiful in the moonlight," he added, smiling and taking a step toward her as he motioned to the marble staircase.

She turned slowly toward the steps. The heat radiating from his body felt stifling in the large, cool library. "All right." She walked briskly to the staircase, hoping to put a few steps between them, but the man kept pace.

"You're from England, aren't you?" she asked as they began their descent.

"Yes."

Something at the edge of her mind urged her to wait a beat before taking the next step.

Not noticing her pause, the man continued on, now a few steps ahead of her. They were almost to the landing. Soon he would be out of here and—her heart skipped a beat—Josh would be waiting for her in the lot.

"What are you doing in Westbury?" she asked.

"I've been at the rare book show in Chicago and wanted to see Highpointe's brilliant collection. I'm a big fan of Alfred, Lord Tennyson."

Sunday stopped midstride, one foot hovering above the next step as recognition flooded over her. He was the proprietor of Blythe Rare Books. "I didn't see your name on the sign-in sheet," she said, her voice barely a whisper. "The collection is in a secure room. I check the log every day."

He peered at her over his shoulder. Even in the dim light, the malice in his eyes was unmistakable.

Move! her brain screamed—but only when he lunged for her did her feet obey. Sunday turned and ran.

Nigel was swift. Two steps up, he caught the lip of her jacket pocket and pulled. She ripped it free but stumbled and the library keys flew out of her hand and sailed over the railing. Nigel grabbed hold of the bun at the nape of her neck and pulled.

She screamed, the sound bouncing off the marble and reverberating through the entire building. She dug her nails into his hand as Nigel yanked her down the steps to the landing. He lost his footing halfway across, and they both tumbled to the floor.

Sunday tore her hair loose and tried to stand, but her hands slipped on a sweet-smelling slimy goo. She started to crawl away from him, but Nigel, on his knees behind her, grabbed hold of her ankle and pulled her back across the slick floor and wrapped an arm around her stomach pulling her up with him. His other arm came around to strangle her, and instinctively she

230

tucked her chin, lodging her face in the crook of his elbow. When he squeezed, she sank her teeth into him and heard his shriek echo across the library.

The door flew open and bounced off the rubber doorstop behind the reception desk almost knocking Anthony back down the steep basement steps. He grasped the doorknob to steady himself and catch his breath when another scream came from the landing directly above him.

He raced to the foot of the marble staircase and saw the librarian thrashing in Nigel's arms.

"Nigel! Stop!" Anthony shouted, and both figures froze.

A dazed face peered at him under a mass of disheveled blond hair. "Professor … ?" The single word croaked out of Sunday's throat, and Anthony dashed up the stairs, taking two at a time.

Nigel dragged her closer to the railing, his legs at awkward angles as he slid across the floor. "You wouldn't do it, so I have to," he hissed, struggling against Sunday's flailing slaps. "She's … got … to … go."

Anthony reached the top stair and rushed at Nigel but lost his footing on the slippery landing. He managed to catch the man's left pant leg on the way down, and he yanked at the fabric. Nigel raised his right foot, bringing it down on Anthony's hand with a sickening crack.

Anthony yelped and released his hold, but Nigel's movement was enough for Sunday to wrest herself free from his grasp. She fell a few feet away from him and crawled to the display niche at the back of the landing to lift herself up.

A furious Nigel grabbed the back of Anthony's jacket, and hauled him to the railing, pulling the professor to his feet.

Sunday snatched a stone bust of Alfred, Lord Tennyson, from the display and landed a solid thud across Nigel's upper back. His fist unclenched, and Anthony jumped away.

Nigel spun to face Sunday and slipped on the slimy floor. The anger on his face suddenly turned to shock, then terror, as he stumbled back into the railing—and tumbled over. His high-pitched scream was cut off by the wail of approaching police sirens as he fell to the marble floor, twenty feet below.

Chapter 43

Lyla rested her book against her chest and snatched her phone from the nightstand on the first ring. "Josh. Is everything all right?"

"Yes—it's better than all right. I'm on my way to pick up Sunday. We're going stargazing."

"I love the sound of that!"

"Would you—would you like to come with us?"

"Of course not," Lyla said. "You don't want to take your mother along on a date."

"You're sure? Sunday wouldn't mind."

"I'm already in bed with my book." Lyla wondered if she should stick her nose into her son's business. She decided she should. "So—you're seeing a lot of each other. Is this getting—serious?"

Josh chuckled. "The line's breaking up. Gotta go."

"Okay, you," Lyla replied. "This line is fine. I can tell when I'm getting the brush off. Have fun tonight."

"I'll call you tomorrow," Josh said before disconnecting the call.

It was nine twenty when he drove past a taxi leaving the library, and pulled around to the employee lot, where only two cars remained. One of them must be Sunday's. He pulled his phone out of his pocket and texted her: *Waiting for you out back. I'm early. Take your time. No rush.*

Maggie heard the click that indicated she had an incoming call. "Hang on, Susan," she said, "I've got another call—the third one since we've been talking. I need to see who it is."

"Take the call. Super news about Frank and Loretta. Talk to you later." Susan disconnected the line.

Maggie tapped her screen and found the chief of the campus police on the line. Her eyes grew wide and her breathing quickened as she listened. "I'm on my way," she said.

John was in the kitchen, giving the dogs their bedtime treats when she raced into the room and snatched her purse from the counter.

"Campus police just called. There's been a break-in at the library. Officers are responding. I think I'd better get down there."

"With what you've told me about those thefts from the rare book collection, I think you're right." John grabbed his coat.

"You've got to get up early for work," Maggie said, thrusting her arms into the sleeves of her coat. "I'll go on my own."

"Not on your life," John said, heading for the stairs. "I'll get my keys and we'll be on our way."

Josh checked the time. It was almost nine-thirty, and Sunday hadn't answered his text. She was always so prompt. He rubbed the back of his neck. He was being silly. She'd be coming out the door any minute now.

He double-checked his text messages; sometimes the phone didn't ping like it was supposed to. He pursed his lips. She hadn't returned his message.

Maybe he should walk around the building. Maybe she needed to set the alarm at the front door and would walk around to the back. He could meet her there.

He got out of his car and walked toward the building when he noticed what he wasn't able to see from inside the car: a broken basement window—and blood. He sprinted up the steps to the back door and found it locked.

Josh ran toward the front of the library. As he rounded the corner, he heard the sirens. By the time he reached the stone steps leading to the entryway, he saw the flashing red lights of police cars.

He took the steps to the front doors two at a time. Josh tugged savagely at the doors, but they remained firmly locked. He pounded on them with his fists and shouted Sunday's name.

Three police cars pulled nose-in to the entrance. Officers piled out of the cars. Red lights ricocheted off the library's stone façade.

"Sir," an officer called to him. "Step away."

Josh continued to rattle the doors.

The officer ran up the steps. "Step away from the doors."

Josh turned. "My girlfriend's in there." He choked on the words. "Somebody broke in from the back."

The officer took Josh by the arm and pulled him aside.

"She's in danger. You've got to get in there."

Another officer joined them and rapped on the doorframe with the butt of her flashlight. The metallic clang reverberated through the night. "Police!" the officer yelled. "Open up."

Maggie and John arrived and parked to one side. Maggie hurried to the officer she recognized as the campus police chief. She cupped her eyes with her hands and looked at the young man that an officer was confronting at the top of the steps.

"Josh!" Maggie cried.

"You know him?" the chief asked.

"Yes. That's my assistant. Josh Newlon."

"Could he be involved?"

Maggie took a step back. "I'm—I'm not sure!"

"Bring him down here," the chief called to the officer.

The officer escorted Josh down the steps to where Maggie and John stood with the chief.

"Sunday's in there!" Josh shouted, but Maggie couldn't hear him above the din of the sirens. "Something's wrong. A window's broken in back. There's blood!"

—·—

Anthony and Sunday stood in stunned silence as the sirens grew louder.

Sunday turned to Anthony, her voice hoarse. "You knew, didn't you?"

Anthony nodded.

"You and—him"—she gestured to the railing—"were in cahoots, weren't you? You were stealing books and selling them to him."

Anthony nodded again.

They heard the sirens in front of the library.

"And he wanted you to kill me because I'd gotten suspicious?"

"That's right." He held her gaze.

"But you didn't do it. You came here to save me." Her eyes grew wide. She took in his battered appearance: the yellowing bruises over his right eye and along his jawline, the blood streaming down the other side of his face. "What happened to you?"

Anthony shrugged. "I was in an accident. At lunchtime."

She drew in a sharp breath. "You were the driver of the car that got T-boned today, weren't you?"

They heard someone pounding on the doors.

"That guy would have hit me—probably killed me." She raked her fingers through her hair. "You pulled out in front of him on purpose, didn't you? You risked your own life. And you saved me." She pointed again at the railing. "Twice."

Their eyes locked as the officers rattled the door.

"You look like you should be in the hospital."

He shrugged. "I just came from there."

"You pushed through all of that pain to come here, to save me. Again."

"How could I do anything else—and still live with myself?"

Sunday tore her eyes away from Anthony and descended the staircase.

"You can tell them everything," he called after her.

She knelt to pick up a set of keys that lay at the foot of the stairs and then looked up at him. "I'm not sure I have anything to say."

Anthony watched her unlock and open the doors, and the flashing police lights almost blinded him. They bounced and reflected off the walls, outlining Nigel's twisted body in screaming red.

The officer at the entrance rushed to Nigel while another radioed for paramedics.

Holding a hand over her eyes, Sunday stepped through the doors into the freezing night. Josh moved forward but an officer held him back.

"Sunday!" he shouted.

She followed his voice and found him standing with President Martin and a man she didn't know at the bottom of the steps.

Maggie spun to face Josh. "You know her?" She didn't have to wait for his answer—his eyes telegraphed his care and concern for Sunday.

Josh started toward the steps, and the officer restrained him.

"May I?" Maggie asked the chief, pointing to the young woman teetering at the top of the steps.

The chief nodded.

Maggie made her way to Sunday.

Sunday hovered at the side of the entrance, her arms wrapped around herself, shivering in the cold.

Maggie removed her coat and draped it around Sunday's shoulders. "What happened in there?"

Sunday swallowed hard and opened her mouth to speak, but the words caught in her throat.

An ambulance arrived and paramedics leapt out, assembled their gear, and raced to the entrance.

"Let's get out of the way," Maggie said. She pointed to where John and Josh stood below with the officer, who was watching Sunday.

Maggie put her arm around Sunday's shoulders, and they made their way down the steps. She caught the officer's gaze and raised an eyebrow, nodding her head in Josh's direction.

The officer stepped aside and released Josh.

Josh met Sunday at the bottom step and swept her into his arms.

She nestled her face against his neck.

"Are you—are you all right?" he murmured into her hair.

She rocked back to look at him, her eyes roaming his face.

A loud clang at the entrance to the library drew their attention. A gurney was being wheeled across the threshold and carried down the steps by paramedics to the waiting ambulance. A breathing apparatus obscured the face of the person strapped to the gurney.

Josh pulled Sunday to him and held her tightly.

She sagged against him.

"I'm so glad that's not you," he said, and his voice cracked. "You're safe. That's all I need to know."

Maggie and John watched as a paramedic slammed the rear door of the ambulance shut and it pulled away, lights flashing.

John pointed to the entrance of the library.

Maggie turned and saw a man staggering down the steps. She took a step forward. The kaleidoscope of emergency lights distorted his face, but something about him was familiar.

She brought her hand to her forehead. The man was Professor Anthony Plume.

"What in the world—" Maggie gasped. She turned wide eyes to John.

"My dear," John said, "you've managed to land smack in the middle of yet another mystery. Life is never boring around you."

The End

Thank You for Reading!

If you enjoyed *Shelving Doubts*, I'd be grateful if you wrote a review.

Just a few lines would be great. Reviews are the best gift an author can receive. They encourage us when they're good, help us improve our next book when they're not, and help other readers make informed choices when purchasing books. Reviews keep the Amazon algorithms humming and are the most helpful aide in selling books! Thank you.

To post a review on Amazon:

1. Go to the product detail page for *Shelving Doubts* on Amazon.com.
2. Click "Write a customer review" in the Customer Reviews section.
3. Write your review and click Submit.

In gratitude,
Barbara Hinske

Just for You!

Wonder what Maggie was thinking when the book ended? Exclusively for readers who finished Shelving Doubts, take a look at Maggie's Diary Entry for that day at https://barbarahinske.com/maggies-diary.

Acknowledgements

I'm blessed with the wisdom and support of many kind and generous people. I want to thank the most supportive and delightful group of champions an author could hope for:

My insightful and supportive assistant Lisa Coleman who keeps all the plates spinning;

My life coach Mat Boggs for your wisdom and guidance:

My kind and generous legal team, Kenneth Kleinberg, Esq. and Michael McCarthy—thank you for believing in my vision;

The professional "dream team" of my editors Linden Gross and Jesika St. Clair;

My genius marketing advisor Mitch Gandy;

To my witty and endlessly supportive attorney friend Howard Meyers, Esq.—thank you for always opening doors for me; and

Keri Knutson for a beautiful cover.

Book Club Questions

1. Have you ever changed careers?
2. What prompted you to make the change—or held you back?
3. Did you have doubts about your new professional direction? How did you handle any second thoughts?
4. If you could have one "do-over" in your professional life, what would it be?
5. Do you have a service dog, or have you ever seen one in action?
6. If you have a dog, have you trained it and how did you do it?
7. What creative outlets do you enjoy?
8. Is there a hobby you're looking forward to enjoying in the future?
9. What activity could you give up so you could enjoy this hobby now?
10. What piece of advice do you wish your 21-year-old self would have listened to?

About the Author

BARBARA HINSKE recently left the practice of law to pursue her writing career full time. Her novella *The Christmas Club* has been made into a Hallmark Channel Christmas movie of the same name (2019), and she feels like she's living the dream. She is extremely grateful to her readers! She inherited the writing gene from her father who wrote mysteries when he retired and told her a story every night of her childhood. She and her husband share their own Rosemont with two adorable and spoiled dogs. The old house keeps her husband busy with repair projects and her happily decorating, entertaining, and gardening. She also spends a lot of time baking and—as a result—dieting.

Please enjoy this chapter from

The Christmas Club—Now on the Hallmark Channel

Readers are hailing *The Christmas Club* as "heartwarming," "uplifting," and "an instant holiday classic."

The heavy revolving door picked up speed, knocking Verna Lind's gloves out of her hand and flinging her from the warmth of the Cleveland bank into the frigid December air. Despite the flat soles of her sensible work shoes, her left foot slipped on the icy pavement, and both she and her large purse came crashing down. The purse's well-worn metal clasp burst open, spilling her possessions across the walk and into West Third Street. Dazed, Verna blinked and began to crawl toward the smattering of five-dollar bills lying in the road when a sudden gust of wind lifted her Christmas savings and sent it soaring into traffic.

Edward Fuller bent his lanky frame into the wind as he dashed down West Third Street, one hand gripping the tan fedora on his head, the other carrying a heavy briefcase. His oral argument before the court had gone well. If he hurried, he'd have time to get something to eat before his next client appointment at two thirty. He hated missing lunch. Being a bachelor, that was his only decent meal of the day.

Edward skirted the mob of people flooding from the bank's revolving door, which was in constant motion this time of year. He was almost past the exit when he saw an elderly woman burst through the door, arms flailing wildly before she tumbled to her knees. A man followed on her heels, stepped over her without offering assistance, and hurried off.

Edward pushed through the crowd to reach the woman sprawled on the ground. "Ma'am," he said, setting his briefcase on the sidewalk and squatting down next to her as she tried to get up. "Are you all right?"

244

Verna nodded. "I've got to get my money." She turned to him as her eyes filled with tears. "That's my Christmas money. I've saved all year. I've got to get it back."

Edward adjusted his heavy black glasses and stared. *Surely, she knew that her money was gone?*

"If you haven't hurt yourself, let's help you get inside the bank," came a woman's voice over his shoulder. An easy-on-the-eyes brunette dressed in a bright red coat with fur collar and cuffs leaned over him and looked anxiously at the woman.

Verna shook her head. "I've got to get it ..."

"We'll help you inside, then we'll come back outside to look for your money," the young woman insisted, placing an arm under Verna's elbow and motioning for Edward to do the same. Together, they helped Verna to her feet and escorted her back through the revolving door. They crossed the bank's lobby to a group of straight-backed chairs along the wall, the young woman's high heels tapping out a staccato rhythm on the marble floor as they made their way. Verna sank into a chair without further protest.

"I'll go look for your money," Edward said. "How much did you have?"

"Thirty dollars. All in fives," Verna said. "A year's worth of savings." She shook her head. "There's no way you'll find it. It'll be long gone by now."

"You don't know that," he said. "I'm at least going to try."

"I'll find someone to bring you some water. Then I'll go help him," the young woman said, gesturing to Edward as he exited the lobby. "Will you be all right here on your own?"

Verna nodded.

"Don't leave until we come back," the young woman said before catching the eye of a banker crossing the lobby. "This woman fell in your doorway," she said. "Would you please bring her a glass of water?"

"Of course," he said, eyeing Verna with concern. "Should I call a doctor?"

"No, thank you. I'll just wait here until my friends return," Verna said, directing a thin smile at the young woman.

Clad in her red coat, the woman emerged from the revolving door of the bank looking like she'd stepped from the pages of a fashion magazine. Edward Fuller stood stock still, taking in the determined set of her shoulders and the graceful curves of her profile. His internal compass responded to her as if she were true north. He would later confess that was the moment. The moment that he knew—Carol Clark was "the one."

She turned her head left and then right, searching for him. He held up his hand, and she flashed *that smile*. He shook his head, and she joined him on the sidewalk.

"Nothing? What a shame," she said. "Seems like an old dear. Still working, I'd say. By the looks of her shoes, I'd guess that she's on her feet all day." She looked into Edward's eyes. "I'm heartbroken for her."

Edward nodded and pushed his glasses up on his nose. "I've had an idea, though. I've got five five-dollar bills in my wallet. I thought I'd give them to her."

"That's terribly kind of you, but I don't think she'll want your charity."

"I don't plan to tell her it's from me. I'll say we found it on the street. Tucked into the corner of a building or something. I know that will leave her five dollars short. I'd be happy to give it to her in ones, but I agree with you—I don't think she'll take it."

She smiled again and the temperature suddenly felt twenty degrees warmer to him. "I have a five in my purse," she replied. "What a nice thing for you to do. I'd be happy to contribute." She retrieved the bill from her wallet and handed it to him.

"I'm Carol Clark," she said, extending her hand once more. Edward took her hand in his own. It was warm and smooth and her handshake, firm and definite.

"Edward Fuller."

"What a lovely little Christmas secret we'll share, Edward Fuller," she said. "Let's go back in there and make that sweet lady very happy."

Verna patted the thick mass of graying blond hair secured in a bun at the nape of her neck and took a sip of her water, all the while keeping her aquamarine eyes trained on the revolving glass door. Her feet ached—as they always did after her shift at the bakery—and she was glad for the chance to sit down. She'd been sending up silent prayers that the two young people who came to her rescue would find her money—her Christmas money. It was December 15, and she'd just withdrawn all the money she'd saved in her Christmas club account.

She smiled to herself as she thought of the amount she'd been able to put aside this year. More customers were depositing their pennies and nickels in the tip jar on the counter. The attorney who came in every morning for two glazed doughnuts left a whole dollar every Friday. The economy in 1952 was booming; all the papers said so. Verna had been able to save most of her share of the tips. And she'd had thirty dollars to prove it. *Imagine that.* Eight dollars more than she'd been able to save last year. Everyone on her list would get something nice. She had next Monday off, and she'd do all of her shopping then—assuming the strangers who had stopped to help her found the bills the wind had swept away.

As the minutes ticked by, she became increasingly anxious. Asking God to help with this small request was a waste of His time. She ought to be ashamed of herself for asking Him. Verna looked at the large clock on the opposite wall. These young people were undoubtedly employed somewhere nearby and had probably already gone back to work. She'd wait another few minutes, then be on her way.

A flash of red in the revolving door caught Verna's eye before the beautiful Carol Clark stepped into the lobby. Edward Fuller was on her heels. The looks on their faces made Verna's heart race. Maybe, just maybe, her prayers had been answered. She put her hands on the arms of the chair and began to rise, but Carol motioned her to sit.

"He's found it!" she cried. "All of it! Isn't he brilliant?"

"What?" Verna gasped. "I never in a million years thought I'd see all of it again. How far did you have to look?"

"Not far, as it turns out." Edward concocted a story on the spot. "It had all gotten caught underneath a trash can across the street, where it was protected from the wind. This must be your lucky day," he said, handing her the neatly folded stack of bills.

Verna took them from his hand and opened her purse, zipping them safely into a side compartment. "I'm not taking any chances," she said, snapping the purse shut and tilting her head to smile up at them. "Thank you for taking the time to assist an old lady."

"We were glad we could help," Carol said. "You really owe it all to Mr. Fuller's quick action."

"I'm so grateful," Verna patted Edward's arm. "And now, I'd better let you two be on your way."

Edward extended his hand and helped her to her feet. "Where are you headed?" he asked.

"Home," she replied. "My bus should be along any minute."

"Let me help you to your bus stop," he said as the three of them traversed the lobby and made a slow exit out of the revolving door.

"It's just down the block, there," Verna said, pointing to a group of people waiting by the curb. She looked from one to the other. "Thank you, again, for your kindness to me. You've been my Christmas miracle. I'll put you in my prayers. And a very blessed Christmas to you both." With that, she set out for the bus stop.

Edward and Carol stood together on the pavement, watching Verna walk away. Carol turned to face him and waited.

Edward cleared his throat. "Well, Miss Clark. Very nice to meet you. Have a good afternoon."

She smiled and something flashed behind her eyes. Was it disappointment? "You too, Mr. Fuller. And a very merry Christmas."

He tipped his hat, and Carol turned and walked away. Edward checked his watch. He no longer had time for lunch and was already late for his next appointment. He set out for his office at a brisk pace, berating himself with each step. *Why hadn't he asked her out to dinner? Or at least gotten her phone number or found out where she worked?* It had been years since anyone had turned his head; he was sorely out of practice.

Edward cursed under his breath and forced his way back through the throng of people he'd just passed, retracing his steps. His long strides ate up

248

the pavement, and his height allowed him a clear view of the other pedestrians. After three blocks he was forced to admit that he'd lost her. He slapped his thigh with his gloved hand and stomped his foot, ignoring the curious glances from passersby. Why in the hell had he been so slow—so stupid? If there really were Christmas miracles, maybe he would see Carol Clark again.

Available at Amazon in Print, Audio, and for Kindle

Novels in the *Rosemont* series

Coming to Rosemont
Weaving the Strands
Uncovering Secrets
Drawing Close
Bringing Them Home

Also by **BARBARA HINSKE**

The Night Train
The Christmas Club

UPCOMING IN 2020

Guiding Emily, the first novel in a new series by Barbara Hinske
The seventh novel in the Rosemont series

I'd Love to Hear from You!
Connect with me online:

Visit **www.barbarahinske.com** to
sign up for my **newsletter** to receive your Free Gift,
plus Inside Scoops, Amazing Offers,
Bedtime Stories & Inspirations from Home.

Facebook.com/BHinske
Twitter.com/BarbaraHinske
Instagram/barbarahinskeauthor
Email me at **bhinske@gmail.com**

Search for **Barbara Hinske on YouTube**
for tours inside my own historic
home plus tips and tricks for busy women!

Find photos of fictional *Rosemont*, Westbury,
and things related to the *Rosemont*
series at **Pinterest.com/BarbaraHinske**.